Train Wreck Girl

a novel

Sean Carswell

Manic D Press
San Francisco

For Joan and the Old Boy

Printed in the USA
Cover photographs: Jeffrey van Daele / Tre Graves

Library of Congress Cataloging-in-Publication Data

Carswell, Sean, 1970-
 Train wreck girl / Sean Carswell.
     p. cm.
  ISBN 978-1-933149-21-9 (trade pbk.)
1. Life change events—Fiction. 2. Bereavement—Fiction. 3. Self-realization—Fiction. 4. Homecoming—Fiction. 5. Cocoa Beach (Fla.)—Fiction. I. Title.
PS3603.A7764T73 2008
813'.6—dc22

                                        2007052537

1
Pink Parkas and Black Eyes

With three minutes left in the millennium, the DJ at Tommy's Bar played the same song that DJs everywhere throughout the Mountain Time Zone played: Prince's "1999." I was so drunk I was dancing. And not just dancing, but dancing like I meant it. Spinning like I thought I was Michael Jackson, pointing a finger in the air like I had Saturday Night Fever. Hell, if the crowd hadn't been so thick, I would've been humping that mud and beer soaked floor like Prince in *Purple Rain*.

My girlfriend Libra tried to dance with me, but mostly she just laughed.

I was not trying to make her laugh.

Libra was a kid. She didn't know. She didn't know what it was like to have been a horny, small town adolescent trying to figure any angle that would work with the girls. She didn't know what the eighties were like to grow up in: all tight pants for boys and big hair for girls. She didn't know what it was like for a thirteen-year-old Danny McGregor in front of his brother's TV, trying to learn to dance from late night videos even though he hated the songs because that's what the girls wanted—to dance to these songs—and all Danny ever wanted was to do his best to be what the girls wanted. Though

I guess Libra did know that last part about Danny. The part about him trying to be what the girls wanted. That was the thing that was perfectly clear about Danny.

The other thing about Danny is that he's me.

The other thing about Libra was that she was just starting elementary school when this Prince song came out.

So that was the big difference between Libra and me: she was at the beginning of her twenties when we danced and waited for the New Year. I was at the end of my twenties. Just a few months from thirty. And, with less than a minute left in the millennium, I flashed back to those days of being that awkward adolescent, hanging out with my buddy Bart at a school dance, taking tiny sips off of stolen whiskey because we thought it was cool and listening to this very same song and me saying to Bart, "Man, that's gonna be one hell of a party when it turns 2000."

"Not for us," Bart said. "We'll be old by then. We'll probably have families and kids."

I said, "Not me. I'll be dead before I'm thirty." I took another sip of stolen whiskey and headed off to dance with Rosalie White, because I had a joint in my pocket and she liked to share her asthma medicine, which had some kind of speed in it, and together we'd be in for a fun night.

I snapped out of the flashback just as the countdown began.

Ten.

It occurred to me that I wasn't gonna be dead by thirty.

Nine.

Or at least the booze and drugs wouldn't kill me before then.

Eight.

And if the booze and drugs weren't gonna kill me, what was I gonna do with the rest of my life?

Seven.

It was a second of vertigo. Like what the fuck?

Six.

I needed something to hold on to so I reached out for Libra and put my arms around her and spun her and kissed her like it was the end of a black-and-white flick.

Five.

Libra laughed a few feet away from me and I opened my eyes and realized that Libra wasn't in my arms at all. That some other girl was.

Four.

I let go of the girl. She slapped me in the face. Her fingernail jabbed my left eye. My vision was too blurry to see what she did next, but whatever it was, it caused her to slip and fall to the mud and beer soaked floor.

Three.

The girl's boyfriend helped her up, then turned to face me. He was a little guy.

Two.

Even though I knew better than to do this, I pushed the girl's boyfriend. Even though I know, never ever push someone in a bar fight. Either start swinging or don't touch the guy at all.

One.

The girl's boyfriend knew this rule. He started swinging. And he knew how to fight. He cracked me once hard in the cheek and kept swinging. I didn't put up my hands to block or fight back at all. He landed five or six punches square to my head by the time everyone else finished screaming, "Happy New Year!" and kissed each other and the bouncers dragged me out and left me sprawling on the icy sidewalk in front of Tommy's Bar.

I walked away from Tommy's and into the Flagstaff night with snow and ice crunching under my Docs and just thinking again and again, damn, I'm a fuck up. A block into the walk, I heard Libra call out, "Danny, wait."

She jogged up to me: pink parka-ed and fuzzy hooded and little clouds of warm breath floating out of her. I wasn't really surprised that she was coming after me. I'd seen girlfriends do this before. All these crazy broads who'll forgive me for the most ridiculous shit. I never understood.

Libra caught up to me. She took my stocking cap out of her parka pocket and put it on my head. She ran her mitten over my left eye, which was already starting to swell. "Are you okay?" she asked. "I think that guy gave you a black eye."

"The girl did," I said. I started walking again, through downtown. Libra and I lived on the other end of it, down the railroad tracks a little. Libra walked with me. We didn't talk. I didn't apologize and she didn't ask me to. All around us, college kids floated in and out of bars, carrying bottles of champagne and blowing noise makers and throwing snowballs and making out against the bricks of century-old buildings.

We walked out of downtown and took the shortcut along the railroad tracks, toward our trailer. A couple of times, trains raced by, and Libra and I walked off the tracks and into the pine forest and waited for the trains to pass, then cut back onto the tracks. Libra carried a snowball with her. She tried to convince me to put it on my eye. I didn't say yes or no. I just kept walking. About halfway down the tracks, I sat down. "That's it," I told Libra. "Tonight's the night I'm not gonna make it. Tonight's the night I'm gonna break down and admit that all of these motherfuckers are better than me. Every one of them."

"Get off of the tracks, Danny," Libra said.

I shook my head. She knelt down in front of me. She pressed her snowball against my eye. It stung enough to feel good. She leaned her face in close, as if she were going to kiss me. The fuzzy hood of her parka brushed against my cheek, right where that first punch landed. I decided right then that it was over between Libra and me.

Within three weeks, I'd breakup with her and buy my ticket back to shit city.

2
Sal Si Puedes

I got to know Sal because of his torch.

Two years earlier, I'd been chugging west on I-40 through the Painted Desert with California on my mind. I'd been feeling like it was time for me to move on and figured that, as long as I was doing nothing with my life, I may as well do nothing with it where the waves were good.

I didn't know anything about Flagstaff then. I had no idea that, in the middle of that giant Arizona desert, my 1973 Ford Galaxie would have to climb a mountain.

Halfway up the mountain, my Galaxie told me just how bad of an idea it was to try to climb this fucker in an old American car. I blew a radiator hose. Stupidly, I duct-taped the hose, refilled the radiator, and kept going. I tried to be careful. I pulled over often and waited for the engine to cool. I reapplied duct tape. I refilled water. I drove slowly. Still, by the time I made it into Flagstaff, something in the Galaxie was seriously fucked. I got a room at a hostel there. The people who ran the joint were okay with me working on my car in the parking lot. I decided to stay a while.

I replaced all the hoses and the radiator itself, and the Galaxie still leaked water. With all that heat going up the mountain, I'd cracked the head of the engine. So I spent a couple of days under the pines in the parking lot, taking out everything on top of the head. Then I walked two blocks down to Sal Si Puedes Auto Shop and asked the owner if he had a welding torch. The owner was this crazy looking chicano guy with slicked-back hair and a devil beard and a body like an upright brown buffalo. He introduced himself as Salvador. He said he did have a torch, but he didn't know how to use it. And this was how we got to be friends.

We worked out an arrangement, Sal and me. Anytime Sal needed any welding, he'd call me and I'd do it free of charge. In exchange, Sal would gather piles of any kind of scrap iron or steel he could get his hands on. I could use the back of his shop to do whatever I wanted with the scraps. So on days when I felt like I needed to spend a couple of hours staring at a single straight flame, welding the shit in my head into some kind of tangible pile of scraps, I'd go to Sal Si Puedes Auto Shop. Sal would call the piles of scraps sculptures. He'd sell them. I wouldn't take the money he made from them. I always knew when he sold a new sculpture, though, because he'd come into my bar and lay down ridiculously large tips. And so it worked out for everyone.

It even worked out for the Galaxie. I drove that old son of a bitch for another year and a half before the transmission gave out, and I just parked it next to a shed in my front lawn. It made me feel like I'd gotten closer to my destiny: living in a trailer with a dead American car in the yard.

So three days after New Year, I went back to see Sal. To weld some shit together and get some perspective. I had two Greyhound tickets in my pocket. One for me. One for Libra. I was heading back home. To Florida. Maybe I'd ask Libra to come with me. Who knew?

Sal was under the hood of a Cadillac when I walked into his

shop. He popped his head out, took one look at me, and smiled. "What happened to your eye?" he asked.

"Ah, this crazy broad slapped me."

Sal grabbed a rag off the Caddy's fender and wiped his hands. He walked over to me and got a good look at the eye. He wagged his finger at me and said, "Looks like you just don't fucking listen."

He walked over to his little dorm-size refrigerator and grabbed a can of soda for himself and a bottle of water for me. We sat in two lawn chairs, back behind the Caddy and commenced to bullshitting.

Sal had gotten a DUI on New Year's Eve night. He told me all about it. Called it a DWM. Driving While Mexican. He'd had three beers and headed home early so that he could ring in the New Year with his kids. The cops pulled him over straight out of the bar parking lot. His blood alcohol level was just barely over the legal limit, and still he went down. "How does that happen, Danny?" he asked. "How do the cops know to pull over the only sober guy on New Year's Eve at nine o'clock? Was I driving too straight? Was all that going the speed limit pissing them off?"

"It's a fucking racket," I said. Sal shook his head.

We talked about other things. Arrests, cops, bad shit. My black eye, fights, more bad shit. At first, I thought that Sal would be in a hurry to get back to work, but he just didn't seem to be. I thought about it and figured that the owner of the Caddy had to be white and Sal had to be still on the clock. I remembered Sal had gone on a rant after his first DWM, shortly after I met him. He told me that he was charging all his wealthy white customers an extra hour's time until his fines were paid, because these fuckers would never have to go through this shit and they had to pony up for their privilege to be white in a white society. I remember asking Sal what race he thought I was and if I had to pony up. "Nope," Sal had told me. "Poor and white doesn't count."

I didn't bring it back up with the second DWM. Sal and I didn't talk much about race and whatnot. We just sat around, bullshitting in the garage until the conversation rolled around to where men's conversations always end up: women.

"I'm gonna breakup with Libra," I told Sal.

"Really?"

"Yeah," I said. "I keep getting mixed up with all these crazy broads. I gotta do something about it. I gotta find a sane woman."

"What's crazy about Libra?"

"She's with me, isn't she?"

"So you're saying that any woman who'd get mixed up with you is crazy?"

"Pretty much."

"And you're looking for a sane woman?"

"Man, am I."

"Good logic, Danny. You're not setting yourself up for failure at all."

I knew exactly what Sal was talking about. It wasn't my logic that was flawed. It was the way I explained it. So I decided to lay it all out for Sal. I couldn't afford a shrink and Sal was my next best bet. Someone was paying him sixty-five bucks an hour. As long as he had nothing better to do with that time than sit and listen, I was in luck. I said, "It goes like this, Sal. There have only been four women in my life who meant anything to me. All of them were crazy."

"Okay, so we'll start with the first one," Sal said. "Tell me about your mother."

See, Sal was just like a shrink. Only he was off with the first question. Because I didn't have a mother. Not really. She died of cancer two months after I was born. So that was it for her. I hardly knew her. I told Sal this and he told me to start with the first crazy broad, then. "Okay," I said. "It was Rosalie White. My first girlfriend. Turned me on to sex and drugs. I dated her for three years. Ninth, tenth, and eleventh grade. She moved away my senior year."

"And what made her crazy?"

"She was black and she grew up in Cocoa Beach, Florida, which is almost exclusively white. It's enough to drive anyone crazy."

"Fair enough. Who's next?"

"Sophie Dunn."

"Another black girl?"

"No. Why?"

"I don't know," Sal said. "What was up with Sophie? Why was she crazy?"

"Because she stabbed me. Three times. In the gut." I lifted up my shirt to show Sal the scars. They were four years old and faded. One of them cut across the first "o" in my "BORN TO LOSE" tattoo. Sal stood up and examined the scars.

"Born to lose," he said. "That's a self-fulfilling prophesy."

"You're really on that kick today, aren't you? All my problems are my fault, huh?"

Sal sat back down. "Well, we know about Libra. That's pretty much your fault, isn't it?"

I nodded.

"And I take it Libra's one of the four?"

I nodded again.

"So who's the last one?"

"Helen Kanako. Sophie stabbed me because I left her for Helen."

"And what was up with Helen?"

I shook my head and said her name. "Helen." I stood up from my lawn chair and headed for the torch. This session was over.

3
Too Late to Die Young

I walked the tracks home from work, so lost in thought that I almost didn't see that freight train until it was too late. Its whistle wailed and snapped me out of my head just in time to take two steps to my right and feel the wind of the train whizzing by. I'd gotten so used to the sound of train whistles that I hardly paid attention to them anymore. They were just part of the landscape. And I had bigger things to think about.

With less than forty-eight hours left in Flagstaff, I had to decide whether to breakup with Libra or take her with me to Florida. I walked next to the tracks and weighed the pros and cons. On the pro side of things, if Libra went with me to Florida, she'd be with me. I'd gotten used to having her around. I liked it. She was a good kid. But more than that, there were moments when she would do things so thoughtful and generous that I would feel, I don't know, more human or something. Or she'd completely drop her guard and let me see the Libra that she was when no one was around. During those times, I could picture a future with me and Libra stretching into old age. So of course I wanted her to go to Florida with me.

On the con side, though, if she came with me, she'd have to quit college, move two thousand miles from home, and get the first job of her life all so she could camp out with a loser like me.

And I guess there was a third option. I could've stayed in Flagstaff. I had a good gig tending bar downtown and I had a cool girlfriend and I had a friend to hang out with and plenty of free time to read and ride my bike around town and sleep when I was tired. But that wouldn't work. This was no time for status quo. I was turning thirty in a few months. It was already too late to die young. And if I had to keep living, I had to come up with a new plan. I had to go back to the place where everything went wrong and start fixing things from there.

The decision about what to do with Libra became more and more clear in my mind. I climbed down off the tracks, hopped the fence into my backyard, and went into my trailer.

Libra paced back and forth across the living room floor. She moved quickly. Her pacing took up most of the room. I had to time it right just to get over to the rocking chair by the wall heater.

I sat in the chair and unlaced my boots. "What's up, kid?" I asked.

Libra didn't stop pacing. She said, "Where have you been all night?"

"At work."

"You smell like a bar."

I pulled off a boot and the wet sock underneath it. "I work in a bar."

"Oh, you've got an answer for everything, don't you?"

I looked up. Libra's pacing was making me dizzy. I said, "You're gonna wear a hole in the floor if you're not careful."

Libra stopped. She looked at me. Her mascara was spread across her eyelids like a fog. The rest of her make up had been washed off, making the freckles on her cheeks all the more prominent. How could I ever leave this girl? I asked myself. And: how could I not?

How could I condemn her to a life with me?

Libra kinda snarled and said, "Don't look at me like that."

I figured I knew what the problem was and said, "Talk to your mother today?"

"What do you think?"

"I think you did. Sit down. Tell me about it."

Libra didn't sit. She crossed her arms and said, "My mom wants me to see a shrink."

"Really?" I let out a little laugh, because for all my talk of Libra being crazy, I always knew that I was the one who really had the problem. So this surprised me. I said, "Are you gonna go?"

"I can't." Libra sat on the couch. She crossed her legs and kept her arms crossed and this made her look so vulnerable that I got a little sad.

"Why not?"

"She made the appointment for tomorrow. I gotta go to the med center tomorrow to get my annual check-up."

As soon as she said this, I got another idea. Because those med center doctors are always good for drugs. I said, "What? Your pap smear and shit like that?" Libra nodded. "Listen, Libra, can you do me a favor when you get there?" Libra looked at me kinda surprised, like it was totally inappropriate for me to be changing the subject right now. Which it was. So I hurried. I said, "Will you tell the doctor that you have really bad cramps? Tell him that you can't sleep some nights because the cramps are so bad. He'll prescribe you some Vicadin, and we can have some fun with it."

Libra drummed her fingers on her bicep. I could see it was about time to wrap things up. I knew I had a long bus ride ahead of me and I wanted two scripts out of Libra's med center visit. I added, "Can you also tell him that your grades have been slipping because you can't seem to focus in class?"

"My grades aren't slipping," Libra said.

"Yeah, but Ritalin is fun," I said.

"I'm not your drug dealer." Libra shot me a dirty look like this was the final word.

I said, "Please."

She said, "I thought we were talking about my mom. And me going to the shrink."

I'd already planted the seeds for the drugs, and that was enough. I figured it was time to let her talk now.

The first thing she wanted me to know was that she absolutely refused to go to the shrink. And not just because of the med center visit. Because, as she put it, "Fuck Mom."

So I prodded her to talk more about her mom's plans. The biggest problem, according to her mom, was that Libra was shacked up in a trailer with me. Even though Libra's mom had never met me in person, she couldn't stand me. She couldn't stand the thought that her daughter was involved with a guy like me: who had never gone to college, had no prospects, no future, no skills, no nothing. I didn't even have a running car.

And there was this other thing about Libra's parents. They were loaded. And not just well off. Loaded. Loaded like Libra would never have to work a day in her life, if she didn't want to. Loaded like they could've bought her this trailer and the property around it and the whole neighborhood around it. Loaded like it was clear that Libra never had to live like this, like the way she lived with me. So Libra's mom was convinced that this whole affair was just a rebellion against her, that Libra was slumming with me just to piss her mother off. That the sooner Libra got rid of a loser like me, the better. And this was why Libra's mom wanted Libra to go to the shrink: to get to the core of the rebellion and end it as soon as possible.

Another thing about Libra's mom was this: even though we'd never met, I pretty much agreed with her. I was pretty sure that Libra was just slumming with me to get back at her mom. I was pretty sure that Libra would come to her senses when she had one semester of college left, and she'd meet a nice, wealthy business school standout and plot her course for the suburbs. And, let's face it, I *was* pretty much a loser with no prospects, no future, and no car.

The only point I disagreed with was the one about me having no skills, because I was a skilled welder. I'd been a union iron worker for four years. I'd gone to all the classes that the union required of me. I built condos all along Cocoa Beach and Cape Canaveral. I'd even worked at Kennedy Space Center. And my welding made that possible. And I'd still be doing it now, only I'm deathly afraid of heights.

But all that's neither here nor there. Suffice it to say, Libra's mom was pretty much right about everything.

Normally, I didn't want to tell Libra this. I usually bit my tongue when the subject came up. But on this night, Libra threw a wrench in the works. She said, "Mom said she was gonna cut me off if I didn't end things with you."

This stunned me. This was serious. Libra's trust fund was huge. I couldn't let her lose that. "What did you tell her?"

Libra lifted her chin, all proud-like, and said, "I told her she could shove her money right up her ass."

"What did she say to that?"

"She said that's it. I'm cut off."

I shook my head. "That won't do," I said. "You gotta apologize."

"Fuck that," Libra said. "I can't be bought."

"We can all be bought," I said. I paused, but not long enough for Libra to interject. "I just... I'm just not worth it."

Libra came across the room and tried to sit on my lap. The rocking chair creaked under the weight of us, and I lifted Libra off me.

"No, kid," I said. "Your mom's right. I'm just a phase you're going through. You may as well get out of this while you still can."

Libra crossed her arms again. "What are you saying, Danny?"

"You don't give a shit about me. I'm just a fling. Someone you can talk about at the country club in a few years."

"That's not true." Libra's eyes watered up again. "I love you."

"No, you don't," I said. And, I didn't want to be mean, but I knew I should be. I knew I should be at least mean enough to make the breakup stick. So I said, "I don't love you."

"You're not an asshole, Danny. Don't act like one."

I got up from the rocking chair and walked to my backpack. It was lying on the linoleum kitchen table. I unzipped it, dug out my Greyhound ticket, and handed it to Libra. "I am an asshole," I said. "We may as well end this now. I was planning on leaving, anyway."

Libra looked at the ticket and saw that I really was leaving in less than two days and a spark flared up in her eyes. It was enough to start the fireworks. Yelling and screaming and throwing shit. She told me I was a loser and a waste of time and the worst mistake of her life. Which was all fair enough. She called me white trash. Which hurt. The "trash" part I can take. But I don't know why she had to throw "white" in there.

I only winced at the insults and didn't yell back. I figured it was her time to lose her temper. She was justified. I guess she took my lack of a response as apathy, though, so she started doing anything she could to get a reaction out of me. She started breaking stuff. That was fine with me. I was planning on leaving it all behind, anyway. She ripped the arm off my record player. She snapped the rocker off my chair. She stuck my boot in the oven and turned the oven on. She heaved my favorite metal sculpture through the living room window. In the midst of her tantrum, I wondered, Could she be The

One? What if she is The One and I'm blowing it right now? Could I stop this?

I decided, no, I couldn't stop it. She'd blown off all her steam already and I needed to get my boot out of the oven before it caught fire and burned the trailer down. When I got back from the kitchen, Libra had exhausted herself. She called her brother Angus to come pick her up.

It only took her brother about five minutes to get to the trailer. I waited out that time on the couch. Libra spent it in the bedroom, packing up shit. I told her that I should be the one to leave, since I was leaving anyway and rent was already paid on the trailer, but Libra wanted to go. Or at least that's how I interpreted all her *fuck yous*.

Angus rattled on the trailer door and I opened it. Libra came flying out of the bedroom with her pink parka on and a backpack slung over her shoulder. She rushed between Angus and me. Angus stood there, glaring at me, looking like he wanted to kill me. I could tell he was thinking about taking a crack at me, but the poor kid was way smaller and younger and dumber than me, and barely smart enough to realize this.

Something in his eyes burned brighter than whatever had been burning in Libra's eyes. At least with Libra, there was some love mixed in with all the hate. Not with Angus. He glared at me like, *one day, motherfucker... One day.*

4

The Fucker in the Room

I still had one scene left to play out with Libra. It came after closing time the next night.

I'd finished my last shift at The Corner Bar. All the night's money was locked away in the safe. All my side work was done: the bar mats had been hosed down and left in the kitchen to dry, all the glasses were washed and stacked in the drying rack, the wells had been wiped down. All the stools but one were stacked on the bar. Sal sat in the last stool, drinking one last draft. I stood on the other side of the bar, drinking my first and last of the night. The front door should've been locked, but it wasn't. It was just before two A.M. My Greyhound left at six A.M. So this was my last nod to Flagstaff. A two-man going away party. Sayonara, Danny.

I'd told Sal all about the breakup. He sided with Libra. I couldn't blame him. I kinda sided with Libra in this one, too. And speaking of the devil, Libra burst through the front door.

She was lit. She leaned on her right leg so hard that her left leg came off the ground and I thought she was gonna topple over. She wagged a finger at me and said, "You're a fucker."

I didn't say anything.

Libra righted herself. She brushed a lock of red hair off her cheek, changed her tone, and said, "Hi, Sal."

"How you doing?" Sal said.

"Not good." Libra shook her head. "Not good." She fumbled through her parka pockets for a second. It seemed to take way too much out of her, like she was wearing herself out just trying to get her hands on something. After a couple of seconds, she dug out what she was looking for. "I just want to give you something, you fucker," she said, apparently to me, seeing as how I was already established as the fucker in the room. She hurled a prescription bottle at me. I caught it in one bounce off the bar. It was Ritalin.

"Thanks," I said.

"I'm not done." She started fumbling again, even more awkwardly. She had her left hand in the right side pocket of her jacket and she spun in a little quarter circle. When she found the other bottle, she whipped it out of her pocket like she was pulling a gopher out of its hole. "Vicadin," she said. "Lucky you."

She threw this one in my general direction, but it hit the leg of one of the stools on the bar and landed on a beer cooler behind the bar. I walked over and picked it up.

"Some of the Vicadin are missing," she said. "I took 'em when I got my tattoo."

"You got a tattoo?" Sal asked.

"I did indeed," Libra said. "Wanna see it?"

Sal looked at me. I shrugged my shoulders. Sal said, "Sure."

Libra staggered across the floor. Part of me wanted to help her. She never got this fucked up, and she wasn't handling herself well. I didn't like to see it. I wanted to protect her, to take care of her, to get her home safely and tell her everything would be okay. But I couldn't. No way. This breakup had to stick. I had to fix my own shit before I could help anyone else. I had to hop that dog at six A.M. I had to get back to Florida. So I let Libra stagger on her own two feet.

She made it up to Sal, put her right foot on the bottom rung of the bar stool, and rolled up the leg of her jeans. She had on a red and white striped knee sock. She rolled the sock down. And just above her ankle danced the sorriest, crustiest little Betty Boop I'd ever seen.

Aww, man, I thought. An ankle tattoo? A Betty Boop one? A picture you got off the wall in a downtown tattoo shop? Libra, you gotta be more original than that. I felt so sorry for the kid. But, really, who was I to talk? I had a dozen bad tattoos. None of them came off a tattoo parlor wall, and none of them were cartoon characters, but they were all mostly ugly. So I didn't say anything. Sal said, "Cute."

Libra smiled and batted her eyelids like she was taking on a new Betty Boop persona. "Ain't it?" she said.

And, see, it just goes to prove my theory that Libra wasn't crazy at all. All of her rebellions were in comfortable, socially acceptable ways. She had the rebel boyfriend in college, but it ended before it got too serious. She got her tattoo, but in a cute and easily hidden way. It was all very safe, very forgivable. It was healthy, even. I'd read that freshman psychology text. I knew exactly what Libra was doing. It was all like that Murray Bowen guy said: you need to differentiate yourself from your family and establish your own sense of self. That's exactly what Libra was doing. It could be explained to her mother very clearly. One trip to a shrink and she'd have her trust fund back. So, okay, I told myself. It's okay.

Libra said, "Do you like it, Danny?"

"No," I said.

"Oh fuck you," she said. "Fucker."

"I am a fucker," I said. "You're better off without me."

"It's true," Sal said.

"Fuck both of you," Libra said. She looked over her shoulder. Her brother and his crew walked past The Corner Bar. "Angus!"

Libra called out, even though he couldn't hear her. "I'm gonna go hang out with my brother," she said to Sal and me. "Fuck you guys." She turned and ran to the door. Just as she got there, she looked back and said, "You're gonna be sorry, Danny." Then she ran off.

Angus and his crew were already out of sight by the time she left The Corner Bar. I couldn't see if she caught up to them or not. But I knew even then that she was right. I'd be sorry.

5

The Evils of Betty Boop

Libra didn't come back to the trailer that night. I assumed she'd slept at her brother's place again. I didn't sleep much myself. Partly because I only had a few hours before my bus left. Partly because Libra had broken out the living room window, so the trailer was literally freezing inside. Partly because, without that living room window, the whistles of the trains passing through my backyard were twice as loud. At five-thirty in the morning, I left to catch my bus.

I had a backpack full of clothes and not much else. I'd mailed one box of records and one box of books ahead to my sister's place in Florida. I left everything else for Libra. Or the landlord. Or whoever got hired to throw it away.

I took one last look at my Galaxie, covered in snow and rusting away by the shed. Underneath that car, I'd buried a little monkey sculpture that I'd done back in high school. That little monkey meant a lot to me. Libra had hated it. I was afraid she was going to throw it away or something, so I buried it out there for safekeeping. But then, with the breakup and quitting my job and thinking about Joe and everything, I forgot about it. I didn't even remember it when I took my last look at the Galaxie. I headed through the backyard, to the railroad tracks, to the bus station.

It was still too early for a sunrise. There was enough of a moon to guide me. And I spent a lot of time out at night, so the walk was pleasant. Up north of town, the snow glowed on top of Humphries Peak. This is a pretty fucking town, I thought, am I making a mistake? Is it too late to patch things up with Libra? To get my job back at The Corner Bar?

It's one thing when you have regrets. Life is full of them. It's another thing when you have regrets in the middle of doing what you're regretting. You think, I could stop this. Right now I could. Just stop it.

But I didn't. I kept walking to the bus station. It really was important to me to get back to Florida. Because, to be honest, there was so much more than my impending thirtieth birthday that was driving me. There was so much more than just getting too old to die young. There was my brother Joe back in Florida. And Sophie who stabbed me. And Helen. And my brother Joe. And, already, though I was in Flagstaff, walking along train tracks and forgetting about trains and lighted by a glowing, snow-peaked mountain, my head was in Florida. I was so deep in my head that I didn't see anything on the train tracks until I tripped over it.

I fell between the tracks on the other side of whatever tripped me. My knees scraped the rocks and the pads of my hands thudded against a railroad tie. First, I brushed myself off. No tear on my jeans. That was a plus. A little something spread across the toe of my boot. I reached down to wipe it away. It was a spatter of blood. I checked myself again. No blood. I had only tripped. Nothing big. So I looked at what I'd tripped over. This lump like a side of beef. But a side of beef between railroad tracks made no sense. I looked closer. It was a torso. Oh shit. My first thought was of Tucson Johnny, this homeless guy who came into the Corner Bar now and then. He never tipped but at least he always paid for his drinks. I liked Tucson Johnny. At least, I liked him enough to not want to see him dead on the train tracks. So I took a closer look, thinking, maybe it's not him. Probably it's not him. I don't even know why I think it is.

A lot of the parts beyond the torso were missing. The head. One leg—the right one, I think. A hand. Everything else was hard to identify since the skin was mostly torn off and the rest of the body unraveled with it. Obviously, several trains had hit it over the course of the night. Bits and pieces were strewn about the tracks for thirty yards. The smell slapped my nose—metallic and a little sweet—and I nearly threw up on the spot. Vomit raced up from my stomach. I felt it coming and did what I could to catch it. A little spilled into my mouth. I choked it all down. The bile burned the back of my throat. My stomach quivered. Little beads of icy sweat crept out of my pores. I took three long, deep breaths. The cold morning air pushed through the pipe where I'd nearly lost my breakfast. After those three breaths, I was still shaken but ready to move.

I started walking. What else could I do? I didn't want to stand and stare. I didn't want to puke on this corpse. If I looked at it again, I surely would. I definitely didn't want to get so lost in thought that I'd ignore a train whistle and meet the same fate. And I couldn't keep thinking the corpse was really a homeless guy I knew. That was just a weird bit of denial. A grotesque little daydream that let me star in my own tragedy without actually being affected by a real tragedy. So, I decided, if I was going to be in denial, why not go whole hog? Why not just deny everything? I walked along and tried not to think. Body parts. Torn jeans. What looked like a pink blanket. A striped knee sock. My stomach trembled with every new discovery. I took deep breaths, tried to exhale my thoughts. I kept sweating through the twenty-degree morning. And then I found the leg.

It was about ten feet off the tracks, down a little hill, leaning up against the fence. I don't know why I climbed down to look at it. But then again, I do know why I did. The top of the leg was crushed.

Tenuous. Kinda crusty. The rest of it was freckled and bare. And right there, just above the ankle danced Betty Boop. Blood clotted along her outline. Her skirt was in a permanent swing. One eye was too big. The smile was lopsided, like she was crazy. Glaring at me. Full of hate. Saying, "This is all your fault, fucker."

I freaked out. It was all so clear now. And I agreed. It probably was my fault. Fucker.

Vomit raced back up in my mouth. I caught it there and put my hand over my lips so that none could escape. With a great force of will, I choked it down again. That just made me feel worse.

I started running as fast as I could along the train tracks, holding everything in. I didn't stop running until I got to the bus station. My Greyhound was fifteen minutes away from leaving. I didn't call anyone. I didn't do anything except show the driver my ticket and settle into a window seat. Filling myself with regret while it was still early enough to change things.

6
Two Days on the Dog

You freaked out. That's okay. People will judge you for this. That's okay, too. If they've never found the destroyed carcass of their girlfriend on the train tracks, then they have no right to judge you.

You're calling her your girlfriend again, even though she was your ex-girlfriend for the last twenty-four hours of her life. But calling her your girlfriend makes things easier. It's easier to deal with the death of a girlfriend than to deal with the death of a girl who, less than two days ago, you decided you had to leave and immediately questioned the decision and rocked back and forth on it and convinced yourself that it was for the better and for her own good. It's too hard for your heart to delineate, to make the distinction between wanting to break up with the girl yet still wanting things to turn out well for her, turn out better than if she were with you. It's all too confusing. Call her your girlfriend. Keep things as simple as possible.

You board the Greyhound. Hop the dog. And ride out of Flagstaff before the sun is up. The sunrise comes when you get about an hour east, with the mountains already at your back. Every second of that first hour, you want to get off this dog. Stop the bus. Go back. Tell someone that Libra is dead on the tracks. But you don't do anything.

When the sun comes up, you start to wonder who will find the body. Surely, one of the train conductors called it in. It couldn't have been the one who hit her. If he'd called the cops, the cops would've gotten there before you did. But surely some conductor would notice the body. Especially now that the sun was up. Someone would call the cops. They'd figure it out. They don't need you. At least that's what you tell yourself.

And then you think: she's dead. She's really fucking dead. Dead. You'll never see her again. You'll never get a second chance with her. She'll never get a second chance at anything ever. She has been robbed of life. She's dead.

The bus stops at a weird little desert travel plaza. An old television show had been filmed there. *F-Troop*. You've never seen *F-Troop*. You've only read the sign that's posted in front of the convenience store. You grab a soda and walk around back and stare at long shadows peeling off of cacti.

Something about the shadows makes you remember that monkey under the Galaxie. It's almost enough to make you turn around. You can't see your brother Joe without the monkey. You wonder what to do, but before you can come up with a plan, an old, skinny dude comes up from behind you. He wants to smoke a joint and offers you some. You accept. This is your second mistake.

You have the sour taste of pot and stomach bile in your mouth. You mix this with an orange soda you'd picked up at the *F-Troop* stop. It doesn't help. You keep thinking, she's dead. She's really dead. The image of the corpse haunts you. You memorize every detail. And now you go back to the Greyhound john. Now, you finally lose your breakfast.

As the bus rolls along, the weed makes you more paranoid. You stare out the window and think about how things look back in Flagstaff. They look bad. Your girlfriend's dead—died a violent death—and you immediately skipped town. The trailer you shared with her is in shambles. Things have been thrown through windows. Furniture is broken. Things got so bad that the last person to visit was a family member who had to pull his sister out of a bad scene. And then you split. On a bus. And you'd bought the ticket three weeks in advance. Things don't look good. Things look like manslaughter. When you consider the advance ticket, though, things get bumped up to first degree pushing a woman into a train.

Your mind spins in circles. The same few thoughts rotate around and around. All of them about Libra and monkeys and dead people. Ritalin and Vicadin help a little. Not enough. And you still have forty-seven hours left on this bus.

You try to pull it together. Have conversations with people who sit near you. But hardly anyone sits near you. It makes sense. You've seen your reflection this morning. You wouldn't sit next to a guy who looked like that.

A Zuni kid boards the bus in Gallup, New Mexico. He's nuts enough to sit with you. He tries to tell you about silver and turquoise jewelry. He's a jewelry maker. He's so cheerful and anxious to talk that it breaks your heart. You try to listen, but behind him, through the other window, a train goes by and you think about Native Americans and trains and your lost girlfriend. It takes everything inside you to keep from crying. The best you can do is stare off into space like a zombie. The Zuni kid gets sick of talking to your blank stare. You tell him, "It's those trains. They're killing us all."

The Zuni kid leaves the bus in Albuquerque, and no one sits by you again until south of Amarillo.

The only rest you get that first night is from Dallas to San Antonio. A huge woman sits next to you. She weighs an easy three hundred and twenty pounds. You're pinned between her bulk and the side of the bus. So helpless and stuck that you finally relax. Let yourself sleep.

Things feel a little better in the morning. You've washed your face and hands and armpits in a bus station sink. You've brushed your teeth and put on deodorant and changed your shirt. It helps. You're not so paranoid, not so shaken. Time is starting to heal things in the slightest little bit. You're still stuck on thoughts of Libra and everything she's going to miss in life. The words *she's dead* still explode in your mind periodically. But at least now it's not the only think you think about. You can even get out of your head enough to focus on a little drama unfolding on the bus.

A young father and his infant daughter are sitting two rows in front of you. They've made friends with a young mother and her toddler son. Most people on the bus probably assume they're a family. You know better. They're all getting along too well: telling stories and playing games and laughing on a Greyhound. Besides, you saw the mother board the bus in Austin, and the father had been riding the dog since Dallas. They make for good eavesdropping, so you eavesdrop. This is what you find out.

Her baby's daddy was never much of a factor. She was raising her son and doing well until she lost her job and unemployment ran out and now she's got to go back to Mobile, Alabama and stay with her mom for a while. He's just dropping his daughter off with his daughter's momma. His baby's momma gets custody for the summer. She lives in Panama City, Florida. He raises their daughter during the school year. The infant, of course, is not in school. This is just the arrangement they made because he'd gone to college and he seemed the more likely parent to prepare their daughter for that.

You're getting wrapped up in this drama. It helps you forget. You have a book on your lap, but you only pretend to read. You mostly listen to the stories of this happy, fleeting family.

Around Houston, they move seats so that the kids sit together and the parents sit together. The toddler son is surprisingly nurturing. He plays games with the infant. He holds her close while she sleeps.

The parents keep a close eye, but they keep talking.

By Lafayette, Lousiana, things are getting a little desperate for the happy, fleeting family. They'll only be together until Mobile. They're talking about how bad it sucks that they met like this and live so far apart. They don't use the word "star-crossed," but you kinda want to teach it to them.

In Baton Rouge, they make a strange move. They talk to you. They say, "Do you have any experience with children?"

This stuns you. You have no idea why they're talking to you about this. The best you can figure, it's because you're the only guy on the bus who's white and looks like he's been employed in the past six months. "Not really," you say. "I was one, once. That's about all the experience I got."

The parents ask you if perhaps you could watch their children for an hour or so at the next bus stop. It seems like a horrible parenting move on their part, but what the hell do you know about being a parent or even about making good moves? You agree to do it. Why not? You're a safe guy. You can take care of two kids.

In New Orleans, they put their plan into action. They take a cab to the nearest motel. You stay at the bus station with the kids. You hold the infant on your lap. She's mostly in and out of sleep. The mother left you some crayons and paper. You draw a picture for the toddler, and he colors it in. He's a quiet kid. Kinda lost. So focused on coloring in that picture that he makes you recognize yourself in him. You know what it's like to be the extra baggage your family has to carry around. You know what it's like to live through a childhood of third-wheel status. You know how to keep your mouth shut, stay out of the way, entertain yourself, acknowledge when you have no control over the situation and just wait it out.

You start to feel so bad for this kid, or maybe for the kid inside yourself, that you want to do something or say something to indicate to him that he'll be all right, that everything will be all right. Then you remember who you are and what your life has been up to this point, and you know you'd just be lying to the kid. So you do the next best thing. You buy a slice of banana cream pie from the lunch counter that's ten feet away from the table. It's tough negotiating your wallet and the pie with this sleeping little girl in your arm, but you manage. You give the kid the pie. He's stoked. So stoked it's a little depressing because you know this kid needs a whole lot more than a slice of pie.

Ah, fuck it, you think. It's better than nothing.

While the kid eats, you look at the little girl. So vulnerable and trusting and a little abandoned. You try to imagine that she's Libra. But no. It doesn't work. Not in a bus station. Not left alone by her mother. Not in hand-me-down clothes. Not poor. Not doomed out of the womb. Not Libra. Still, you look at this baby girl and think about Libra and you realize that someone's gonna be coming after you before too long. People can accept it when kids like these two are lost. People can accept it if *you* die before your time. But pretty, rich, white girls? They don't stay dead for long before everyone starts looking for someone to blame. You can't forget that.

In Mobile, the parents break off. The mother leaves the bus. She hangs out in the bus station until the bus is leaving again. As you pull out of the station, you see the father holding his daughter up to the window. The daughter is waving. The mother and son stand outside the bus, waving back, crying. You watch for a few seconds and go back to looking at your book and thinking, I can't believe she's fucking dead.

The father leaves the bus in Panama City. You still have another night and morning left on your trip. You do your best to sleep. The bus empties out in Tallahassee, and you can stretch across two seats. But you're a few inches over six feet tall and on the border of your thirtieth birthday. There's no real stretching out or deep sleeping for you on these little seats. You nod off until the cramps or nightmares wake you up, switch positions, nod off again, repeat.

You get off the bus in Titusville, Florida. It was the longest two days of your life. You walk out of the station and into the warm January sun. Ocean breezes aren't far off. It would seem like things would get better, but you're still Danny McGregor. You're still facing a horizon full of crazy broads and dead people.

7
Forget the Car, Remember the Spare Tire

Well, it's true I'd left things badly in Flagstaff. But now I was in Florida and that was my new problem. I hadn't been back to Florida in four years. Not since Sophie stabbed me. And, on the whole, I hadn't left things much better in Florida than I had in Flagstaff.

The only person from home I'd kept in touch with during my four years away was my brother Joe. I knew he wasn't around when the dog parked in Titusville, so I tried the next best thing: my sister Janie.

I dropped a quarter and a dime in a pay phone and dialed her number. She picked up on the third ring. I said, "Sister Janie, this is Brother Danny." Not that she was a nun and I was deacon or anything like that. I just got into the habit of calling her sister and myself brother because, if I didn't, Janie would always say, "Danny who?" And that kinda hurt my feelings.

"Knucklehead," Janie said, because that's what she always called me. "So you are alive."

"Alive and stranded at the Greyhound station in Titusville."

"And I suppose you want me to pick you up."

"If you don't mind."

Janie sighed and let the line fill up with silence until I fully understood how much this was putting her out. Finally, she said, "I'll be there in a couple of hours."

Which was Janie's way of fucking with me. I knew this. Janie's a big believer in justice or karma or whatever. If the universe didn't mete it out, she'd do it herself. We both knew good and goddamn well that there was no reason for her to take a couple of hours to drive the twenty-five minutes to the bus station. It was seven in the morning. Unless things had changed drastically since last I heard—which they hadn't—she still didn't have a job to go to or kids to take care of. How busy could she be? So I bluffed. I said, "No sweat. I can take a cab. Will you be around?"

"Forget it," she said. "I'm leaving right now."

Janie saw me before I saw her. I was leaning up against the wall of the Greyhound station, reading the last chapter of an old crime novel. She pulled up in her big-ass Land Rover. She rolled down the window and hollered, "Daaaammmn." Long and slow. And then: "Who ate my brother Danny?"

Because, yeah, I'd gained about twenty or twenty-five pounds in the past four years. It was all that free beer at The Corner Bar. Plus, we served hot dogs there. Beer and hot dogs. Libra called it my Babe Ruth diet. It worked exactly how you'd expect it to.

I picked up my backpack and climbed into the Land Rover. "Hey, Sister Janie," I said.

Janie pulled out of the Greyhound station. "What happened to your Galaxie?"

"I left it in Flagstaff."

"Funny." Janie patted me on my belly. "You forgot your car but you remembered the spare tire."

"Go on," I said. "Pick on the fat kid." Which was actually okay with me. I'd rather Janie pick on me than talk about the real shit that we probably should've been talking about.

Janie asked me how my car ended up in Flagstaff and I told her I'd been living there for a couple of years. Janie said, "Well, it was nice of you to come back for your brother Joe's big send off."

"I didn't know until it was too late," I said.

"So you did know?"

I nodded.

Like I said, I'd kept in touch with Brother Joe. He was kinda like a father to me. The long story short is this: my mother died two months after I was born. I don't know much about it. All Joe told me was that she died of some kind of "woman's cancer." My dad died when I was four. He'd always been a heavy drinker and big eater and he was sixty when I was born, so his heart attack wasn't really a surprise. Janie was sixteen at the time. Joe was nineteen. He was in Vietnam when Dad died. Janie and I were put in a foster home. Janie promptly left me and stayed with friends until she could get a job and apartment of her own. I stuck it out at the foster home until Joe got back and took custody of me. So Brother Joe was the closest thing to a parent that I had.

And Janie, well, she was always just a lesson learned the hard way.

Keeping up with the trend, Janie said, "Look, you can't stay with me."

"I didn't ask to," I said.

"You sent me two boxes of stuff... There better not be drugs in them."

"There aren't."

"Okay, so you send me two boxes. Are the boxes for me? I don't think so. I think they're for you. And you come off a Greyhound with nothing but a backpack. And I guaran-fucking-tee you're planning on staying in Cocoa Beach. So you'd need a place to stay, right?"

"Yeah."

"So I'm just telling you. You can't stay with me."

"Okay," I said.

"You can take a nap. And you can eat some food out of my refrigerator, if you don't eat all of it. But my husband gets home from work at five-thirty. And you'll be gone by then."

I nodded. I had my ultimatum. It was fair enough. It was pretty much what I'd expected out of Janie. It was actually about a nap and a snack more than I'd expected out of her. She must be softening in her old age, I thought.

The Land Rover rolled down US-1. The Indian River flanked us to the east. I rolled down the window and took a whiff of that hometown smell: swamps and salty air. And everything looked familiar. We turned east on State Road 528. From the top of the bridge as we crossed the Indian River, I could see the Vehicle Assembly Building. To my right was Merritt Island. We'd cross that and cross the Banana River and I'd see the launch pads of the Space Center from that bridge and I'd see Port Canaveral ahead of me and I'd feel like I was home. I rode along and waited until I was back on the barrier island that is Cocoa Beach. My home city.

When I was there and feeling comfortable enough, I said to Janie, "You're not still in touch with Sophie, are you?"

"Of course," Janie said. "I love Sophie."

"That's why I didn't call you for four years. 'Cause I knew you'd tell Sophie where I was."

"And why shouldn't I?"

"She stabbed me," I said. "You know that, don't you?"

Janie took her eyes off the road and glared at me. Her eyes always seemed so big to me. Chocolate brown, but they were like baking chocolate. Not sweet at all. Janie said, "I heard that rumor. I don't believe it. Sophie said it's not true."

I lifted my t-shirt up over my spare tire. "I got scars to prove it."

As if she didn't believe her eyes, Janie ran her fingers across the scars. At first, she seemed surprised. The smart-ass in her came back quickly, though, and she said, "Well, those ain't liposuction scars."

"Is Sophie still around?"

" 'Born to lose,' " Janie said. "I remember when that tattoo went straight across your belly. Now it's got a nice curve to it."

I pulled my shirt back down and asked again, "Is Sophie still around?"

Janie shrugged. Obviously, she wasn't gonna answer.

I said, "Please don't tell her I'm back."

"Of course I'm gonna tell her," Janie said. Because that's how she was. Fucking Janie.

8
The Fat Kid and the Phantom Ice Cream Truck

I guess my self-esteem wasn't low enough, because I decided to go surfing.

Janie had taken off, gone to an aerobics class or some shit. I'd had my nap and snack and it was still before noon. I felt like I had time. I checked Janie's garage and she still had my old Rainbow surfboard there, so I stole a pair of baggies from Janie's husband—who, luckily, was rocking a spare tire about the size of mine—and walked the seven blocks down to 3rd Street North.

Everyone out surfing was wearing a wetsuit, but I wasn't worried. I'd just rolled down the mountain from Flagstaff. My body was still used to snow and sub-freezing temperatures. Sixty-degree water wasn't gonna kill me. Besides, the waves were good. A solid chest high and pretty good form. I remembered enough about Cocoa Beach waves to remember that this wasn't all that common. It was almost like things were looking up for me.

I strapped my leash on my ankle and ran for the water and, just like a grommet on his first day out, I tripped over the leash and fell on the sand. Things got worse from there.

My board slid out from under me the first time a wave came my way. By the time I was back on the board, a new set was coming in and I got crushed by every wave of that set. My timing was off. I would try to duck under the wave and start too early and pop right into the undertow. Or I'd duck too late and get spun around by the whitewash. One wave after another. It was ugly.

It took ten minutes for me to finally get out to the line-up. By then, I was huffing and puffing like a fat kid chasing after an ice cream truck.

The worst thing about it was that I knew I used to be good at surfing. I did this shit every day in high school. I'd catch rides with friends down to Second Light, right by Patrick Air Force Base, and I'd hold my own with the best surfers in the area. High school girls would come out and watch us and dig it and say to me things like, "How'd you learn to do that three-sixty?" or "I saw you totally spray that kid," or "That was pretty gnarly." And I'd try to ride it for all it was worth. It was all I had at seventeen.

And now, here I was on the verge of thirty, hardly able to make the paddle out and so chubby that, when I sat on my shortboard, it was completely submerged.

That's okay, I told myself. It's sunny and the air is warm in January and there are waves and I'm out here now.

The line-up wasn't too crowded and before long, a wave came right for me. I timed it right, paddled right into it, and promptly nose-dived. This kinda set the tone for the next twenty minutes. I took off too late on the next wave and got dumped. I stood on the next wave, tried to cut up off the lip, and wiped out. I stepped on my leash when I stood on the next wave and slipped off my board. And so on.

Thirty minutes into my session, I was exhausted and a little frustrated. I felt like even the ocean was fucking with me. Which was ridiculous. The ocean didn't give a shit about me one way or another. It was what it was. I just needed to relax.

I took several deep breaths. I counted to ten. Out of principle,

I let a wave pass underneath me. When the next wave rolled in, I timed it right, caught it just ahead of the break, and stuck with the face of the wave. I was too heavy for my board. I felt like the wave was dragging me more than pushing me. Water lapped over the tail of the board, and I didn't have a whole lot of speed. But I was surfing. That was all that mattered. I rode the wave all the way in to shore.

As I walked out of the ocean, I noticed an older longboarder heading out for a session. He had short, spiky hair on the top of his head and long, curly locks in the back. He looked kinda like my brother Joe. So much so that I did a double-take. Of course he couldn't be Brother Joe, but just seeing this old longboarder made me feel good.

I walked across the sand and toward the boardwalk. A young, black girl was sitting there. She made me think of Rosalie White. And, of course, she couldn't be Rosalie, either, because this girl was only eleven or twelve years old and Rosalie was my age. But still, I liked it. I liked seeing ghosts of Joe and Rosalie and walking out of the ocean and feeling like I was back in that time when people were still alive and the future felt promising.

I climbed up the boardwalk. The girl said to me, "Where'd you get that little board?"

"It's mine."

The girl said, "Oh, I thought you stole it from your son or something. It's way too small for you."

This hurt. She could've have said she thought I stole it from my little brother or something. She didn't have to say my son. Because was I really old enough to have a son who rode a six-foot shortboard? It's one thing to call me fat. I can take that. But she could've left my age out of it. I said, "What's your name, little girl?"

"Taylor."

"Is that your first name or last name?" I asked, knowing that surely it was her first name and this question would probably piss her off. It did.

She said, "Fuck you. I'm not the fat guy trying to surf on a potato chip."

"No," I said. "You're the little asshole who's afraid to paddle out."

I thought I was just holding my own with this girl. She was the one who started it. Calling me fat and old. Right out of the blue. Right when I was finally feeling good. But I guess I was more than holding my own. I was being the bully, because as soon as I said what I said, little Taylor started crying. Just like that. In a flash. Tears coming out before she could stop them. She turned and ran down the boardwalk, away from me.

I should've felt bad for making that little girl cry. I should've felt like a bully. But I didn't. Not really. Later, I would. In a few months, this would become one of those moments that I really wish I could relive, that I could go back and fix. At the time, though, it didn't really bother me at all. Instead, the whole scene made me think of Sophie: the way a girl could hit me right on my sorest nerve and run away crying like it was all my fault. That was Sophie's trademark.

And at that moment when I should've been chasing down a little girl to apologize, or at least thinking about Sister Janie's five-thirty ultimatum, I sat on the handrail of the 3rd Street boardwalk. Looking out at the ocean. Wondering where Sophie was and whether or not I could get in touch with her.

9
Hurricane Sophie

I thought I had it made in Kill Devil Hills until that hurricane blew in and brought Sophie with it. This was back in '92. This was how Sophie and I met. She rode in on a storm.

Before the hurricane had really hit, six of us headed for Jennifer's place to ride it out. The night still looked like a typical summer thunderstorm, with palm trees bending nearly in half and sea oats pushed flat to the dunes and street signs flapping back and forth as if the signposts were stuck between huge, nervous fingers. The real destruction would come later. Later, porches would tumble down the street and roofs would get ripped off of houses and streets would flood. In the meantime, it was the rain and the wind and six drunk kids in my Galaxie, me drinking a beer as I steered toward Jennifer's.

I'd only known Rick before the storm came in. Rick was from Cocoa Beach. He'd moved up to the Outer Banks of North Carolina the year earlier. When iron working got to be too much for me down in Cocoa Beach, Rick helped me move to Kill Devil Hills. He helped me get a job as a bar back, too. The other four drunks, I'd just met them. The two girls and guy in the back seat were friends of Rick's. Two of them, Marigold and Christian, nuzzled against each other like lovers. Marigold wore a hemp necklace and Birkenstocks and argyle socks. She had a tattooed flower on her shoulder. Christian had white boy dreadlocks and a face that was, to be honest, kinda pretty. Like he should've dressed in drag or something. Together, they looked like some Woodstock fantasy. Marigold wore a ring on her left ring finger. Christian didn't. I took that to mean they were engaged.

The other woman in the back was Sophie. She stared out the fogged up window as if we were on a sunny Sunday drive, not on the edge of a hurricane. She was decidedly not-hippie, so I liked her all the more.

A drunk chick named Jennifer sat in the front seat, between Rick and me. She'd been sitting at the bar all night. I'd fed her drinks for free, and now at the end of the night, she'd volunteered to shelter us all until the hurricane passed. She told me to turn right the next time I could. I pulled the Galaxie into Jennifer's front yard.

Jennifer ran through the stinging rain first. She fought the pounding wooden screen door until she got the big front door unlocked. The other five of us ran from the Galaxie into Jennifer's beach shack. We all got soaked on the run. The place was dry inside.

Jennifer lit a bunch of candles and set them up on the hardwood floor. I went into the kitchen with one of the candles. The electricity was already out. I found a cooler and filled it with beers I'd stolen from work and dumped all the ice from the freezer into the cooler. By the time I got back, everyone was sitting in a circle on the floor. Obviously, a decision had been made.

Sophie looked up at me with big brown eyes and said, "Strip poker, Danny." Her voice dripped like watermelon. I started to slip. Sophie shuffled the blue Bicycle cards one last time, then dealt them. I tried my best to turn away from her and remember that I'd spent all night trying to seduce Jennifer.

Jennifer went into her room after the first hand. She came back out after the second hand with a boom box. Rather than try to tune in news about the storm, she played a Willie Nelson cassette. Rick and Marigold complained. Sophie said she liked Willie, but she'd rather listen to the storm. I agreed. Christian said, "Willie Nelson is the perfect rainy day music."

Jennifer gave Christian a drunken smile. Marigold shot Jennifer a dirty look. Jennifer flipped her peroxided hair off her shoulders. Marigold turned her glare to Christian. He didn't seem to notice. The game went on.

We listened to Willie and the screen door banged itself into splinters and hurricane shrapnel pelted the house. We played slow games of draw poker. No bets. Just the one with the worst hand shedding one article of clothing. Rick was the first big loser. The poor kid was naked while most of us still had on shoes or at least socks. To make matters worse, when he dropped his briefs, he had a hard-on and a weird curve to his dick. Sophie said, "Jesus, Rick, you could stand at the toilet and piss in the sink with that thing." Jennifer nicknamed him "Boomerang." Rick lay on his belly until the hard-on went away.

It took a while for the next one of us to get naked because, for some reason, Rick kept losing. Finally, we made the rule that if Rick lost the hand, the person with the next worse hand had to lose some clothes. This led to Jennifer's nudity. She hadn't been wearing a bra and had lost her panties a few hands earlier. She took off her shirt and sat on her knees. Her posture was perfect, probably because she was a little chubby and her belly looked flatter if she sat straight up. I liked the chubbiness, though. It made her full and round and that much prettier. Rick made a crack about her not being a real blond. She said, "I'd throw you out for that, Boomerang, but you'd just come back."

The card game went on. Sophie lost her clothes, but seemed

glad to be rid of the wet rags. She was a lean girl. Not thin like she had an eating disorder or fit like an athlete. Just young and lean. She seemed real comfortable being nude, too, sitting like we were in an art class and she were the model. Or at least it's what I imagined it would've been if I'd ever taken an art class.

The Willie Nelson cassette ended. Jennifer stumbled drunk—but sexy anyway because she was naked—back to her room. We played another hand that left Marigold without her summer dress, but with a bra. I got up and went to the bathroom. When I got back, Christian was gone. We played another hand. I lost my boxers. We played another hand. Marigold lost her bra. Neither Jennifer nor Christian came back to the game. The screen door kept slamming. The windows rattled. Drafts of wind crept through the house, making the candlelight dance. Sophie gathered the cards to deal another hand. Marigold stared down the dark hallway toward Jennifer's bedroom. Sophie finished dealing. We all picked up our cards. Marigold stopped looking at the dark hallway long enough to look at her cards. We were all naked at this point. I didn't know what the stakes were. Marigold slammed her cards against the dirty hardwood floor and said exactly what I'd been thinking for the past ten minutes. She said, "Goddamn it! They're fucking in that back room, aren't they?"

No one said a word and that said it all. "Goddamn it," Marigold said again. "That goddamn little whore. I'm gonna kick that little whore's ass!"

Sophie, very calm with a hurricane and Marigold raging around her, touched Marigold's arm. "Come on," Sophie said. She led Marigold away from the dark hallway and toward the kitchen. I could barely hear what they talked about.

I was pretty pissed, too, because I'd spent all night at work trying to hook up with Jennifer. And I could've come back here without Rick and his friends and had Jennifer to myself. But no, I had to let everyone tag along. And look where it got me. But as I thought that, I looked to see where it got me, and realized that it got me into a room where I may have lost one girl, but there were still two naked ones hanging around. So I did some figuring.

Marigold was a lost cause. I wouldn't have gone after her even if she weren't. There was something crazy about her. Her wild, curly hair or those big biceps. I don't know. I was only twenty-two at the time, but I'd had my share of crazy broads and wanted someone who was calm and together, just like Sophie seemed. And I'd been digging Sophie all night, her whiskey brown eyes and the way her slender fingers dealt the cards. I also realized that Rick was lying on the floor right by me, and he probably had his eye on Sophie, too. So I said to him, "Dude, what's up with you and Marigold?"

"What are you talking about?"

"Don't tell me you haven't noticed the way she's been looking at you."

"No way," Rick said. "Marigold's Christian's girl. They're getting married."

Of course, Christian was back in Jennifer's bedroom, fucking her. It wasn't a long shot to bet that the wedding was off. But I didn't point out the obvious. I said, "Is that why she kept playing cards while Christian was back there fucking Jennifer? Is that why Marigold didn't lose her temper until *after* she was naked?" I gave Rick enough time to think about this, but not enough time to answer. "This is all an act," I said. "It's all for you, Rick. Step up to the plate and take a swing."

Rick looked like he was trying to think it over but like thoughts were hard to come by this late and after this much drinking. He finished his beer, grabbed a new one from the cooler, took a long pull off it, and staggered into the kitchen on two sleeping legs.

He leaned against an ancient gas stove and paused. I worried he'd lose his nerve, but he didn't. He said something to Sophie and

Marigold. I watched the three of them chat in the kitchen: a normal sight made bizarre with the nudity and candlelight and hurricane. I closed my eyes and listened to the storm, the whispers, the vague traces of sex in Jennifer's room.

When I opened my eyes, Sophie was standing above me. She had a fat, orange candle in one hand and Jennifer's cassette player in the other. "Let's clear out, Danny," she said. I stood and followed her into a bedroom. She shut the door and locked it behind her. I could barely see around the room. Clothes were scattered in lumps and piled on the bed. The candlelight flickered. I looked around three times to make sure, then said, "There are no windows in here, are there?"

Sophie said, "There's no closets, either. It's probably supposed to be, like, a dining room or something." She handed me the candle. "Maybe you could pick out some music?" She walked away from me and sat Indian style on the middle of the bed. I held the candle up to the cassette racks. The cassettes were arranged alphabetically. I didn't recognize most of the bands. When I saw the double whammy of New Edition and New Kids on the Block, I gave up my search. I couldn't imagine liking anything in those racks.

I walked over to the night stand and set the candle down. "I have a better idea," I said. "Let's listen to the storm."

Sophie blew out the candle. We lay beside each other on the bed. Destruction surrounded us, muffled through the walls, pounding on the roof. "Are you tired, Danny?"

"No."

"Promise you won't fall asleep on me?"

"Yes."

"Then try this," Sophie said. "Listen real closely. Don't pay attention to the air on your skin or the beer aftertaste in your mouth or Jennifer's roommate's smelly clothes or anything you can see. Just listen." She stopped talking and took four deep breaths. "What do you hear?"

"You breathing. Me breathing. The mattress creaking."

"Exactly," Sophie said. "First, you hear what's closest to you. Keep listening. What do you hear next?"

Sophie stopped talking. I listened for about thirty seconds. I said, "Rain on the roof. Bare feet on the hardwood floor. Angry knocking. Marigold must be going after Christian."

"Don't worry about them. Stay with me. Listen. Tell me what you hear. Only what you hear."

"Glass bottles falling... yelling... wind through hollow places... trees breaking up."

"Exactly. Did you notice that you always move from what's right in front of you to what's far away? From your head to the world outside as far as you can hear? It's weird, isn't it?"

I nodded. I realized Sophie's eyes were probably closed, just like mine, so I said, "It is weird."

"Now come back," Sophie said. I listened to the screen door crashing. Voices. Jennifer and Marigold yelling. The lid of the cooler slamming. "Come closer," Sophie said. She exhaled through her nose. My heel scraped the blankets. The bed stand groaned. "Come closer." To the white noise inside my head. Muscles in my neck straining. Blood flowing. I opened my eyes but still listened. Sophie only breathed.

"Open your mouth," she said. I don't know if she hypnotized me or put me under a spell or what. Whatever it was, I was ready to do whatever Sophie said. I opened my mouth. "Stick out your tongue." I stuck out my tongue. She placed a tiny scrap of paper on it. It tingled. I braced myself for the trip. What followed flowed naturally, like big wave riding on a longboard: all grace and power.

We groped for matches and lit the candle and watched the flame. We chatted for a bit about nothing. Sophie nuzzled close to me. Her nipple grazed my bicep. I immediately got an erection. Sophie reached down and grabbed it. "Look what we have here," she said, straddling me. I reached between her legs. She was already wet and ready. I slid right in.

Afterwards, Sophie found a Replacements cassette and we listened to the whole album. Sophie sang along. I watched her mouth and listened to the guitar. The album ended. We listened for the storm, but it was gone. The others in the house had long since passed out.

Sophie and I walked out into the breaking morning, the sun shining through the eye of the hurricane. No birds flew around. The fronds that still hung off palm trees hung loosely. Jennifer's yard was covered in torn shingles and shutters and a Big Wheel that would never ride again. Not even a light breeze blew. The air was wet hot like a jungle. Sophie and I started toward the beach.

The streets were deserted. Fences had been ripped apart. We passed a house without a roof. A broom handle was stuck in a palm tree, half in and half out like those gag arrows we used to wear on our heads as kids. We walked through the wreckage of the day. Everything sunny and wet and ominous. The storm was only half done.

We walked all the way down to the beach, where we caught the first glimpse of the second half of the storm. Rain clouds stampeded from the east, fast and angry and climbing over themselves. The ocean frothed white and rabid. We started back for the shack. The rain pelted us from the side, as if it were being shot out of a low flying fighter jet. A baby doll flew past Sophie's head.

The house was only a hundred yards away. I could've sprinted to it in seconds. But not without Sophie. Sophie walked. A palm frond nailed me in the back at fifty miles an hour. It left a welt. I grabbed her hand and made her run with me. Sophie ran.

10
Knucklehead Chronicles

ITINERARY FOR FINDING A PAD IN COCOA BEACH

1:30 P.M. Stop daydreaming about Sophie. Either it won't happen or it'll be a bad idea if it does.

1:31 P.M. Walk back to Janie's house. You'll see Taylor on the way home. She'll flip you a bird. Wave back.

1:43 P.M. Get to Janie's. Nod when Janie says, "I'm fucking serious, Knucklehead. You have to be out of here by 5:30."

1:44 P.M. Nod again when Janie says, "Are those my husband's baggies you're wearing?" Stop nodding when she adds, "You little shit."

1:45 P.M. Take a shower. Notice the granite walls of the shower. Wonder when your sister got so rich. Tell yourself, "I didn't want to stay in this bourgeois pad, anyway."

2:01 P.M. Leave Janie's house. You will have a few ideas as to where to go, but none of those ideas are good ones. Just start walking.

2:12 P.M. Get to Woodland Avenue. Pay attention to everything you've come to associate with Woodland: weedy lawns, concrete apartments built in the sixties with names that celebrate the ocean or the Space Center north of town, scattered duplexes in the shadows of these apartment buildings, junk cars in carports or on the weedy lawns, rusty beach cruisers locked to skinny palm trees, a big kite surfing kite stretched across a live oak, yellowed surfboards behind the screens of front porches, stained mattresses by the dumpsters, the detritus of blue collar lives in trash bins as people upgrade or downgrade from one block apartment to the next depending on the winds of the local economy. Everything about this neighborhood screams out Danny McGregor. It's your old neighborhood. A wave of optimism will build on the horizon. You'll paddle for it, but you won't catch it.

2:13 P.M. Begin an hour of up and down Woodland Ave. Notice that there's a new library at one end of Woodland. Remember when there used to be a movie theater there. A draft house. The place that would sell you beer when you were only fifteen years old. The place where you could go see stoner movies after midnight and make out with Rosalie while everyone else slept through the last hour of *Tommy* or *The Wall*.

2:59 P.M. Knock on the front door of a duplex. Your friend Rick used to live here. When an elderly woman answers, understand that Rick no longer lives here.

3:13 P.M. Knock on the last front door that used to belong to a friend. Find a third stranger opening the door. Decide to give up.

3:21 P.M. Pull up a stool at Sullivan's Tavern. Order a screwdriver. You may not feel like drinking, but the bartender will actually squeeze fresh orange juice into your drink. That alone will make you feel better.

3:22 P.M. Think about your brother Joe. He was a regular at Sullivan's. Raise your drink to Joe. Ignore the strange look from the bartender.

3:27 P.M. Stop thinking about Brother Joe. Notice that there's an arcade basketball game behind you. Don't turn to look at it. Just listen. Someone will be playing the game. Listen to ball after ball sink into the net. Hear the computerized voice repeating, "Three, three, three," for ten seconds. Realize that the guy playing just won a free game. Listen to his next game. A minute of balls dropping into a hoop. Remember your old buddy Bart Ceravolo, the hometown basketball star. Remember when Bart had been the next white hope, playing Division I college hoops at the University of Tennessee, only six foot tall and slow, but with a killer outside shot and enough three pointers to make the all-SEC team two years running. Wonder what's become of Bart. Wonder if he's still drunk and broke and homeless like he was when you left Cocoa Beach. Wonder whose couch he's sleeping on tonight.

3:29 P.M. After listening to two more games of arcade basketball, ask yourself how many basketball stars Cocoa Beach has produced. How many of those basketball stars became drunks? How many of them would be in Sully's at 3:29 in the afternoon, playing an arcade basketball game and winning so many free games that he can play all day on three quarters? Decide to turn around.

3:30 P.M. See that it is Bart playing the arcade basketball game.

3:31 P.M. When the next game ends, stand behind Bart and say, "Look at you. A man your age. Drunk every day by noon. Why don't you get a job?" Hope he gets the *Barfly* reference you're making.

Bart will say to you, "I got a job: killing the cockroaches in that place of yours." Understand that Bart did get the reference, but wonder for just a second if you and Bart are still friends. He'll turn from the basketball game with a serious look on his face. He'll ask you, "What's up, Danny? Are we cool or what?"

Remember that things were left shaky with Bart. There'd been a lot of backstabbing and sleeping with the wrong people. You were implicated. So was Bart. So was Sophie. And, of course, Helen. But that was four years ago. Too much shit has gone down since then. You can't worry about all that. Give Bart a smile. But not a fake smile with all your teeth showing. A genuine one. The kind that starts on the left side of your face and stops halfway to a grin. The kind of smile that says, "Are you fucking kidding me?" Let the smile do your talking.

Recognize the look in Bart's face. He's either gonna be macho and punch you in the arm or he's gonna be open and hug you. You'll root for the punch. Bart will opt for the hug. Don't be surprised. Or be surprised, but don't let it show.

3:32 P.M. Withstand a barrage of questions, like, "What are you doing back?" and "Where have you been?" and "Have you talked to her?" and "Have you heard from him?" and "Did you know this or that?" The questions will come at you fast. Don't worry if you don't answer them. Hold tight until Bart asks you, "Where are you staying?"

Tell him, "Nowhere, yet. I was thinking about getting a hotel room tonight."

Bart will recognize that you're bluffing. He'll recognize that you're too proud to point out to Bart that he slept on your couch for an entire summer, rent free. He'll appreciate that you don't bring up the jobs you hooked him up with and the several hundred dollars you loaned him five years ago, both of you knowing that neither of you expected it to be paid back. Bart will not need to be reminded of this. You'll know that, if Bart has room, he'll take you in. Bart will say, "Don't be crazy. Stay at my place."

3:35 P.M. After Bart plays his last two free games, clear out of Sullivan's. On the one-block walk to Bart's, gather three important bits of information: 1.) Bart had been living with a girlfriend. They had a two bedroom apartment. She left him three months ago. Rent was cheap enough that he didn't move out. The second bedroom is yours, if you want it. 2.) Bart works for Space Coast Medical Services, a medical transport company. Part of his job requires him to drive mentally challenged adults to and from a care facility. He's on break right now. He'll leave soon to drive them home. 3.) At nights, Bart picks up dead bodies. This is the other half of his job at Space Coast. He gets a pager and he's on call from 10 P.M. to 6 A.M. If someone finds a dead body outside of the hospital during that time, Bart picks it up and brings it to the Medical Examiner. He gets paid eight bucks an hour the whole time he's on call, whether he picks up a dead body or not.

3:40 P.M. Be sure to get an apartment key from Bart before he changes his mind.

3:41 P.M. Bart will sing a line from a Dead Milkmen song: "Boring day, got nothing to do? Get a load of retards, take 'em to the zoo." Then he'll convince you to go with him on his short bus route.

3:42 P.M. Ride to Janie's house with that Dead Milkmen song stuck in your head. Sing with Bart, "Wooo-oooo-ooo, take 'em to the zoo. Wooo-oooo-ooo, take 'em to the zoo."

3:53 P.M. Pile all your earthly possessions into the front seat of the bus. You will have with you your backpack, your old Rainbow surfboard, one box of records, and one box of books. For a fleeting moment, you'll feel like things might work out after all.

3:54 P.M. Slowly realize that you're riding around in a short bus with one of the problems you fled Cocoa Beach to escape.

II
Adventures on the Short Bus

So there was Bart cruising along in his short bus, singing "Takin' the Retards to the Zoo." All my worldly possessions rode in the seat directly behind him, and I rode in the other front seat. Bart stopped singing and pointed to a shoebox full of CDs that was under his seat. He said, "Dig through that box there. I'm pretty sure I've got *Big Lizard in My Backyard* in there."

Big Lizard in My Backyard is the album with "Takin' the Retards to the Zoo" on it.

"You have that album in the bus?" I asked, though I didn't need to, because there it was, right in Bart's shoebox.

"Of course," Bart said. "The clients love that song."

"Who are the clients?"

"My short bus riders."

"The mentally, uh…" and I couldn't think of what to say, what the proper term was now. If they were mentally retarded or mentally challenged or whatever. Bart solved it for me.

He said, "The retards, yeah."

"You don't call them retards, do you?"

"No," Bart said. "I call them short bus riders." He reached into the pocket of his white and blue striped work shirt. He pulled out a packet of cigarettes. In all the years I'd known Bart, I'd never known him to smoke a cigarette. I was pretty sure he hadn't started. And, sure enough, he opened the pack and pulled out a joint. "Wanna smoke out?"

"No," I said. "I'm good."

"Not me," Bart said. "I got a little buzz on. I shouldn't have had that fourth beer at Sully's." He lit the joint and inhaled. I handed him the CD. He slid it in the stereo and let it start from the beginning.

I knew this CD well. I knew where we were and what our route was and it didn't take much math to know that the short bus riders would be riding when the "Takin' the Retards to the Zoo" came on. I said, "What do the short bus riders think of that song you were just singing?"

"They love it. They sing along to all the wooooo-ooooohs. It's fun."

"They don't get offended."

"Hell, no," Bart said. "They're fucking retarded."

I let the subject drop. Bart smoked his joint. A cloud of silence floated around the short bus. It had nothing to do with what to call Bart's clients. It had nothing to do with Bart's drinking or the joint. It had everything to do with the last time Bart and I had hung out: the night when Sophie stabbed me. And really, it had everything to do with the year leading up to the night when Sophie stabbed me. Because there was that shit that would always be between Bart and me. That shit that comes from friends dating the same girl. And here was the crux of the problem:

I was dating Sophie and getting sick of her. Bart was heavily lusting after Helen. Helen didn't dig Bart. She did dig me. Sophie and I broke up. I started dating Helen. Bart started dating Sophie. It all seems logical and clean, but there's nothing logical and clean in the affairs of the human heart. And here was our problem. From Bart's perspective, I should've stayed away from Helen. I knew he was infatuated with her. From my perspective, though, I knew that he didn't have a chance in hell of dating her. Besides, he didn't even ask her out. I mean, Jesus, you have to shoot if you want to hit something, right? Not for Bart. He just sat at her bar and drooled over her and got nowhere. So when I saw my chance, I took it. I don't see that as a betrayal. Bart does. This led to the Sophie situation.

See, maybe I was broken up with Sophie and dating Helen. Still, there was a lot of history between Sophie and me. A lot. Years of a relationship, different towns, breakups and reconciliations, brutal fights, bruised hearts, everything. And the way I see it, Bart shouldn't have jumped on that shit the minute we broke up. He should've given it more time. Or, in fact, he shouldn't have done it at all. Friends don't date their friend's ex-girlfriends. Not if they want to stay friends. So there was that, too.

Anyway, it was all years ago and probably a moot point. I figured it was best to just bring it up and clear the air. I said, "So what's up with Sophie? Is she the chick who just moved out on you?"

"God, no," Bart said. "Sophie and I broke up right after she stabbed you. When Joe told me what she'd done to you, I made a rule for myself: don't date any chicks who stab their ex-boyfriends."

"Good rule," I said.

"Fucking-A."

"So where is she now?"

"She moved to Atlanta. She lives with her mom up there. I heard she cleaned up her act. She's sober, working a nine-to-five, the works. At least that's what I hear."

Bart sounded like he didn't believe what he was saying, so I asked, "Do you believe it?"

"Hell, no. That bipolar girl? It doesn't matter what way she swings. It's just a matter of time before she swings back."

"Fair enough," I said. "What about Helen? What's up with

her?"

"She got married," Bart said. Just matter of fact like that. *She got married.* I winced. That phrase made me feel like someone was making a lasso out of my small intestine. I don't know why. I don't know what my intentions with Helen were. But, married? That's so fucking permanent. Or long-term, anyway.

"Shit," I said. "That sucks."

"She's divorced now," he added. He kinda smiled. I knew the score, here. He wanted to make me wince. He paused on purpose.

Still, I didn't feel relieved to hear that she was divorced, because the next thought crept into my head. "She didn't marry you, did she? She's not the girl who just moved out on you?"

"Nah," Bart said. "She married some fag."

This meant nothing to me, because of course Bart wouldn't like anyone who married Helen. And it's his own damn fault. You can't go around getting mad at other people just because they have the balls to ask out girls you wish you had the balls to ask out.

Anyway, it didn't matter. The air was clear, now. Clear enough.

We pulled up to the care center where Bart's clients spent their days. Bart stopped the bus, opened the door, and said to me, "Come on out. You gotta meet this crew."

I climbed down from the bus.

About a dozen mentally challenged adults were standing around in the front yard of the care center. Bart called out, "Huddle up, team." His clients gathered around him. Bart put his hands on the shoulders of the two who were closest to him. "I'm gonna introduce you to someone. His name is Danny. He's my oldest and closest friend. He's riding with us today. I want you to welcome him onto the short bus and show him love. Okay?"

The clients answered with smiles and head nods and descended on me. They circled around and patted me on the back and stroked my face and two or three of them hugged me at once. They looked up at me with big, mad grins and *hi, Dannys* and one poor woman was even drooling a little. I suddenly felt like I'd been picked for the Special Olympics. It was a great feeling. Better than you'd imagine.

Bart said, "All right. That's enough. Line up."

The short bus riders formed a single file line outside the door. An older white guy took the front of the line. Bart said to him, "I need a hoot, Little Johnny. No one rides until Little Johnny gives me a hoot."

I guess Little Johnny knew what Bart was talking about, because he waved his hands over his head and yelled, "Woo-hoo!"

It was pretty loud and sounded good to me, but it wasn't enough for Bart. He said, "C'mon, Little Johnny. That's bullshit. I want a hoot."

Little Johnny took a huge breath and arched his back and stuck his chest out and bellowed, "Wooooooo-hooooooo!" And, just in case that wasn't enough, the rest of the short bus riders bellowed with him.

I started laughing. Bart said, "That's what I'm fucking talking about. Now get on the bus, you crazy sons of bitches. Load up."

The short bus riders filed in, and we drove off.

About five minutes into the ride, just as I'd predicted, "Takin' the Retards to the Zoo" came on. Just as Bart predicted, the clients sang along to all the "woooo-ooooohs." You have to give the guy credit. He had fun with this crew. They loved him.

When the song was over, Little Johnny said, "Mr. Bart, isn't that a bad word that they use in the song?"

"What the fuck are you talking about, Little Johnny?" Bart asked.

"That word in the song. Ain't it a bad word?"

"Which one?"

"I can't say. It's a bad word."

"Don't be a pussy," Bart said. "Just fucking say it. We're all adults here."

"Retard," Little Johnny said. "Mrs. Munroe told us that was a bad thing to call a person a retard."

"Now, that depends, Little Johnny," Bart said. "Retard has two meanings. On the one hand, you can make fun of people and call them a retard and that's a bad word. On the other hand, retard can just mean a person you take to the zoo. So in this song, it's not a bad word because it's just talking about people you take to the zoo. Understand?"

Little Johnny nodded.

"Now give me a hoot," Bart said.

Little Johnny cocked his head back and hooted. Bart smiled. I remembered this about my old, close friend Bart Ceravolo: don't ever trust the guy.

After we dropped off the short bus riders and Bart smoked another joint and I put in an old Clash CD, *Give 'em Enough Rope*, Bart said to me, "So what are you running from, Danny?"

"Weed making you paranoid?" I asked.

"Just a little inductive reasoning, my friend. Everything you own fits in a seat on a bus—and the surfboard you got from your sister's house this morning. You took a Greyhound from Flagstaff. A fucking Greyhound. No one rides a Greyhound if they don't have to. You're still the same guy I always knew. So add it up. You got into some shit in Flagstaff and you're running away."

Of course, Bart was right, but I wasn't surprised enough to not be suspicious. I said, "How'd you know I was in Flagstaff? I didn't tell you that."

"I saw Janie this morning," Bart said.

"Where?"

"It's Tuesday. Janie and I fuck on Tuesday mornings."

Bart paused. I knew he was full of shit. I hadn't been away so long that I forgot about his sense of humor. I said, "Where'd you really see her?"

"At the Circle K, but that's not the point. What happened in Flagstaff? What are you running from?"

What I was running from had obviously been on my mind nonstop for days now. Not a minute passed when I didn't think about Libra or see that fucked up leg and that bad tattoo in my mind. Not one minute. I had to tell someone sooner or later, so I just came clean. I said, "I found my ex-girlfriend's dead body a couple of days ago. I freaked out and came here."

Bart jammed on the brakes and swerved into the nearest parking lot. He turned off the engine, took the keys out of the ignition, and spun in his seat to face me. "Wow," he said. "I was expecting something fucked up, but, wow."

"It's not as bad as it sounds," I said.

"Well, it can't be good."

"No, it's not good," I said, "but it's not as bad as it seems." I laid out the story for Bart, from my New Year's Eve fight to my decision to breakup with Libra to the final fight and the tattoo and the leg on the railroad tracks. Bart just stared at me with big, bloodshot eyes. Occasionally, he'd nod or say, "yeah, yeah." But mostly he just stared.

When I got done, Bart said, "How rich was this girl?"

"Well, she wasn't rich. Her parents were."

"Obviously, but how rich were her parents?"

"Rich."

"How rich?"

"Her dad owned banks."

"What do you mean, he owned banks?"

"I mean he owned a bunch of banks in Phoenix. I don't remember how many. Ten. Maybe a dozen. A bunch."

Bart rubbed his short, curly hair. "I don't get it. How do you own a fucking bank?"

"You just own it," I said. "Someone has to own it."

"I thought corporations owned banks."

"I think they do, now. They own Libra's dad's banks, anyway. He sold the whole lot of them to Bank of America a few years back."

"Goddamn," Bart said. "How much do you get for a fucking bank? Wow. You're fucked, Danny."

"How do you figure?"

"This guy's got ten or twelve banks' worth of money and his daughter's dead and you're the last one who saw her? You're going to jail."

Of course, this exact thought had occurred to me. I didn't want to spend too much time thinking about it. I used my typical excuse. "She got hit by a train. I wasn't driving the train. How are you gonna blame me?"

Bart counted the reasons off on his fingers. "You're poor. You're the ex-boyfriend. You skipped town. It doesn't matter what the police find. You're going to jail."

I shook my head. "Nah," I said. Because I'd thought about it. They'd have to do forensic tests. They'd have to realize that she was already lying down when she got hit. You can figure that out from the angles of the wounds and all. Plus, they'd have no real evidence. Not enough to build a case on. There'd be no way they could prove I did it. So I made my case to Bart.

Bart kept staring at me with those bloodshot eyes. "They won't get you for murder. That's true. They don't have much of a case. And, anyway, you did the right thing running away. They won't be able to drag your ass all the way back to Arizona for questioning. But someone will come after you. A bounty hunter. A P.I. Someone. And if they do get you to Arizona, they'll bust you for something."

I tried to argue this point, but what was the use. Besides, before I could say much, Bart had cranked up the bus and was driving again. He mumbled to the windshield, "I wonder if there's a reward."

And I knew I shouldn't have said anything.

12
The Whitest Girl in Florida

You're back in the Vehicle Assembly Building, indoors but three hundred feet off the ground. The air up here is dead and thick. You can't stop sweating. You're laying down the final weld on the handrail that surrounds this platform. Even though you're kneeling on a platform rather than standing on the typical narrow I-beam, even though this handrail is all around and you know it will stay in place because you built it, the height scares the hell out of you. You try to ignore the fear. You push everything out of your mind except the flame at the end of your torch and you finish the weld.

While the metal is still glowing hot, you turn down your flame, stand, and lift your mask. The sight beside you on this platform startles you. It's Libra. She's wearing a shear little sundress. She's dry but everything else about her looks fresh out of the shower: no make-up, her auburn hair tucked behind her ears, her freckles sparkling under the fluorescent work lights. This is the Libra you know best. No airs. Nothing done to prepare her for public. Just Libra. You're not sure why she's on this platform with you, three hundred feet off the ground, but you figure it's just as likely as any other scenario in your life right now. You say to her, "Hey, kid. What brings you here?"

"I wanted to show you my new shoes," she says. She lifts her leg so you can see her sandals. The straps are leather and every part of the shoe that touches Libra's skin is made out of a fluffy wool. They actually look pretty comfortable.

"Very nice," you say.

"I got them for Florida. To celebrate us coming here. Aren't they fun?"

You've never understood how a shoe can be fun. You've never understood why Libra would get so happy just from purchasing an item at a store. It's never had an appeal to you. Still, you recognize the joy in her eyes and you nod. "Fun."

"Do you like the colors on my dress?"

"I do," you say. And you're not just humoring her. Her dress is yellow with little pink and orange flowers on it. Very girly, but the colors are somehow comforting. The dress drapes her torso, soft and free, barely hiding everything that you've come to memorize underneath.

"I'm thinking of painting our house these colors. The insides. Add a little life to those white walls. What do you think?"

"I could do without the pink."

Libra gives you a coy smile. "No pink? I love pink! Maybe we could just do the bathroom in pink. Or, you know what? I'll paint my closet pink." She raises her eyebrows and gives you a look like she's just discovered radium.

You find it charming. You don't know if you've ever had this optimism, if you've ever fallen into a smile this easily. It's fun to live vicariously through Libra's joy.

Libra looks down at her leg. A little cartoon birthmark seems to be growing on her ankle. She says, "I think I'm the whitest girl in Florida, but I don't want to get a tan. Tans give you wrinkles."

"You're a beautiful girl," you tell her. You reach out for her hand but forget you're still holding the torch. The flame slices through her wrist. Her hand drops on the sheet metal platform. A hollow echo rings through the VAB. You know welding torches don't cut through skin like this, but you've seen what you've seen. How else can you make sense of it? You reach out to tell her you're sorry, but the torch is still in your hand. It slices through her leg, just below the hip. Her leg starts to fall. You move to wrap her in your arms. The torch won't stop cutting. It strips her skin from her chest. Libra's coming to pieces in front of your eyes. The platform below you starts to give and fall. Libra quick reaches for her head and pulls it off her shoulders. You and all the pieces of Libra tumble into the hole. You fly around, chasing the leg and the hand, trying to weld the skin back together, stretching it over the moist and sticky muscle beneath. The ground races up toward you. Libra's head remains in its place three hundred feet in the air. You try to swim up there, but gravity works the same for everyone. It drags you down. You start to fall for real and do everything you can to save yourself.

Just when vertigo is about to take over, you land in your bed on Woodland Avenue. Your sheets are covered in sweat. The green light of the smoke alarm stares down at you. All the pieces of Libra have been replaced by empty air.

13

The Face that Launched a Dozen Greyhounds

Bart took me to Duke's. That was the last big thing that happened on my first week back.

He had insisted on taking me on a bar tour of Cocoa Beach. Hitting all the old joints. Re-acclimating me with my hometown. Mostly, I think he wanted to go out drinking and was happy to have a partner in crime. We ran through a series of sports bars and dive bars and crusty beach joints full of local barnacles stuck to the barstools and we ended up at a Duke's down around 22nd Street. The joint was actually called Duke Kahanamoku's—after the surfing legend—but the locals couldn't be bothered trying to learn all the syllables in Kahanamoku's. So Duke's.

We walked into the tiki and bamboo and straw, and I caught a glimpse of the bartender. She was a short, tough, half-Japanese chick in baggy jeans and a tight, white tank top. She had a tattoo of a big-headed, big-eyed doll on her shoulder. The tattoo matched her just right. Who else could it be but Helen: with the face that launched a dozen Greyhounds?

I had no idea how this scene was going to play out. I hadn't seen Helen since a few hours before Sophie stabbed me. Last she heard from me, I'd left her house, told her I'd call her the next day, and disappeared for four years. Now, I didn't know whether to expect a smile or a slap in the face.

Bart pulled up a barstool. Helen saw him and smiled. She took a mug from behind the bar and started pouring him a draft. Once the tap was flowing, she looked up and saw who Bart's friend was. She stopped the tap. "Holy fucking shit!" she said.

I was up to the bar at this point. Helen climbed onto the beer cooler, kneeled on the bar, and leaned in toward me. I braced myself. Helen gave me a big hug. This surprised me. I squeezed right back. Took a deep breath to smell her hair. Oh yeah, I thought, I remember that Helen smell.

She whispered in my ear, "I'm never gonna sleep with you again." She let go of me and climbed off the bar.

I thought, hey, I'm just saying hello, here. Let's not get ahead of ourselves. But I was too stunned by the comment. And besides, don't you know I was thinking about it?

A group of tourists walked in right about then, all flowered shirts and sunburns and socks and sandals. Helen said, "We'll talk soon." And she was back to tending the bar.

She finished pouring Bart's draft and gave me the same without asking, then took the tourists' orders. The bar was fairly crowded. Helen floated around behind it, mixing drinks, pulling drafts, telling jokes, listening to stories, popping a drunk guy in the head when he tried to get a free refill off the taps, making sure everyone at the bar knew everyone else. She was a natural. I couldn't keep my eyes off her. I started thinking way too much about the past, about the year we'd spent together and all those old feelings and those daydreams I had about her and me. It was kinda overwhelming. I watched Helen and thought, I can't believe I left this woman just because I got stabbed a few times. I'm such a pussy.

I did not drink the beer she poured for me.

By about eleven o'clock, the bar had pretty much cleared out and I was drinking soda and Bart was drunk and playing pinball. I'd talked to Helen on and off all night. It was good to be near her again. She came up to me at the end of the night and handed me a deck of tarot cards. "Mix these up," she said. "Get your energy in them." She handed me a bar towel.

I wiped up the bar in front of me and pushed the towel aside. I looked at the tarot. It was an erotic deck. All the cards had artfully drawn naked people on them. Some of the people were having sex. I shuffled the cards a few times. I laid them all out on the bar, mixed them up, picked them up, and handed the deck back to Helen.

Helen shuffled the cards once and broke the deck into three equal stacks. She dealt three cards, one off the top of each stack. She flipped one card at a time, starting from the left and working her way right. She looked at the cards quickly, said, "That makes sense," and put the deck away.

I figured that she was doing the reading for me, since she'd had me handle the cards. I said, "What did the cards say about me?"

"Do you want to know your future, Danny?" Helen asked.

"Yeah," I said, though, really I didn't want to know.

"Things'll get worse before they get better."

"Is that what the cards say?"

"No," Helen said. "I did that reading for me."

"Then why do you say that? Why are things gonna get worse?"

"Because I know you," Helen said.

And damn if she wasn't right.

14

Superheroes and Sidekicks

By April—two months after I'd gotten back to Cocoa Beach—I had a sidekick and a shadow. The sidekick was Taylor, the little girl who I'd made cry on my first day back. I'm not sure exactly why it happened, but she latched onto me almost right away. And, yeah, maybe it was weird to be spending so much time with a preteen girl. I was cool with it, though.

Taylor started by shouting out insults every time she saw me. I never responded other than to smile and wave. Because there was no way I was gonna make her cry again. Not on purpose. She teased me a lot about my surfing that first week. But by the end of that week, I was back in form. I could even get some speed out of that little board. And, for some reason, Taylor seemed to be down at 3rd Street North every time I surfed.

By the second week, I could do some tricks again. Taylor noticed this and stopped ragging me about my surfing and started ragging me about my belly. That was okay by me. I was happy with my belly.

On my fourth week back in Cocoa Beach, Taylor showed up at my house just as I was about to head out surfing. I'm sure she timed it that way. I surfed every afternoon at three o'clock. Right after work. Taylor had on this red spring suit. It was too loose on her to really keep her warm. She also had a fat, purple, twin fin surfboard. Between the wetsuit and the surfboard, she looked like the "don'ts" half of a "dos and don'ts" section in a surfing magazine, circa 1985. "Will you teach me how to surf?" she asked.

"Where'd you get that set up?"

"My stepdad," she said. "He told me you used to be the best surfer in Cocoa Beach. Will you teach me how?"

"Who's your stepdad?"

"Paul Stromme. He's says he went to high school with you."

I ran the name through my head a few times, but it didn't sound familiar. "I don't remember him."

"He's kind of a redneck," Taylor said.

I chewed on this for a second. Was her stepdad a black redneck? Not that there was no such thing. I'd spent enough time in Florida to know a few black rednecks. I thought of one guy in particular who was in the union with me when I was an iron worker. I tried to remember his name. It wasn't Paul. I was pretty sure of that. And I didn't go to high school with him. And, while I was at it, there was no reason for me to think that Taylor's stepdad had to be black. It was probably more likely that her mom had married a white redneck.

Taylor snapped me out of all of these thoughts. She said again, "Will you teach me to surf?"

I shrugged. What the hell? I was heading out, anyway. I grabbed my board, and Taylor and I walked the three blocks to the beach.

I'd never successfully taught anyone to surf. I'd tried a few times, but it didn't really work out. I didn't know how to teach it. I told Taylor to just follow me, and I told her everything I was doing and why. The first couple of days were rough for her, but really, she got the hang of it in no time.

By the time I'd been in Cocoa Beach for two months, Taylor was already pretty good. Partly because I'd made enough money working at a metal shop to buy a new board for myself. Since I was still too big for my old shortboard, I gave it to Taylor. Well, I didn't quite give it to her. Bart convinced me that people would see it as creepy enough that I was hanging out every day with a twelve-year-old girl. If I started giving that girl presents, he'd start calling me Humbert Humbert. So I sold the board to Taylor for ten bucks. She skipped her school lunch for a week to save up the money. I felt kinda bad for her, missing meals. It was better in the end, I thought, because now she could feel like she earned something and maybe it would inspire her and maybe when she got better than me and better than most of the girls on this coast, she could go pro and have a great story about this fat, weird guy in her neighborhood and how she bought her first board off him.

So Taylor and I were out surfing and she was really taking to the new Rainbow. She couldn't do any tricks or anything, but she had learned how to catch waves early and how to ride the face of the wave and that's most of the battle. Once you learn that, everything else is gravy.

It was a pretty good day to be out. The water was warm again and the waves were kinda small, just over knee high, but they had good form and enough power to push my fat ass. I was having a lot of fun out there until I looked back to shore and saw a dude in a wheelchair sitting on the boardwalk.

I didn't know the dude. I didn't know anyone who rode a wheelchair. But I sat out there in the ocean, keeping one eye east for waves creeping across the horizon and one eye west on the wheelchair guy. He was my shadow. He seemed to show up everywhere I went. He'd been to the metal shop where I worked and he'd been to Helen's bar and I'd even seen him sitting in a van outside of the duplex that Bart and I shared. He had long, sandy brown hair and a green army jacket. It was a bit warm out for the jacket. He looked like a Vietnam vet.

As I waited for the next wave, it occurred to me that, when I was a kid, I used to see guys like him everywhere: wheelchair vets. Brother Joe had fought in Vietnam and he had a couple of buddies like this guy in the chair. But those guys were gone now. All the vets I used to see around seemed to be gone. I sat out in the ocean and tried to figure out what happened to them all. Had they died off? Were they in VA hospitals? Were they hanging out at freeway onramps with cardboard signs? Had they assimilated back into society so completely that you'd never recognize them if they didn't happen to take a nap around you and wake up screaming? Does PTSD wear off? It was all a mystery to me.

What was not a mystery to me was the reason why this dude showed up everywhere I went. I felt pretty certain he was the private investigator that Bart had predicted.

I was so wrapped up in my head that I missed two sets of waves and may have missed a third set if Taylor hadn't said, "Danny, this is your wave."

I caught the wave. As soon as I felt the momentum of the ocean, I stopped thinking about the wheelchair dude. I stopped thinking at all and let instinct take over, ripping a big cut off the lip and curling into the whitewash and whipping back into the wave. I rode for a few seconds there. When the wave closed out, I rode the whitewash into shore.

I sat on shore and watched Taylor while the wheelchair dude watched me. I'd been keeping an eye on him while I was surfing, but I didn't notice a camera then. When I sat on the beach, the dude pulled out his camera. I knew this because I was looking straight at him when he took my picture. He had to be a P.I. Had to be.

I tried to ignore him until I could figure out what to do. If he hadn't been in a wheelchair, I would've just walked over and punched him. I would've hit him enough times for him to get the point that he should stop following me. But I couldn't do that to a guy in a wheelchair. Especially a veteran, which, of course I didn't know if he was one or not, but still. I couldn't hit him and I'd have to figure out a different way to handle this. For starters, I stopped looking in his direction.

I watched Taylor instead. She caught her last wave. The kid was doing all right. She had a funny way of standing on her board: she leaned forward with her knees hardly bent at all. It reminded me of the way girls used to dance a few years earlier. There was even an R&B song where the singers danced like that in the video. Every time Taylor would stand on her board like that, I'd start singing to myself, "Don't go chasing waterfalls." Which was the only line from the R&B song that I knew. It drove me nuts.

Anyway, my own mania notwithstanding, Taylor was doing pretty well out there on her surfboard. She wasn't great, yet. But give her a year. Maybe she'd become the superhero and I'd be the sidekick.

I kept watching waves and thinking too much and not really thinking at all until Taylor was sitting on the beach next to me.

"You're getting the hang of this surfing thing, huh?" I said.

"Starting to." Taylor unhooked her leash from her foot and wrapped it around the tail of her board.

"Having fun?"

Taylor nodded. She looked out at the ocean. This was my little ceremony after surfing. Whenever I was done, I liked to sit on the beach and look at the waves. To try to understand what I'd ridden and how I could've ridden them better. To try to make sense of what I saw under me in the ocean, and what it would look like from shore. I don't know if Taylor was doing the same thing or just imitating me, but she'd usually sit down and stare east, too.

After a couple of minutes, Taylor said, "Are you losing your belly, Danny?"

It was true that I had lost a little bit of bulk since I'd been back in Florida. Fewer hot dogs, almost no beer, a lot of surfing. I hadn't been on a scale to see what the weight difference was, but I did have to tighten my belt one notch. "Maybe a little," I said. "I hope I don't lose too much."

"Huh?"

"Lose your belly and you lose your center," I said. "It makes surfing tougher." Taylor looked at me like I was crazy and I guess she didn't get that I was kidding around. I let it drop. I kept staring in the direction of the ocean, but really, I was obsessing on that wheelchair dude. I tried to convince myself that he had nothing to do with the rich, white girl I'd left dead on the tracks in Flagstaff. I tried to ignore the reality that stabbed me in the gut every time I thought about Libra.

After a couple of minutes, Taylor said, "Why do you have so many tattoos, Danny?"

" 'Cause I think they look cool."

"What do they mean?"

I shrugged. "Point at a tattoo and I'll tell you what it means." Taylor pointed to the hula girl on my left forearm. "That one doesn't mean anything," I said. I balled my left fist and squeezed it a couple of times. Not much happened to the hula girl. "She was supposed to dance, but she doesn't really."

Taylor pointed to my right shoulder. "Why do you have the number forty-two on your arm?"

"That's the answer."

"To what?"

"The ultimate question of life, the universe, and everything."

Taylor was really starting to master her *you're crazy, Danny* look. I knew she didn't get the joke. I let that dangle, too.

Taylor pointed at my chest, the left side, just above the heart.

I had a tattoo of two machetes crossed and under the head of a monkey.

"That was my first tattoo," I said. "My brother Joe drew it. It had something to do with Vietnam. He and all his buddies got this tattoo. Kinda like a gang, but not really. I was like their mascot. So Brother Joe asked me if I wanted one, too, and of course I did, so he used a homemade gun and gave me this sucker when I was fifteen."

"Fifteen!" Taylor said. "What did your parents think?"

"I didn't have parents," I said. "Brother Joe raised me."

Taylor looked at me to see if I was full of shit. Of course, I wasn't. Taylor said, "I don't have a dad."

"Who gave you that crappy wetsuit and board, then?"

"My stepdad."

I nodded. "What happened to your dad?"

"Who knows?" Taylor said.

I could tell that she still wanted to talk about this, but I didn't really know how to draw it out of her. I kept looking at the ocean. I figured that, if I just waited long enough, she'd say something else. She did.

She said, "Do you know what the most confusing day in Harlem is?"

"No," I said.

Taylor said, "Father's Day."

I didn't laugh. I'd heard that joke before. Live long enough in blue-collar Florida and you'll hear every racist joke. I didn't think this one was funny the first time, but it was even less funny when a little black girl who'd been abandoned by her father told it to me.

"Laugh," Taylor said. "It's funny."

"It's bullshit," I said.

Taylor stood up and grabbed the Rainbow. "You're a fucking jerk," she said. She started to walk away. I got up to follow her. The wheelchair dude snapped our picture.

"Wait," I said.

Taylor paused. "What?" she said.

"I'll make you a promise," I said. "If I ever meet that son of a bitch dad of yours, I'll kick his ass."

As quickly as Taylor had gotten mad, she calmed back down. She even smiled and waited for me to walk up to her. "It's a deal," she said.

We crossed the beach and headed up the boardwalk toward home. The wheelchair dude rolled over to one side so that we could pass. Taylor walked by him first, then me. I nodded to him as I scooted past. He said, "Danny McGregor?" Like he'd just realized who I was. Like he hadn't been following me for a month. Or, I guess more like he just wanted to be sure that he had the right guy.

I said, "Yeah?"

And then I asked myself, why are you so fucking stupid?

15
Does PTSD Wear Off?

You're tending bar in the worst of dives. It's all ancient beer signs and bad lighting and chipped linoleum and torn vinyl seats. You're by yourself, doing your best to keep the joint clean when Brother Joe walks in with his buddy Paddy. You haven't seen Joe since the morning after Sophie stabbed you. You haven't seen Paddy since you were in high school.

Paddy is a moose of a man. When you were a kid, he was a giant. In your mind, he ducked when he walked through doorways. Now, with age and perspective and yourself grown to full height, he's less of a giant. He's barely two inches taller than you. Still, Paddy and you would be the two tallest guys in most rooms. Paddy has so much hair on his face that it's hard to find any skin there. On his left shoulder, he has a professionally done, full-color tattoo of a woman. Below the tattoo is the word "Tina." Full color, professionally done, too. Below that is a homemade, chicken scratch tattoo that says, "is a whore."

One time when you were a kid, you worked up the nerve to ask Paddy about Tina. "She's a whore," Paddy told you. "I would've made that more clear, but I'm left-handed."

It took you a long time to get his joke. You thought and thought on it. Finally, you saw Joe give himself a homemade tattoo and you knew what Paddy had been talking about.

Brother Joe looks exactly like he did the last time you saw him: leathery skin, stringy muscles, hair gray from age and dirty blond from the sun. As always, he's wearing a collared shirt. It's a bowling shirt, but he still looks sharp. Brother Joe always does his best to look sharp.

Paddy and Brother Joe had both been in the Vietnam War. They hadn't known each other then. They both spent the decades after the war working manual labor and drinking to forget. When you were an adolescent, they usually took you to the bars with them.

You didn't drink.

Anyway, seeing Paddy and Brother Joe finally makes you feel like you're home. These guys are your childhood. To most people, they're white trash guys. Most bartenders would see two guys like this walk in and the bartenders would try to remember if that baseball bat or pistol was still down by the cash register. To you, these guys are heroes. Especially Brother Joe. He's the guy who pulled you out of the foster homes and made you feel like you had a family, even if there was only one other member in said family.

It's never a mystery what these guys are drinking. You pull two bottles of the cheapest domestic beer, pop the top, and set them in front of Joe and Paddy. "If it ain't the Machete Monkeys," you say.

"Fucking-A," Paddy says.

"I thought you were dead," you say to him. Because you vaguely remember a phone call from Brother Joe back when you lived in Kill Devil Hills. Something about Paddy and a motorcycle accident.

"He just smells that way," Joe says.

You smile. Now you really feel at home.

No one comes into the bar for some time. You hang out and chat with Paddy and Brother Joe. You talk about the things you always talked about with these guys: women, Florida State football, drinking stories, Vietnam, women. When Paddy and Joe are six or seven beers into the afternoon, a group of women about their age walk in. You stroll over and serve them. A margarita, a gimlet, and a Tom Collins. They ask for a menu. "Sorry," you tell them. There's no food in this dive and you wouldn't want to serve it if there were.

You keep chatting with Brother Joe and Paddy. One of the women is giving Brother Joe the eye. She has hair so blonde it's almost white and a tan so dark that, in the bar light, she looks like she could be from India or something. Paddy gets up to play pinball. Brother Joe pats you on the arm. He says, "Watch this, Danny. I'm gonna score with this broad."

That was Joe's M.O. way back when you were a preteen and Joe'd take you with him on a Saturday bender. You'd go to his favorite bar, Barnacle Bills. He'd make sure everyone knew you were his kid brother and not his son. He'd drink and tell stories and feed you, then try to "score with a broad." When you first started heading down there, you'd bring a book and go out onto the rocks of Port Canaveral and read while Joe tried to work his magic. Which wasn't magic. He'd always stumble out a few hours later, drunk and alone. He did woo the women at first, but he never knew when to stop drinking and he'd hang with the women until he got ugly. You started putting your bike in the back of his truck so that you could split when he tried to pick up women. You hoped that, without you around, he'd quit drinking earlier and actually score. He almost never did.

So now with Joe looking across the bar at that one woman and her smiling at him, you feel like you're back in 1982.

Joe smiles to the woman. He says to you, "See that broad over there. She's pretty hot, huh?"

You nod, though that woman is not hot. You never went in for those skinny, blond beach chicks.

Joe says, "She might be too good for me, right? I'm just some drunk asshole in a bar. I mow lawns for a living. Why would a broad like that want a guy like me?"

"Don't run yourself down, Joe," you say. "You're a good guy." Also, you're thinking: that girl's nothing special.

Joe says, "No, it's true. I'm a drunk and I'm an asshole. But I will pick up that broad because I know something that no one else in this bar knows."

"What's that?" you ask, even though you've heard this speech a thousand times. It's classic Brother Joe. You wait for it. Joe looks around as if he's giving out national security secrets.

He stage whispers, "She took a big shit this morning."

You laugh.

Joe smiles. He says, "I'm not kidding. All these fuckers in this world around us, they think they're better than a pair of white trash bastards like you and me. Because they own the houses they live in and have money and good jobs and parents and shit. And we don't have any of that. But we know this, Danny. We know that they all get up in the morning and take a smelly shit and they hate the way they smell inside. Just like you and me. They're no better than us. We're just a bunch of fucking monkeys sitting around eating and shitting and trying to get laid. Don't you ever forget that."

You never have forgotten that. You've tried to forget, but you haven't forgotten. Now, you're a little happy about it. Other people can keep their money and families and things. You have Brother Joe and monkeys and the world on a toilet. God bless that fucking guy.

Joe grabs his beer and walks around the bar. He pulls up a stool next to the blond woman. She flips her hair over her shoulder and looks down at the bar like she's being coy. Within five minutes, Joe and the woman are talking and laughing and doing shots.

You try to keep busy and give them space. You wash some glasses. You wipe the linoleum bar. You dust the bottles in the well. You fill the ice bin. You keep your head down and work.

The cow bell on the front door bounces off the glass. You look up to see who's walking in. You can hardly believe it.

It's Libra.

She saunters in like it's nothing. Like she's been here a thousand times. She's wearing her winter clothes: pink parka and gloves and everything. Last you checked, we were still in Florida in the springtime. Things are making less and less sense.

Libra sits in a stool away from Joe and the women and even Paddy and the pinball machine. You walk up to see what she needs, even though you're certain that she's dead. You saw the corpse.

Libra reaches under the bar and snaps her leg off her hip. She slams the leg on the bar and says, "What the fuck, Danny?"

And the night sweats come back.

16
Ripping Off Guernico

Bart told me he'd take me to Joe. I knew what he meant, but I was still down for it.

He picked me up at work at around one-thirty. I'd been working at a metal shop that was about ten blocks from the duplex Bart and I lived in. Bart wanted to check it out before we hit the road.

I introduced him to my boss—a guy named Duane. Duane and I had worked together out at the Space Center a decade earlier. He'd been working in a crane about fifteen feet away from me one day inside the Vehicle Assembly Building, which is the warehouse where rockets are built. We were indoors, but about five hundred feet off the ground. It was a one of a kind type situation, working in there. You heard all kinds of crazy statistics about that huge warehouse, like that you could fit Yankee Stadium and all its parking lots on the roof of the VAB. Or that the VAB had more square footage than Vatican City. Crazy things like that. I don't know if any of it was true. It was a weird joint to work in, though, because you'd have to work higher than anywhere else locally. Like, if you built a condo on Cocoa Beach, you generally wouldn't get any higher than about seven stories, but when you were up seventy or eighty feet, there'd be a pretty mean wind blowing in off the Atlantic. It'd be easy to lose your balance. There was no wind inside the VAB. It was easier to walk the beams there. But if you fell, you fell five hundred feet, not eighty. The result of either fall would probably be the same, so I guess it shouldn't have mattered much to me.

Only, one day Duane and I were working. He was safe in his crane and I was out on the beams, welding. I leaned over a little too far and my tape measure fell out of my tool belt. At first, I tried to reach for it and almost lost my balance. It freaked me out. My heart started racing. I could feel my blood fill with adrenaline. I squeezed my thighs tight on the beam and breathed as slowly and deeply as I could and I watched that tape measure fall and fall and fall for what seemed like forever. The whole time, I was thinking: that's me. That's me falling all that distance. And that's the difference between falling eighty feet and falling five hundred. You're gonna die either way. Either way, you're gonna think about dying for the rest of your short life. But five hundred feet gives you a long time to think about dying.

I finished welding that beam, walked over to Duane, said, "I quit," and rode the elevator down.

A few years later, Duane opened this metal shop in a warehouse off Brevard Avenue and found a way to keep his feet on the ground, too. When I got back to Cocoa Beach, Duane was the first guy I went to see about a job. He hired me as a freelancer. I could use his tools and he'd pay me by the job. Most welders wouldn't work like this—because you didn't get benefits or workman's comp and it was tougher to make good money—but I worked faster than most welders and I appreciated being able to make full-time money without having to work full-time.

Plus, Duane paid me under the table. In cash. There was no record of me working there, so I felt like I'd be harder to find, should the Flagstaff police come looking. Which I guess didn't matter because the wheelchair dude had already found me. He was sitting outside the shop in his van when Bart came by to see me. I knew this because Duane had told me. He told me that he knew the wheelchair dude was after me for something. Duane said that, if I didn't do something about the wheelchair dude, I was going to have to find another job. He told me that the wheelchair dude made him nervous. I knew the feeling.

Bart came inside the metal shop. I showed Bart the things we were making. Some kind of cellular phone sub station antennas. Bart asked, "Are you still doing sculptures?"

I pointed to some over by my work station. "Nothing special," I said. "Just something to keep me busy while I'm waiting for supplies and shit."

This wasn't exactly true. I worked on those sculptures every day. They were the most important thing in the world to me. I don't know why I always downplayed that, always acted like they didn't matter.

Bart walked over to the biggest of my sculptures. It was about sixteen inches high and thirty inches wide and six inches deep. I'd made it out of galvanized wire cloth and some strips of sheet metal and straps that carpenters use to brace trusses against hurricane winds. There was a bull, kinda, and a sort of horse looking thing and some fucked up looking people reaching for the sky. A total rip-off of Picasso's *Guernica*, only I hadn't seen *Guernica* for a few years and just went by memory, so maybe people wouldn't even know what I was ripping off. I think there was enough of my style in it to make it distinctive, too. I was actually pretty proud of that one. Bart said, "You could probably sell this for a decent amount of money."

"Nah," I said. "It's crap. Let's go."

Bart tried to take the sculpture with him, but I told him to put it down. And, anyway, we didn't have a lot of time. We had to make it out to north Merritt Island and back in time for Bart to drive his four o'clock bus route.

Bart drove deep into the swamps and orange groves of Merritt Island, to that weird, rural redneck moat that surrounds Kennedy Space Center. We turned onto a dirt road lined by retention ditches and citrus trees. Wind blew through the groves, kicking up that smell of orange blossoms. An ibis fed on insects in a freshly mown section of grass. I hung my hand out the window of the car and let it float up and down. It was all white noise and peace. I felt like I was a world away from civilization out there.

At the end of the dirt road was an ancient little chapel and a little graveyard. Bart parked the car. We got out and started walking.

Of course, all that was left of Joe was a sorry little slab of a tombstone. Not even a tombstone, really. A grave marker. The kind that you could run the lawn mower right over. Which I guess would be cool with Joe, because if there was one thing Brother Joe hated, it was running a weed eater. I'd hate to think that sister Janie would've bought a big ass tombstone and doomed a new generation of guys like Joe to run a weed eater.

That was the first thing I thought about when I saw Joe's grave marker, too: oh, good, no one's gonna have to weed eat around this shit.

The second thing I thought was: oh, shit, he's really dead.

The next thing I did was laugh. Not long and hysterical. Not even loud. Just that little quick laugh that I always let out when I saw Joe after not having seen him for a bit.

Because, in my mind, it's crazy, but I kept thinking that maybe it wasn't all true. Maybe he didn't really have that heart attack. There was something about that story that I never believed. How does a forty-four-year-old guy have a heart attack? Especially one that kills him? And what kind of cause of death is a heart attack? Doesn't everyone's heart attack at the end? Isn't saying someone died of a heart attack the same thing as saying someone died of death? It didn't make sense. Why should I believe it?

I'd first heard the news back in November. I happened to call Joe the day after it happened. Some broad I'd never met answered the phone. She had this rough, lifetime smoker's voice. I wondered what bar Joe had picked her up at and how long she'd been around. I asked for Joe and she said, "No, honey, he's dead." Just like that.

She gave me the details, but it all seemed unreal. I didn't want to believe it. And part of me didn't believe it.

But here I was, standing over Brother Joe's grave marker. Reading it. They even got his name right: Joe Cully McGregor. None of that Joseph shit. He was never a Joseph. Not even on his birth certificate. Just Joe.

And the marker was here in the cemetery of St. Luke's Episcopal Church. Joe was right there with the rest of my family. My dad's marker was there. My mom's. My oldest brother, who died in Vietnam before I could get a chance to know him. My grandparents, who were old memories before I was born. McGregors and Cullys stretching back to the late eighteenth century. All gathered around under these ancient live oaks and the hanging Spanish moss and the shadows of the old chapel. That's it, I realized. It's just me and Janie now. There were six of us when I was born. Now there were two.

I don't know if it was tougher to see Libra mutilated and dead on the tracks or to see nothing left of Joe but a grave marker. I don't know which was worse. Or maybe they were equally bad. Just different. I don't know.

Bart stood next to me. I wondered if he'd ever brought a forty out here and poured beer on Joe's grave. That old tribute kinda thing. Probably not. Bart dealt with death all the time at his second job. He probably knew how to deal with it. Better than me, anyway. Better than always running from it and denying it. I don't know. At least Bart knew not to say anything until I did. Not to make a joke or pat me on the back or anything. He just stood there until I said, "You're not the one who picked up the body, are you?"

"Nah."

"Are you sure?"

"Yeah. It happened during the day. I work nights." Bart knelt down and picked off the grass that hung over the marker. "I think Joe made it to the hospital, anyway. I think he died there."

"That's too bad," I said. I don't know why I said it.

Bart and I stood there for a little bit, just looking at Joe's name and "1955-1999." Too young to die. Too old to die young. Finally, I said, "You think you could hook me up with your night job?"

"Really?"

I nodded.

"Sure," Bart said. "You could probably start next week."

I took one last look at Joe, then walked away. Maybe picking up dead people would help. Maybe it was exactly what I needed.

17
Bart's Homemade Death Tests

I'd seen exactly three dead bodies outside of caskets. The first was when I was twelve. My buddy Rick and I were hanging out at his house after school. I went into his garage to grab us a couple of sodas from the refrigerator there. I found his dad's body hanging from the garage door opener, an orange electric chord around his neck, a puddle of urine at his feet. I added my own puddle of vomit to the garage floor.

The second was an old man. He'd been driving in front of me when he lost control and slammed into a telephone pole. He flew through the windshield of his car and headfirst into the pole. By the time I got to the scene, he'd stopped breathing and had no heartbeat.

Both of these bodies haunted me for a while, but they were nothing compared to the third body I found. Libra's. Libra still infested my dreams and clouded my thoughts. And it wasn't just the horror of finding her body. Let's be honest, if I'd seen Libra alive that morning, just sitting on the tracks as I walked to the Greyhound station, *that* would've fucked with my head. A lot of things about Libra being on those tracks bothered me, not just the fact that she was dead. And this is what I thought about on my first day of grim reaping.

Bart and I stood over the body of an old lady. We were in a bedroom in a nursing home. Bart had shut and locked the door behind us because, as we'd walked through the nursing home, every old bastard in the joint stopped us to ask who died and what happened to her and to tell us their life stories and a million other things. It was a pain in the ass.

Now, Bart and I stood over this dead lady. I was thinking about Libra and death. Bart was talking away.

"The first thing you want to do," Bart said, "is make sure the patient is, in fact, dead. There are a few ways to make certain. The first is to take the patient's pulse. Like this."

Bart picked up the lady's flaccid arm and placed two of his fingers just below the woman's wrist. He explained to me about how to find the pulse.

I said, "Come on, man. We're not paramedics. They've already checked her. She's dead."

"They made sure someone was dead," Bart said. "What we have to be sure of is that we put the right body into the body bag." I looked at Bart like he was full of shit. He shook his head. "I'm serious," he said. "When I first started doing this job, the guy I worked with was a total fucking numbskull, and I didn't know what I was doing yet. We went into a nursing home to fetch a corpse. I was just following him. I figured he knew where we were going. We walked into a room and there was this stiff old man in the bed. I grabbed the feet of the guy and Numbskull grabbed the shoulders and, just as we lifted, the old bastard started kicking and screaming. I almost shit my pants."

"Really?"

"It's no lie. So let's go through this." Bart picked up the arm again. "First you check the pulse. Try it."

I put my two fingers below the woman's wrist. No pulse. Rigor mortis was starting to set in. The woman was turning blue. She had soiled herself. She didn't stink yet, but I didn't want to stick around until she did. Bart kept guiding me, telling me to put my ear over the dead lady's mouth, to blow into her eyes to see if she blinked, that kind of thing. I kinda doubted these were even really tests. I reckoned they were just things Bart had made up to make sure a corpse didn't kick. Still, I humored him.

After we'd gone through four or five of Bart's homemade death tests, Bart said, "Okay, take a step back." I backed away from the dead lady. Bart stepped forward. "There's just one more test." Bart turned, lifted his leg, and farted on the dead lady's head.

I didn't want to laugh. I really didn't. But I couldn't help myself. A wave of nervous giggling wiped me out. Bart laughed, too. That made things worse. I couldn't look at him without laughing harder.

Right in the middle of this, someone knocked on the door. "Everything okay in there?"

Bart composed himself long enough to say, "Everything's fine." Then he burst out laughing again, trying to keep as quiet as he could.

I could hear people talking outside the room. Saying things like, "What's going on in there?" "I don't know. Are they trying to resuscitate her?" "I thought she was dead." "Maybe not." And so on. The more the people outside the room said, the more nervous it made me, and the more it made me laugh. I couldn't stop.

Bart was just as bad. His face was glowing red and he was gasping for air. Still, he pointed to the lady's feet and grabbed her shoulders. I grabbed her feet. Bart said, "One, two, three."

I lifted the dead lady's feet. Bart ripped another fart. I started giggling again.

Someone knocked on the door again. "What's taking so long?"

"We're almost done in here," Bart said.

We wrapped the body bag around the lady, zipped her up, strapped her into the gurney, and started wheeling her toward the door. I was laughing the whole time. Bart was, too. The murmur of voices came through the door. Just as we got to the door, Bart said, "Okay. You've got to pull it together."

I closed my eyes and took a deep breath. A quick burst of breathless giggles slid out. I took another deep breath. Okay. Composed. I looked at Bart. He'd stopped laughing. He wasn't even smiling. I took another deep breath.

"Ready to go outside?" Bart whispered.

I nodded.

"Here we go." Bart put one hand on the doorknob, lifted one foot off the ground, and ripped another fart.

"Goddamn it," I whispered, giggling again. Bart, at this point, was doubled over. Someone knocked. I couldn't take it.

All I could think was that someone outside might actually have hope that this old blue corpse might breath again, and the longer we sat in here, the more hope that someone got. The more I thought about this, the worse I felt, and the worse I felt, the more I laughed. It was crazy. I reached over and punched Bart in the arm. Not hard. Just enough to let him know that we had to get out of there. Bart nodded and stood straight up. I started taking deep breaths again. I resolved to avoid looking at Bart until we were out of that nursing home.

Bart grabbed the doorknob again. "Ready?" he asked.

I nodded. He opened the door. We wheeled the corpse out.

I didn't say a word to anyone until I got to the van, and by then I felt all right.

We hauled the corpse over to the Medical Examiner's office, dropped the van off at Space Coast, picked up Bart's car, and headed home. It was just after five-thirty in the morning. By this point, Bart had farted again and again enough times to make it an old joke. The giggles had passed. I kept my window down and mostly ignored him.

"Jobs like this are gravy," Bart said. "They're almost as good as the nights when we don't have to pick up anyone."

I nodded, but I was already done thinking about it. The sun was just beyond the horizon, about to rise but not quite there yet. I didn't have a whole lot to do at Duane's metal shop that day. I wasn't due in until eight or so. I figured I'd get back to Cocoa Beach and join the dawn patrol out there on the ocean. I hadn't seen the sun rise while surfing in a long time. This would be a good morning for that.

Bart kept talking about the job. "It can't all be fart jokes," he said. "Some nights, you see some fucked up shit."

"I bet," I said, but really, my mind was on surfing. Not on farts; not on dead people. I had no idea what I'd signed myself up for.

18

A Holiday in the Past

ITINERARY FOR RECONCILIATION

6:47 P.M. You'll once again have a crush on Helen. You'll want to go see her at her bar, but you know from experience that the worst way to try to hook up with a bartender is to sit at her bar every night and drool over her. Pace yourself.

6:48 P.M. There will be no food in your apartment. Helen serves food. You haven't been to Duke's in two weeks. Decide it'll be okay to go there now.

6:49 P.M. Give your bike a quick once over. You rescued the bike from someone else's trash. It's a beach cruiser. You had to replace the bearings and the chain, but everything else seems okay. Still, check the brakes before leaving.

7:01 P.M. Take a stool at Duke's. All the regulars will be there. Wonder briefly if you look like just another in this row of lonely guys, just another barnacle stuck to a barstool. Tell yourself, I'm different. Tell yourself: my brother—who was really my whole family—died four months ago and my girlfriend—who, sure, was my ex-girlfriend, technically, but still—died just over two months ago. I'm in mourning. The last thing I need now is another relationship.

7:02 P.M. Tell yourself, besides, I'm not just any other guy. I'm Helen's ex-boyfriend. Decide that makes matters worse. Say hello to Helen. Order food without looking at a menu. Order water to go with your food.

7:14 P.M. The bar will start to fill up. Don't pay much attention to this.

7:21 P.M. Start eating your dinner. A surfer-looking guy about your age will sit next to you at the bar. You will recognize him, but you won't remember his name.

7:25 P.M. Helen will introduce you to the guy. His name is Benji Clarke. You went to high school with him. You and Benji will both have a moment where you're like, oh shit, I didn't realize that was you.

7:26 P.M. Say to Benji, "Are you still surfing?"

Benji will laugh and say, "Now and then."

There will seem to be some joke that you're not getting. There is. Benji surfs professionally. In fact, he's one of the top surfers in the world. He was a close runner up to world champion two years earlier. He's back in town to sponsor a surfing contest. It's been in all the papers. You didn't notice any of this, partly because you've spent so much time since high school drunk or high or both. Partly because you never paid much attention to pro surfing. Partly because you see reading newspapers as tantamount to weed eating.

Helen will explain some of this to you. She'll tell you about Benji being a pro and second in the world and sponsoring the contest. This will make you especially happy when...

7:27 P.M. Benji will say, "I'm still pissed off that you beat me in that Easter contest back in 1986." Shrug and say, "It was a fluke."

7:45 P.M. As you finish your dinner, you will notice the bar is now packed. Helen will be so busy you can't get her attention to pay her and leave. Shaggy will be losing his mind in the kitchen. Benji and his crew from the surf contest will take up half of the dining area. The other half of the dining area will be full of guys from a local longboarding club who just happened to pick this night and this bar to have their annual party. They'll all be so excited to meet Benji Clarke that chaos will ensue.

7:46 P.M. Recognize that only two people are working in this packed bar and restaurant. Decide to help Helen and Shaggy.

7:47 P.M. Actually get up to help Helen and Shaggy. Bus your own plate. Walk behind the bar. Gently touch Helen in the small of the back and say, "I'll wait tables. You take care of the bar."

Helen's eyes will not be able to focus on anything. Stray hairs will be stuck to the sweat on her forehead. She'll take a deep breath and nod. This will be your only indication that she understands. Pick up a pad near the cash register. Walk into the kitchen and say to Shaggy, "Tell me the table numbers and where to run the food." Shaggy will point to a diagram on the kitchen wall. It shows which table in the restaurant adheres to which table number. It's all pretty logical.

Shaggy will say, "Take the lau lau, chicken katsu, and kalua pig to table seven."

You've waited a lot of tables in your life. It's all old hat to you. You pick up the three plates, double check with the diagram, and run the food.

7:48 P.M. On the way back to the kitchen, take food and drink orders from three tables. Treat them as if they are all one table, getting all the orders before going back to the kitchen.

7:49 P.M. Run food. Take orders. Pass the orders on to Shaggy. Get drinks yourself from behind the bar. Write everything down on the pad. Let Helen ring up the tickets when the time comes. Bus tables when people finish. Get extra sauces from the refrigerator. When the wheelchair dude shows up, treat him like any other customer. Take his order. Bring him his food. Keep his water glass full. Help Shaggy with the dishes when they pile up too high. Refill Helen's ice. Make more iced tea. Switch out the syrup once on the soda gun. Keep your hands clean. Continue to do these things for the next hour. You'll get the same frazzled look as Helen and Shaggy, but no one will lose their mind.

8:49 P.M. You'll like this frazzled feeling. You haven't been in the weeds like this for a few months. You haven't waited tables for a few years, but since you no longer do it every day, it's kinda fun. It's like taking a holiday in your own past. You'll feel like everything is working out okay. Food service will slow down. Your duties will gradually switch to running drinks and collecting money and cleaning up.

9:32 P.M. The crowd won't really thin out, but they'll stop ordering food. This rush will be over. Helen and Shaggy will have things under control. It's almost time for you to head home, anyway.

9:33 P.M. Helen will say, "You saved my fucking ass. Your dinner's on me." When she looks away, put the tips you made that night into Helen's tip jar. Shaggy will see you do this. Put your forefinger in front of your lips in a universal symbol of, *keep your mouth shut, Shaggy*.

9:34 P.M. You have to get home to be on call for your night job. Explain this to Helen briefly. Wave goodbye to Shaggy. Walk to the door.

9:35 P.M. Helen will call out to you, "You're my hero, Danny McGregor." Start glowing.

11:17 P.M. Your pager will go off. Things will turn nasty that quickly.

19

Dead Guy All Over It

The first thing I had to do was drag Bart's drunk ass out of a bar. This was actually part of the plan. First light bulb that went off in Bart's head when I said I wanted to work with him picking up stiffs must've been: cool; if Danny can drive me to Space Coast and drive the van, I can get as drunk as I want.

Bart had been drinking a lot more since I started driving us to get the dead bodies.

He was in Sullivan's. He had his pager, too. He was supposed to come outside as soon as the pager went off. Still, I had to park Bart's car, go inside, and get him.

Sullivan's was as packed as Duke's had been. I noticed some of the crowd from Duke's had filtered down. A DJ worked on weekends. Spinning the same songs he'd been spinning for a decade, more or less. Mostly disco. It was like he was the musical embodiment of the guy who tells a joke so many times that it goes from funny to ridiculous to funny again. Or, at least the disco at Sully's had gone through various stages of funny to ridiculous to funnier to more ridiculous and so on. And where was Bart? Getting down on the dance floor.

He was flanked by two young women. He was dancing with

them, but they didn't seem to be dancing with him. He was that drunk. I paved my way through the dance floor, grabbed Bart by the ear, and tugged enough so that he knew he really had to go. He followed my trail off the dance floor. He chugged the last of his beer.

When we got to the door, I worried for a second that Bart would make a run for it. Go back for the two broads on the dance floor. I turned to make sure he didn't. As I did this, I caught a glimpse of her at the bar. Summer dress. Mary Janes. Bangs cut high up her forehead. Still lean. Still looking peaceful. Drinking wine. Sophie.

I thought my mind was playing tricks on me. Sophie waved. I looked at Bart. Bart waved back. I waved, too. Then I pulled Bart out of the bar.

We got into Bart's car and headed for Rockledge to pick up the van. "You see me with those two girls?" Bart asked. "Out on the dance floor?"

"Yes I did," I said.

"Aww, man, I was in there. Did you see that?"

"You're the mack."

"Shit," Bart said. "Hell of a time for someone to die." Bart fumbled through his glove compartment. Down in the bottom of it, beneath the registration and sunglasses and map and rolling papers and lighter was a cassette tape. He pulled it out and put it in the stereo.

At first, I didn't believe my ears. A few notes played. I looked at Bart. He was dancing in his seat. My ears weren't lying. My punk rock buddy was playing the *Saturday Night Fever* soundtrack. Not only was he playing it, but he owned it. What kind of crazy shit was this?

I tried to ignore it as we drove out of Cocoa Beach. I wanted to think, anyway. I wanted to think, what the fuck was Sophie doing in Sullivan's? Where did she come from? Bart told me she'd moved back to Atlanta to live with her mom. What was she doing in Cocoa Beach? She didn't have family down here. Except for her dad. That's right. Her dad moved down to Orlando when he finally decided that Atlanta wasn't big enough for him and Sophie's mom. A move I guess I could relate to. So he lives in Orlando now. That's pretty close. She could be visiting her dad and decide to come to the beach for a weekend. It could have nothing to do with me. And I guess this would be a good time to visit family. Spring. Right around Easter, maybe. Was that it? Was this Easter weekend? I asked Bart, "Hey, Travolta, when's Easter?"

"Last Sunday," Bart said.

Oh shit, I thought. He's right. But that was okay. Last weekend would be close enough. It would make enough sense for me to relax about Sophie being in town. It could possibly be a coincidence. Nothing to do with me. Sophie comes down to visit her dad for Easter and visits Cocoa Beach the next weekend. Easy enough.

And it only bugged me because I happened to see Sophie on the exact same night when it seemed like I may have a chance with Helen again. It felt like that DJ was spinning my life, letting it go from funny to ridiculous and back again. All the while, still playing the same old tunes.

By now, I was driving across Merritt Island. Bart had his window down. His hand was out the window, snaking up and down in the wind. He started calling out the names of all the places we passed. "Wal-Mart. McDonald's. Applebee's. Steak and Shake. Outback. AMC Theaters. Barnes & Noble. Toys R Us. Blockbuster. Circuit City. Chili's." And so on. This stretch of Merritt Island was Generic Town, USA. I noticed this every time we drove to Space Coast to pick up the van. I never said anything about it. I knew it bugged Bart, though. He said, "Remember when we were always talking about the meaning of life?"

I said, "Yeah."

Bart didn't say anything. The *Saturday Night Fever* soundtrack danced on. We drove past another dozen or so chains.

I said, "Why'd you bring that up?"

"I was just looking at all these joints along this strip here. And I was thinking, you know, about the meaning of life and why we're here and where we're headed right now. To pick up dead people. And I was thinking, because we're always sad when people die. But how bad is death, really, if all it cheats you out of is another shitty meal at Applebee's or another crappy movie rental at Blockbuster? It's not so sad then, is it? If all you were gonna do on your last day on Earth was go shopping at Wal-Mart, then, shit, you might as well die a day earlier, right?"

I saw my opportunity here and I went with it. "Exactly," I said. "It's like, if all you're gonna do is listen to the *Saturday Night Fever* soundtrack one more time, what's the point?"

Bart gave me the dirtiest look I'd ever seen him give me. I smiled. He ejected his tape and threw it out the window. I immediately felt guilty. We didn't say anything again until we picked up the van.

The dispatcher at Space Coast said two things to me when I picked up the van and got our instructions. She said, "Bart needs to sober up." Which was true, but I wasn't gonna let on that I agreed. She also said, "You got a nasty one tonight."

Bart and I climbed into the van. I drove to the Merritt Island Airport.

It was pretty obvious where the bodies were. Two fire trucks were parked in the field west of the runway. A cop car was there, too. Red and blue lights swirled around, bouncing off the remains of a plane. I parked the van next to the fire trucks, got out, and walked to the back of the van. I started to unlatch the gurney but Bart said, "No." He grabbed two body bags and handed one to me. "Those wheels will just get stuck in the grass. We'll use these," he said.

The plane and the bodies inside it were about twenty yards across a field, west of the runway. The door to the plane was open. The grass surrounding it was black, moist, spongy. Outside the cockpit was all charred metal and flakes of burnt paint. It was a small plane. A two seater. The body of the pilot leaned on the controls. He was black. Not brown like an African. Crispy black. Burnt.

Bart and I walked up to the plane together. Bart said, "Remember when you were in high school and you'd walk into the locker room and that smell of ass would just hit you?"

"Yeah," I said.

"Well, now it's the smell of death."

And Bart was a pro at this, or at least his timing was perfect, because as soon as he finished saying this, that sweet, rotten stink slapped me in the nose. The kind of stink that seems to glue itself to your nose and esophagus and lungs and just keep stinking. I nearly puked right there in the wet grass by the plane.

Bart watched me gag and smiled.

"Don't you fucking fart," I said. "It smells bad enough as it is."

Bart laughed a little. We kept walking toward the plane. Bart reached into the pocket of his plaid bermudas and grabbed a handkerchief. "You'll learn to carry one of these," he said.

I lifted the collar of my T-shirt up over my nose. It didn't do much good. The stench of smoked plane and charred flesh was too strong.

There were two bodies in the plane. A pilot and a passenger. Bart took his body bag around to the passenger side. I worked on the pilot.

I grabbed the his arm. It felt like a burnt turkey leg. Like something you were planning on serving, but you left it in the oven too long. I pulled on his arm, but he hardly budged. I made a rookie mistake. I put my foot up on the edge of the plane, got a good hold on the arm, and yanked with all my might. The arm popped right out of the socket. The arm and I flew ass backwards into the wet grass outside the plane. Water seeped through my t-shirt. I got back to my feet and looked at the arm. Cooked meat and tendon stuck out of the shoulder. I put the arm in the body bag and went back for more.

Bart was on the other side of the plane. He couldn't budge the passenger. He said to me, "Don't take him apart piece by piece."

I gave Bart my best no-shit look, then turned my attention back to the pilot. I had no idea how to get this bastard out. His skin seemed to have fused to the leather of the seat. And it wasn't that I was squeamish about touching him. I wasn't. A few days on this job and you realize that there's a big difference between dead people you know and dead people you don't know. Dead people you don't know don't have a history for you. They come with no baggage. It's easy to accept their mortality. They're just the corpse in front of you. Part of the job.

I guess I got jaded pretty quickly, too, because I was looking at that burnt pilot stuck to his seat and wondering where I could get a spatula to pry him out. As I was thinking of this, someone walked behind me and said, "Damn, Bart, where'd you find this loser?"

I turned around and looked at the guy who'd spoken. He was a cop. In the darkness, I could barely make out his face. He stepped closer and put his hand on my shoulder. "It's good to finally see some black folks around here," he said. As soon as he said this, I recognized him. Dante Jones.

We'd gone to high school with him. He and my ex-girlfriend Rosalie were the only black kids in the school. Whenever Dante saw me and Rosalie, he'd say that line about seeing black folks. At first, I thought he was just talking about Rosalie. After a while, though, he started saying it to me when Rosalie wasn't around. I didn't really get his joke, but I liked it, anyway. It always feels good to be included.

I gave him a big smile. "Holy shit," I said. I held my hand out to shake his.

He said, "I'll shake your hand after you wash it, you nasty motherfucker." He squeezed my shoulder. "How the hell have you been?"

"Up to my ass in dead guys right now," I said, "but pretty good otherwise."

Bart said, "Hey, Dante, you got a knife?"

"Yeah. Why?"

"These bastards are stuck to their seats. We have to cut them out."

Dante reached into his pocket and grabbed a Leatherman. He handed it through the cockpit to Bart. "Try not to get dead guy all over it," he said.

Bart opened the knife and started cutting the passenger out of his seat.

Dante turned his attention back to me. "I heard you were back," he said.

"Who told you?" I asked.

"The Flagstaff Police Department."

This surprised me. This actually freaked me out more than the crispy guys in the plane in front of me. "Huh?" I said.

Bart stopped cutting the passenger out and looked up.

Dante said, "I got a call about a month ago from the Flagstaff Police Department. They'd called the station a few times asking about you. They said you were involved in some kind of shit back there. Somehow word got around to me, so I talked to them. They said some white chick died back there. Said they wanted to talk to you about that. You know anything about that?"

I shrugged. "What did you tell them?"

"I told them that you wouldn't have anything to do with white girls."

"If I had any sense, I wouldn't," I said.

Dante put out his fist. I touched it with my fist. "No shit," he said. He looked down at the spongy grass around his police black loafers. "Anyway, you didn't kill any white girls, did you?"

"No," I said. "I haven't killed anyone." I looked at Bart. He was back to cutting up the seat. He'd cut open the side closest to him, and now he was leaning over the body, cutting the other side. "Is that what they thought? That I'm a killer?"

"Nah," Dante said. "They thought you were more of a manslaughterer."

I laughed a little nervous laugh. "That's better, huh?"

Dante smiled. He told me that he'd looked into it. He said that, if the police department really had anything on me, they wouldn't have been calling him. They were just trying to shake me down. "But if you go back to Flagstaff, they'll probably throw your ass in jail," he said.

By now, Bart had his dead guy cut free and stuffed into the bag. He handed me the knife. I started cutting the pilot's seat. Dante kept talking. He said to Bart, "Do you know where Flagstaff is?"

"Arizona," Bart said.

"Did you know that before this motherfucker told you?" Dante pointed at me. Bart shook his head. "I'd never heard of that town," Dante said. "I had to get out a map and look that shit up. I didn't even know which state to look in. What were you doing way the fuck out there?"

I shrugged and kept cutting. As I started getting around the pilot's legs, I put my hand on the floor for balance. I felt something hard and metal under the seat. It was a flask. "What's this?" I said. I handed the flask to Dante. He opened it and took a whiff.

"I think it's whiskey," he said. "I better make sure." He lifted the flask over his mouth and poured about a shot of whiskey down without touching his lips. He swallowed and shuddered. "I can't be sure." He handed the bottle to Bart. "Taste like whiskey to you?"

Bart did a shot, too. "Yep," he said. "It's whiskey."

Bart tried to hand the flask to me, but I wanted to get the dead guy free before I hit on any of his hooch. I kept cutting and Bart and Dante both did another shot. I got the guy free, dragged him into the wet grass, and stuffed him into the body bag.

"I'll take one of those now," I said.

Dante handed me the flask. I downed a little whiskey. Bart said, "Danny, why don't you ask him about the wheelchair dude?"

"Who's the wheelchair dude?" Dante asked.

"Some dude who's been following Danny around. Danny thinks he's a P.I.," Bart said.

I shook my head. "I'm probably just being paranoid."

"No, sir," Dante said. "That's Clay Barker. He used to be on the force until he got that spinal." Dante took another shot. "Look out for that guy."

I had more questions for Dante about Libra and the wheelchair dude, but I also kinda wanted to just catch up with him. I'd always liked Dante. So I asked him what he'd been up to, if he was married, if he still played soccer, that kind of thing. Dante told some stories and that led to me telling some stories and Bart telling some stories. We stood around that burnt out plane with two dead bodies in the wet grass below us and bullshitted like we were in a bar. I won't lie to you. It was a little weird. It was also nice to run into an old friend like Dante.

After a bunch of stories and a few shots, Bart picked up the body bag at his feet. "Enough chit chat," he said. "We should go."

He started dragging the bagged body toward the van. I tried to hand the Leatherman to Dante. "Fuck that," he said. "I don't want that nasty shit." He took another shot from the flask and put it in his pocket. I picked up one end of the body bag and started dragging.

Dante patted me on the shoulder again and said, "Good seeing you again, man. We should hook up, get a beer sometime."

"We should," I said.

Dante turned and walked toward his cruiser. I dragged the body over to the van.

On the way home, Bart stopped at a convenience store to get beer. I almost got some beef jerky until Bart said, "You know what that looks like?" I thought about the dead pilot and put the jerky back and got some peanuts. We drove on. We didn't talk much about the pick up, other than Bart saying a few times how fucked I was about all that Libra shit. I tried to ignore him and just drink my beer.

By the time we got to Cocoa Beach—I hate to admit this—I was only thinking about one thing: what the fuck was Sophie doing back in town?

20
Pink Speedo Lambada

Sophie looked at me and asked, "Do you know what's on TV?"

The television was not on.

I was sitting on the couch in my living room, reading a Jim Thompson novel. A great Jim Thompson novel, all about a small town Texas sheriff who may or may not have been the second coming of Jesus. The sheriff's killing spree was almost over and I was wondering if this really was how it would be: would Jesus return as a mass murderer? Crazy shit. But there was no reason for me to know what was on TV. I said, "Leave me alone."

This was the beginning of the end between Sophie and me. It was roughly three years after that hurricane in Kill Devil Hills and one year before Sophie stabbed me and five years before Sophie showed back up in Cocoa Beach. That would put us at 1995.

Sophie said, "What's wrong with you?"

What was wrong with me is that I was ten pages away from finishing one of the best books I'd ever read and I had this crazy broad asking me what was on TV. But more than that. Insanity was brimming all around me. For one thing, Sophie was too broke to support her cocaine habit, so she was in the midst of an ill-advised crystal meth bender. She hadn't slept a full night in weeks. She was not fun to be around. For another thing, it was the start of summer. Whenever it gets that hot in Florida, people start showing their ass. Sometimes, it's good. Usually not. But the start of summer meant the Start of Summer Block Party in Cocoa Beach, which meant everyone on Woodland Ave. and into downtown Cocoa Beach and really for nine square blocks would get drunk and go nuts for the next three days. And I lived right in the middle of those nine square blocks. And for the last thing, I lived in a duplex on Woodland, and on the other half of the duplex were a bunch of drunks from Merritt Island. They were fun to hang out with, but they'd been drunk when I left for work at nine-thirty that morning, and they were still drunk when I got back at four that afternoon. So all I wanted to do was read a little Jim Thompson before it started. I said, "Please, Sophie, leave me alone."

Sophie didn't say anything. She sat on the other end of the couch, facing me, her knees curled up to her chest, her shoes on the cushions. I went back to reading. The sheriff started his long soliloquy. Right at the beginning of it, though, Sophie's foot came flying through the book, knocking it out of my hands and bruising my knuckles. "Jesus," I said. "You jerk."

"You're so mean," Sophie said. She stormed off toward my bedroom.

The next door drunks were blaring music on their side of the duplex. Almost loud enough to shake the walls. Sophie crashed around my bedroom. Breaking shit, probably. Throwing shit, probably. Trying to get my attention any way she could. I felt like I'd been suddenly swept up into a wave of chaos. I figured I'd just ride it. I got up, walked over to the record player, and put on a Minutemen album. A little chaos to balance the chaos. I picked up my Jim Thompson book, sat down, and went back to the sheriff.

The sheriff thought he was Jesus. I wasn't so sure. I wanted to believe it. I wanted to think good and evil could be that complex, that indelibly wrapped. I got so sucked into the novel that I didn't notice Sophie until she walked over to the turntable, yanked my record off, and snapped it in half. Damn it. Adios, *Double Nickels on a Dime*.

"I want you out of here," Sophie said.

Which was ridiculous because Sophie didn't live there. It was my apartment. "If you want to go, kid, just go," I told her. I looked at my broken record on the floor. "Just go."

Sophie dropped to the floor. She sat Indian-style there, with her elbows on her knees and her face in her hands. Her back shook. She was crying. I wasn't going to comfort her. She brought all this on herself. Her madness was not my fault. I thought, if she wanted comfort, maybe she could listen to the Minutemen. Damn it. I picked up my book again and tried to read, but it was all too crazy.

After a couple of minutes, Sophie looked up at me—red-eyed and red-nosed—and said, "What's the point?"

"Exactly," I said. Thinking she was asking whether or not there was a point to our relationship. A reason to go on. Hoping she'd come to the conclusion that there wasn't.

"There is no point, is there?"

"Probably not," I said.

"So that's it? My whole life has no meaning? Is that why your fucking book is so precious and you don't care at all about me?"

"Don't be so dramatic," I said.

"But you said it. You said there's probably no point to my life." What should've been the whites of Sophie's eyes glowed like red coals at the bottom of a fire pit.

"That's not what I meant. I'm sure your life has meaning."

"What is it, then?" Sophie asked. "What meaning does my life have? That's what I want to know."

"I don't know. What meaning does anyone's life have?"

"None!"

"Oh, quit it," I said. "Just because you don't know the answer to something doesn't mean it doesn't exist."

"But what is the answer?" Sophie asked. Like I was holding out on her. "What's the meaning of life? That's what I want to know. If it didn't all seem so pointless..." Sophie drifted off. She grabbed half of the broken record on the floor and started breaking it into pieces. I don't know why it bothered me. It wasn't like I could've played the record ever again. Still, did she have to keep breaking it in pieces? Was I supposed to come up with an answer for the meaning of life while I watched her destroy my record?

I couldn't come up with anything to say. I just stared at Sophie. She broke the record into bits.

The music from next door had stopped. I heard their screen door slam shut. Three seconds later, there was a knock on my door. I didn't move to answer it. Neither did Sophie. Before we could've gotten to the door, it opened anyway. It was Swoboda, one of the next door drunks. He had a bottle of beer in one hand. He stood on my living room floor like it was a ship at sea, swaying back and forth. Rocking there. He pointed one finger in the air and said, "To the bar."

Sophie looked up from the floor. She smiled. "I'm in." She hopped to her feet. "I'm young. I deserve to have a little fun," she said. "Hang on a second, Swoboda." She walked back to the bathroom to clean up.

Swoboda looked at my broken record. He looked at me. "To the bar?" he asked.

I shook my head. "Nah." I stood up and walked into the kitchen. Someone had left a bottle of Rumplemintz there, and I was trying to get rid of it. I poured a shot for Swoboda. Sophie walked past the kitchen and into the living room. I poured a shot for her, too, and brought both shots out to them.

"Dan the man," Swoboda said and drank the shot. Sophie drank hers. She threw the glass at me. I batted it down. She grabbed a record out of my stacks. The Pixies. *Doolittle*. She pulled the record out of the sleeve, broke it in half, and walked out the door.

Swoboda looked at me, stunned. I waved to him. "Have fun," I said.

He nodded and left.

I looked for my Jim Thompson book. It was gone. Sophie must've palmed it.

I went back to my bedroom. Dresser drawers were on the bed, one of them missing its face. The top of the dresser was empty and everything that had been there—surfboard wax and a couple of books and a zine and some cash—had all been swept into a trash can. I saw my favorite sculpture. I'd made it a few weeks earlier. I'd taken steel and shaped it into a waterspout and put a thick weld around it to look like it was foaming water and I'd made these little people out of bolts and wire coat hangers and scraps of steel, and the people were hanging onto the waterspout, riding it for all its worth. Only hurricane Sophie had knocked a couple of those little people off the waterspout. And the waterspout was now impaled through a longboard that my brother Joe had given me. Sophie knew enough to throw the metal through the stringer of the board, so even I couldn't fix it. There was more carnage around the room, but with the fucked up longboard and broken waterspout, I didn't even want to look.

The sliding glass door to my bedroom was open. Hot air from the backyard blew in. Most of my clothes were scattered around in the backyard. I went out there to pick them up. The sad thing, I thought as I picked up the clothes, was that this wasn't the worst of Sophie's bouts. One time, back in Kill Devil Hills, she'd taken scissors and cut open every t-shirt I had. From the collar to the bottom. Every single one. And I only had t-shirts at the time, so I literally had no shirts. I had to walk barechested into a store and buy some. I went to a tourist place and got the three-for-ten-dollars deal on shirts that said "Outer Banks, North Carolina" on them. I wore nothing but those stupid tourist t-shirts for months. One other time, she'd taken all of my records—not just a Pixies one and a Minutemen one, but all of them—threw them in the bathtub, poured lighter fluid all over them, and lit them on fire. They didn't burn very well, but they did melt into a mass of crap. And there were forever instances of her palming whatever she thought was valuable to me, and I'd never see those things again. Mostly, though, she only attacked my things. She never, up to that point, had been violent toward me. She'd never hit me or slapped me or anything. She just trashed my things.

I'd usually breakup with her after attacks like that. The breakup would stick for a couple of weeks or a month, depending on where she was in her cycle of drug abuse and whether or not she was back in therapy. I kept taking her back, though. I don't know why.

I guess I do know why. I just don't want to get into it.

Anyway, I was out in the backyard, picking up my clothes when one of the next door drunks, Lester, popped his head over the fence. "Getting thrown out?" Lester asked.

"I'm throwing myself back in."

"Crazy Sophie," he said. "I hope you don't mind me saying, but that chick is nuts."

"Who's crazier: her for being the way she is or me for staying with her?"

"That's a good question." Lester looked at all my clothes in the backyard. "Fuck all that shit," he said. "Come over here and have a beer."

I threw my handful of clothes through the sliding glass door. "I think I will," I said.

"Oh," Lester said, as if he really were just remembering it. "Bring beer."

Typical of the next door drunks. It was all feast or famine with those guys. They had a full refrigerator and shared with everyone or they had nothing and bummed off of me. There never seemed to be an in-between. It didn't matter to me, though. People were always partying after hours at my pad. They usually brought more beer than they drank, pulling that old two A.M. trick of buying a case, drinking two beers, and passing out. I grabbed a six-pack of Miller Lite—because that was a better beer to give away than it was to drink—and went next door.

Lester sat in the backyard, smoking a joint. He had a set of golf clubs back there. He handed me the joint. I took a hit and handed him a beer. Let the weekend begin.

"So Swoboda and Sally and all of them are in the family room, having a fucking twist contest and I'm sitting back here, trying to get some peace and quiet," Lester said. "And what should I see but the next door neighbor's underpants flying out his back door. What kinda crap is that?"

I took another hit off the joint and shrugged my shoulders. I handed the joint back to Lester. I opened a beer for myself.

"So I start trying to reason things out for myself. I think, well, maybe Sophie is kicking Danny out, right? But what I can't figure out is, when did Sophie move in?"

"She didn't," I said.

"So, again, what kinda crap?"

I ran my hand along the fake leather golf bag. "What's up with the clubs?"

"Swoboda says he stole them," Lester said. "But Sally says that he bought them at a garage sale for ten bucks."

"Does he golf?"

"No."

"Do you have balls?"

"The biggest pair you've ever seen."

I looked at Lester. He was all grin. I reached for the joint. He passed it. I asked, "Golf balls?"

"There's a whole shitload of them in that side pocket."

"So what you're telling me," I said, "is that we can stand back here and drink beer and launch golf balls into downtown."

Lester stood. "That's exactly what I'm telling you," he said.

And that's exactly what we did. I reached for the biggest club I could find. It had a wooden head. Lester took it out of my hands and gave me an iron club. He showed me how to stand and how to swing. He shot a few balls first. We lived behind a nightclub called Sandals. His first few balls landed on the roof of Sandals. I took some swings. My first ball shot in a line drive into the fence and came screaming back at us. Lester shook his head and gave me more pointers. I hit the side fence one time, but the rest of my chip shots landed on the Sandals roof. In my head, I pictured the happy hour crowd at Sandals hearing the thumps on the roof and coming up with conspiracy theories. Hail. Martians. Terrorists. Errant mints from airplane toilets. Two stoned guys golfing.

Lester pulled me out of my head and said, "I know it's none of my business, but you seem like a normal guy, Danny. Why don't you breakup with that crazy chick?"

"See, that's the problem," I said. I handed him the club and stepped away from the ball. My beer sat on the air conditioning unit. I picked the beer up and took a sip. "Whenever I leave her, she chases me. I always give in and take her back."

"It doesn't make any sense."

"No," I said. "No, it doesn't."

Lester held the club in his hand. A golf ball sat on the ground between us. Teed up. Lester didn't take a swing. He said, "So, what? You're waiting for her to leave you?"

"Exactly."

"How's that plan working?"

"Good," I said. "Maybe today's the day she'll leave."

Lester kinda sang that last line. "Maybe today's the day she'll leave." He stood in front of the ball, adjusted his feet, took a phantom swing, stepped closer, and whacked the ball deep into downtown.

I couldn't hear the ball land. Lester smiled. I thought, maybe today's the day she'll leave.

About an hour later, I ran into Bart in front of Miguel's. He was in a bad way. Glowing red sunburnt, feet coated in beach sand, and so drunk that his left eyelid sagged down like he was trying to sleep, one half of his body at a time. "What's the rumpus, Danny?" he said to me. "Where's your girl?"

"Possessed," I said. "I'm ready to call the priest and exorcise those demons."

Bart put a hand on my shoulder, either to comfort me or to keep himself from falling. Probably a little of both. "Let's get a beer, then."

I wanted to do just this, or really do anything but be back at my apartment when Sophie got back. Lester had split earlier to have dinner with his dad on Merritt Island. I needed a partner in crime. Bart was a good one. I knew he wanted to go to the Casablanca. Helen was working there at the time, and Bart spent a lot of hours sitting at her bar, making an ass of himself. He was too smitten. I couldn't stand to watch it. I said, "I'm not going there."

Bart stood up straight. "Then we're at an impasse."

I looked up at the sign for Miguel's. Bart did the same. We decided to go in for dinner.

Miguel's was a Cuban diner. A hell of a greasy spoon. We ate there all the time. And there was a server at Miguel's who Bart had been drooling over. At the time, Bart had a sad little schoolboy crush on just about any woman who'd serve him beer. He made me wait until he figured out which section was his favorite waitress's, and we sat in her section.

The waitress came over. She was a pretty woman. Shiny black hair. All hip sway when she walked. A lot of cleavage and a gold cross right in the middle of it. Probably every drunk guy on the beach had a little crush on her.

Bart stared directly at her cleavage and ordered a soda. I looked her in the eyes and ordered the same. She walked away.

Bart picked at a tear in the black vinyl booth. He said, "So the drugs ain't doing Sophie any good?"

I assumed Bart meant the Prozac and not the crystal meth. "They were," I said. But the truth was, I wasn't sure about it. Sophie had been on so many drugs over the years, it was hard to tell. I took a lot of them with her. And when you're fucked up yourself, it's difficult to gauge how the other person is doing. Some shit seemed to do okay for Sophie. She was good on Ritalin. I think only because it saved her the trouble of having to go out and buy speed. And I'm sure Ritalin was better for her than your garden variety crank. Sophie on Prozac was a nightmare. It would blank her out completely. She'd be calm and peaceful, sure, but not pleasantly calm. Zombie calm. She was like a Stepford wife on that shit. I preferred the insanity. But Sophie had a lot of control over her vices. She'd have an appointment with a shrink and say, "I think I'd like some Xanax today." And she'd think up a story for the shrink that would get her Xanax. She got so bad—or good, depending on your perspective—at this that she bought a copy of the *DSM III* and learned how to fake symptoms of various mental disorders just for the drugs she could get out of it. I hate to admit this, but I actually helped her. I know that I should've encouraged her to actually get healthy with all the therapy her dad was paying for. I know I should've been supportive. I tried to be. But I liked the drugs, too. And I doubt she would've listened to me, anyway.

I didn't want to tell Bart all this, so I just said, "She fine when she doesn't drink. But the last few nights." I paused.

"What did she do this time?"

"She tried to kick me out of my apartment."

"Out of *your* apartment?"

I nodded.

"That makes no sense," Bart said.

The waitress brought our drinks. Bart and I ordered dinner. We watched her walk away again. I said, "She told me she'd quit it all and straighten up if I could tell her what the meaning of life is," I said.

"The waitress did?"

"No, dumbass. Sophie."

"What'd you tell her?"

"I told her I'd ask you and get back to her."

Bart grabbed a piece of Cuban bread out of the black wicker basket on the table. He slathered butter on it and put the whole piece in his mouth. He chewed for what seemed like forever. He gulped down most of his soda in one trip to the lips. The waitress came back with a pitcher and refilled his drink. I glanced at a map of Cuba on the wall. I waited for Bart to answer, because, if there was one thing I knew about Bart, it was that he'd thought about this question. He had probably written a paper on it when he was in college. He probably had his "meaning of life" essay sitting in a box in his mom's attic. He probably hung out with other philosophy majors at the University of Tennessee and debated the issue. He probably sat in bars, staring at the condensation on his mug of beer and letting the question drift like a yellow fog through his brain. And he probably ran through a million visions and revisions in his theory. But what did Bart say when I asked him? He said, "How the fuck would I know?"

"I don't know," I said. "But Sophie likes you. She told me that you're the smartest guy she knows."

"If all the people you know in the world are idiots, and one person is just a little less of an idiot, he'd seem like a genius, wouldn't he?"

"What are you saying?" I asked. "That we're all idiots?"

"No," Bart said. "Just me and Sophie."

And me, too. Let's face it. Bart didn't want to say it, but I was an idiot, too. I gave Bart time to wolf down another piece of bread and said, "So what is it, Bart? If pressed to come up with an answer, what would you say the meaning of life is?"

"I don't know," Bart said. "Carbon?"

Was he trying to fuck with me? Did he think I was a college professor looking for a cute answer? I'd asked for meaning and he gave me a definition.

Luckily, our food came before I could get too mad. Pork chops and black beans and rice and plantains. A little heaven on a plate. I hadn't realized how hungry I was until I started eating, but I chowed down. I was sopping up the last of the black bean juice with flat bread when Bart was still working through his first chop.

I watched Bart eat. He was so dehydrated from the booze and from hanging out at the beach that he could hardly finish a bite of food without drinking half of his soda. The waitress had to keep coming back to our table to refill his drink. And the more Bart ate, the higher his left eyelid lifted. I could see the guy coming back to life with all the sugar and caffeine and grub. This could end up dangerous. If he hadn't eaten, he probably would've just passed out early and not hurt himself too badly. As it stood, though, he'd get his second wind and blow himself into a night of wasted money and bad decisions.

As he finished up his food, he started talking again. He said,

"If you think about it, Danny, carbon isn't a stupid answer. Because if you take the whole universe and break it down to atoms—which you can do. All the world is is a random collection of atoms. They come together and break apart. Making things. Destroying things. And the only collection of atoms that all life has in common is carbon. So if all we are is a random collection, then that's what we mean. That's all life is. It's random. Chaos."

So there it was. Bart really had gone through all his decisions and revisions and come up with his meaning of life. It wasn't carbon at all. It was random events and chaos. "I can't tell Sophie that," I said. "Her life is too random and chaotic as it is."

"Well, hey, man," Bart said. "So's mine, and that's the belief that keeps it going. I'm doing fine."

"Doing fine, huh?" I asked. I didn't bring up the point that he lived out of a duffel bag and slept either on my couch or in the backseat of my Galaxie most nights. I did say, "How much money do you have, Mr. Doing Fine?"

Bart pulled a wad of crumpled bills out of his pocket. He flattened the bills and counted them. "Almost two hundred bucks."

"How much do you have to your name?"

Bart smiled. "Almost two hundred bucks."

I nodded. "You're doing great," I said. "Dinner's on me." I picked up the tab and walked over to the cash register to pay it.

When I got back, Bart told me he'd gotten a date with the waitress. That made me feel even more sorry for Bart. I knew that the waitress was a Jesus freak. She'd tried to sell me on her church one day when I was in Miguel's, eating alone. Mixing a meaning-of-life-seeking Bart with the god squad in the middle of a bender weekend could be a recipe for disaster. Maybe it was all chaos.

My roommate, Rick, had a party going back at my place. People were everywhere. Someone brought a keg and set it up in the carport.

I planted myself in a lawn chair beside the keg and commenced to drinking and chatting with whoever got a refill. Someone brought a spiked watermelon. People flowed in and out. I knew most of them. I hadn't seen some of them since the last summer's party. Some folks went to bars and others came back from bars. Some set up a game of quarters on the white plastic lawn furniture. Some smoked joints in the backyard. A few golf balls flew over the house and into the front lawn. One drunk girl walked into a closed screen door and fell back down the front steps. One really sunburnt guy passed out in the driveway. Two girls took a permanent marker and drew all over him. For a while, a game of hoops took over this section of Woodland Ave. The party started to get too big, so I decided to leave. Half of me hoped my apartment would still be there when I got back. Half of me hoped it would all burn down.

I cut through the backyard and across the Sandals parking lot. Someone screamed out, "Heads up!"

I ducked. Lester walked up behind me, laughing. Nothing fell out of the sky.

"Where are you going?" Lester asked.

"I'm not sure. What about you?"

"The Bungalow."

"The Bungalow?" I have to say, this surprised me. The Bungalow was a strictly tourist joint. The kind of place that had wet t-shirt contests and classic rock cover bands. It was three blocks from where I lived and I hadn't been there since back when I was way underage and it was the only place that would honor my fake ID. "Why are you going there?"

"The whole sick crew is there." Lester reached into the pocket of his baggy, plaid shorts. He pulled out a can of beer and handed it to me. I would've turned it down, but Lester had a second beer in his other pocket. He raised his drink. "Maybe today's the day she'll leave," he said. I drank to that.

We walked along the dark streets of downtown Cocoa Beach. A warm, nighttime breeze blew in off the ocean. A police cruiser drove by. Lester waved his beer in front of the cruiser, saying, "These are not the droids you're looking for."

The cruiser kept driving.

"The force is strong with you," I said. Even though Cocoa Beach cops never busted people for drinking in the streets. It didn't matter whether the drunk was a Jedi or not.

The next door drunks had taken over the Bungalow. They'd pulled a bunch of tables together and looked like they were having a banquet next to the dance floor. The table was covered in empties. One of the crew was on stage, singing a karaoke version of "Soul Man." A couple of guys in the crew had apparently been spending too much time at a topless bar, because they were shirtless on the dance floor, giving lap dances to a couple of tourist girls. The girls kept laughing and smacking the guys' butts. One of the guys even had a bra on. Swoboda was out on the dance floor. His upper body didn't move much, but his feet went non-stop. I had to watch him a while to figure out what he was doing. But I remembered him telling me that he used to play soccer, and I realized he was going on an imaginary dribbling spree through all the dancers. The rest of the crew sat at their banquet table, drinking, doing shots, pointing at one dancer. Laughing. Pointing at another. Applauding.

When Lester and I walked up, Sally poured us two beers from a pitcher. Sally was the next door drunk who actually lived and paid rent at the place next door. The glasses she handed us were not clean. I didn't care. Sally said something to me. I couldn't hear her. I shrugged. She gave me the thumbs up. What was there to say, really?

The song ended. The karaoke kid launched into a version of "Mustang Sally." Sally jumped up and ran out onto the dance floor.

One of the topless dancers gave up his tourist girl and led Sally in some ballroom dancing. Not to be outdone, Swoboda dropped to the floor and scooted on his butt as if he were rowing a boat. A few more dancers followed him. Lester got up and joined the crew team. Pretty soon, the whole lot of them were up and dancing. The goofiness was contagious. I joined in.

The karaoke kid didn't give up the stage. He ran through the complete soundtrack of *The Commitments*. Everyone in the joint was up and dancing. The floor was packed and hot. Smelling of smoke and suntan oil and booze sweating out and perfume melting away. Sally snuck behind one of the next door drunks and pulled his pants down. He was wearing a pink speedo. He grabbed Sally and did the lambada with her. Lester kept pointing and screaming, "That's the forbidden dance," until finally someone else pulled the guy's pants back up and the pink speedo lambada ended.

I danced a few songs with a short, blond girl who was part of the whole sick crew. I knew she was married. Her husband sat at the banquet table and rooted for me. He even bought us shots. When the karaoke kid sang "Chain of Fools," I let the guy dance with his wife and scooted over to Sally.

"Where are your speedos?" she asked.

"Next time," I said. I didn't do the lambada with her, either. But I did break out all my best Prince moves. About halfway through my jig, one of the other next door drunks came over to me. She said, "You're Sophie's boyfriend, aren't you?"

I nodded.

She said, "She's passed out in the bathroom stall. If I get her out, will you take her home?"

I nodded again. Fuck it, I thought. At least Sophie's finally sleeping.

Sally went into the bathroom with her friend. They both came out a minute later. Sophie had an arm over each of their shoulders.

She looked confused and tired. She had red hand prints on her face and red elbow prints on her knees. I put my arm around her.

"Can you walk?" I asked.

"A little."

"Just lean on me," I said, and I walked her home.

She apologized a dozen times on the way home. "I'm sorry, Danny," she kept saying. "I'm sorry."

It was exactly what I needed to hear. But it was also the last thing I needed to hear.

The next morning brought chaos. You could say Bart had predicted it. But Bart created a lot of the chaos, too, so it was more of a self-fulfilling prophecy than a prediction.

He woke me up at seven A.M. to do shots. We drank until he had the date with the Jesus girl. He stole Sophie's car to take the girl out. The people passed out on my floor came to life. I could hear the next door drunks milling around. Everything became a mass of movement: trips to the grocery store and breakfasts acquired and showers taken and more booze purchased and trips to Sullivan's for fresh-squeezed screwdrivers and a general migration to the front lawn and tables set up and a keg tapped and guests arriving and basketball games commencing and by the time noon had rolled around, the party was in full swing again. Sophie slept through most of it, thankfully. I was glad she was sleeping again.

Bart came back early from his date. He'd found out the hard way that the Jesus girl was after his soul. Nothing more, nothing less. He also found out the hard way not to steal Sophie's car. She attacked him as soon as he got back to my pad. Jumped on his back and started swinging at him, closed-fisted. I let her take a few shots. She deserved it. He had taken her car without asking. When enough was enough, I pulled Sophie off Bart and convinced her that she'd said it was okay for him to borrow the car. She looked at me to see if I was lying. I could see in her eyes that the meth bender was far from over. I let her go. She started really drinking.

Bart had managed to score some weed and acid during his trip to the church. He rolled a joint and told the story and drank a beer and someone handed him a bottle of tequila and he turned it up and guzzled about four shots' worth. He staggered out onto the part of the street in front of our house that had been designated as the basketball court. He was barely able to stand. Rick called out that Bart was on his team. A couple of guys on the other team laughed at Bart. As soon as the ball was in his hands, though, Bart was back in form. A star again. He dribbled until he could shoot, then shot. Eleven baskets in a row. No one else even got to touch the ball. Bart got kicked out of the game. He went back to my bed to pass out.

By this time, Sophie was wired and drunk and I'd had enough. I took her into the backyard to have a heart-to-heart. I kept it simple. "I've had enough," I said. "You and me are over."

Sophie's glance darted around the backyard. She looked like a trapped cat. I started to walk away. "Wait," Sophie said. She started talking. She told me everything that was wrong with me. I agreed. She told me a whole lot more. I decided I needed new friends. I walked out the back of my backyard and across the Sandals parking lot. Alone. I walked all the way to the beach.

A few of the next door drunks were at the beach. They had lawn chairs set up and a cooler. Lester waved me over. There was an empty lawn chair. He invited me to sit in it. He gave me a can of beer. I said hello to everyone in the group. Helen was there.

"I thought you were having a party at your place," she said.

"I think the party was having me," I said.

Sally raised her beer. "I'll drink to that."

I took off my shirt and kicked off my flip flops. All of those random and chaotic events from my place were getting to me. It felt good to sit in a small, calm group with no drama around me. Or, there was probably drama among the next door drunks, but I didn't know what it was, so I didn't have to care.

Lester reached over and tapped my beer with his, like we were toasting. "Maybe today's the day she'll leave," he said.

I smiled. "Today's the day she did leave."

"Your crazy girlfriend?" Helen said. "Really?"

"Really," I said.

"Did you kick her out?" Sally asked.

"Yeah, but I think she was sick of my shit, anyway."

"What did you do?" Helen asked.

"It couldn't have been what Danny did," Sally said. "We found her passed out on the toilet last night. Danny had to carry her home. It was the saddest thing."

"Really?" Helen asked.

"Really," Sally said.

"So what happened?" Lester asked.

"Near as I can tell, when she was beating up Bart for stealing her car, she decided she was in love with him," I said. "At least that's what she told me after I told her we were quits."

"Bart? Your buddy Bart?" Helen asked. "The one who's always drunk at my bar?"

"One and the same," I said.

And that was it. Helen started telling Bart stories. Lester started telling Sophie stories. Sally told next door drunk stories. And so on. Nothing mean, but enough to laugh about. Things settled down. I stayed away from the chaos for a little while.

That night, I found myself surrounded by the whole crew of next door drunks. We were in the middle of the block party—among the beer tent and the carnival games and the food stands and the mass of people—taking over the dance floor. Pink speedos abounded. Apparently, Swoboda had been at the dollar store and found a clearance bin full of the pink men's bikinis. Two for a dollar. He'd bought twenty and passed them out to anyone who'd actually put it on. I'll admit it. I got mine.

The goofiness from the Bungalow abounded once again. Swoboda on his dribbling spree. Alex—the guy who'd been in the bra the night before—rocked the sprinkler. The karaoke kid was breakdancing. Sally and the original pink speedo guy—who was wearing regular baggies at this point—were dancing in that old New Wave style: all swinging arms and kicking feet. And I danced with Helen.

We'd been hanging out all day. Now she nuzzled close to me, grabbing my belt, unhooking it, and dropping my pants. I joined the pink speedo armada. I did my best lambada. I put my hand on her hip and swayed back and forth with her. She stood on her tiptoes and kissed me.

That was the real beginning of the end.

21
The Funny Thing about Regret

The nagging id inside me wanted to beat up the wheelchair dude. I spent a lot of time trying to figure out how I could do that and still feel good about myself.

The past was weighing on me too heavily. It was too much. I'd left one ex-girlfriend dead on the train tracks in Flagstaff. I had another ex-girlfriend—the one who'd tried to kill me—back in town, floating around in the same circles I floated in. I couldn't think about either one. I couldn't bring myself to think about all the life that Libra was missing. I couldn't bring myself to think about Sophie stabbing me. I couldn't bear to let these thoughts run through my mind one more time. Really, with problems like this, it just made sense that all my anger should be directed toward someone safe, like the wheelchair dude.

What's more, the past wasn't so much the past. At the very moment when I tried to rationalize reasons that would allow me to beat up a guy in a wheelchair, two very significant people from my past hung out with me. Bart and I were having lunch at Duke's. It was about two in the afternoon.

Bart was giving me shit about Taylor. He did this in a very Bart way. He told Helen about it, in front of me. He said, "What do you think of a thirty year-old man who spends all his time with a twelve-year-old girl?"

"I'm not thirty," I said. "I'm twenty-nine."

"Okay, Helen," Bart said, "what do you think of a twenty-nine-year-old man who spends all his time with a twelve-year-old girl?"

"What do you think of it, Bart?" Helen asked.

"I think it's creepy. They hang out all the time. They're probably gonna hang out after lunch."

Helen looked at me. "Are you?"

I nodded. "We're going surfing in about an hour," I said.

"And, watch, she's gonna come over to our house wearing next to nothing and Danny's gonna invite her inside and I'm gonna have to sit there like, oh shit, there's an underdressed adolescent in my living room."

"She's not underdressed," I told Helen. "She wears what girls wear when they go surfing."

"Which is what?" Helen asked.

"Bikini top and board shorts," Bart said.

"That is next to nothing," Helen told me.

"She's a kid. We go surfing. That's it," I said. What I didn't say was that there was a little more to it. Part of the reason I liked Taylor was because I had no history with her. Nothing bad had happened between her and me. No issues needed to be skated around. I couldn't say that about any of my other friends.

"What do her parents think about you hanging out with her all the time?" Helen asked.

"We don't hang out. We go surfing. And it's not all the time. It's just sometimes."

"What do her parents think about you surfing with her sometimes?"

"I don't know. They're cool with it, I guess. They must be. Her dad's the one who told her to take lessons from me."

"And who are her parents?" Bart asked. "Do we even know? Has Danny even met them? Ask him that, Helen."

"Have you met this girl's parents?" Helen asked.

"No."

"And ask Danny if this girl looks like Rosalie," Bart said.

"Who's Rosalie?"

"Rosalie is Danny's old high school girlfriend."

"Is that true, Danny?" Helen asked. "Are you hanging out with a little girl who looks like your old high school girlfriend?"

"We don't hang out," I said. "We go surfing. And, no, she doesn't look like Rosalie. Bart just thinks that because they're both black girls."

"No, dude. That little chick looks like Rosalie," Bart said.

"Something's fucked up there," Helen said.

"Nothing's fucked up," I said. "You guys know me a little."

"I know this," Helen said. "You're gonna make that little girl fall in love with you. Because that's what girls do with you, Danny. They fall in love and you break their fucking hearts."

So that was it? The past was really closer than I thought? We weren't sitting there talking about Taylor at all. We were talking about me and Helen and Bart and Sophie being back in town and all that shit all over again. I dropped a ten dollar bill on the bar, left my burrito half eaten, and said, "Fuck you guys. I'm going home."

And on my bike ride home, I tried to think of justifications for beating up the wheelchair dude.

It was typical crappy, blown out Florida surf. Taylor and I stood on the shore in front of the 3rd Street walkway, looking at the ocean. "Should we even go out?" she asked.

I watched the waves peak and close out. I knew what it meant to go out there. I figured it would be good for Taylor to ride these waves. You could learn a lot about how waves build and form on days like this. I nodded. "It's worth it," I said.

I paddled out into the chop. Taylor followed.

A day like this meant that you had to paddle all the time. Chase every little peak and chop. I went after a little peak, caught it, rode it for about five seconds, and it closed out. I saw Taylor right behind me, trying to do the same thing, missing the peak. I paddled back out and showed her how to do it. I pointed out the way the peaks built. I swam into the right position. She tailed me. I told her when and where to paddle. She caught a little wave. It only lasted a few seconds, but she was stoked.

"I didn't know you could ride waves like this," she said. "It's awesome."

And, see, that's the other reason why I liked surfing with Taylor: everything was brand new to her. She could ride these crappy waves and think it was awesome. She could learn something. She could find a way to have fun with shit like this. I could still have fun out there, but it would never be new to me again.

After about an hour, I'd had enough. I'd gone out surfing to try to forget about Sophie and Helen and Libra and all that. Surfing helped a little. It distracted me, but it didn't free my mind. I caught a little peak that actually turned out to be a half-decent wave. I rode it nearly into shore, then swam the rest of the way in.

Taylor was still out. I'd leave it to her to catch her own wave in. I walked up onto shore and sat down. I cast a glance up at the 3rd Street walkway, and, sure enough, the wheelchair dude sat there. He had his camera with him. He looked away when I looked at him. I really need to kick that guy's ass, I thought. I still hadn't come up with a good rationalization, though, so I just sat on the beach and watched Taylor.

She had a hard time catching a wave without me to guide her.

She paddled back and forth up the coast, chasing chop and getting frustrated. She started to just swim in, apparently thought better of it, and swam back out. She sat on her board and caught her breath. While she was doing this, a wave came right for her. She swung her board toward shore and started paddling. It was perfect. Waist high and enough face to ride. She rode it for maybe seven or eight seconds, pumping on the wave, trying to carve a little, getting all she could until the wave closed out and her session was over.

A few minutes later she was sitting on the beach with me, looking out at the waves. She said, "I can't believe how fun that is."

"You never know until you paddle out," I said.

"I guess not. I guess you have to try things."

"That's the funny thing about regret," I told her. "It's better to regret something you have done than something you haven't done."

This brought out Taylor's *you're crazy* look. "Did you make that up?"

"Nah. I got it from a Butthole Surfers song."

"A what?"

I remembered that Taylor either wasn't born or was just an infant when the Butthole Surfers were good. I didn't want to explain. I let it drop. We sat in silence. I stared out at the choppy water. No one else was out surfing. Just little peaks and close-outs. A lot of wind.

After a minute, Taylor said, "What do you regret, Danny?"

"Everything," I said.

"Be serious."

"I am being serious," I said. "Lately, I'm regretting it all."

"What's the big one? What's your number one regret?"

"What's yours?" I asked. Because, really, when someone asks a question about something like that, isn't it because they want you to ask that question of them?

Taylor bit her lip and looked east. I could see she was thinking about how to say it. "Okay," she said. "There's this guy at school, Chip Summers. I hate him. He's like, this total asshole. And he's got this super expensive mountain bike that he's always bragging about. I get so sick of him. Like he's the king shit because he's got an expensive bike. And he's got one of those fancy locks for it. Like the horseshoe shaped locks. So I took some super glue and I squeezed it into the keyhole of the lock. Now he can't get his key in the lock. The bike is just stuck there at school. And I'm like, who's the queen shit now." Taylor was all grin.

"You don't look like you regret that at all," I said.

"I do," Taylor said, still smiling. " 'Cause it wasn't enough. I wanted to get at him worse."

"Do you have a crush on Chip or something?" I asked.

"Gross! No!"

"Then why are you doing this stuff to him?"

" 'Cause he called me a nigger," Taylor said.

"Okay," I said. "So now we have to find new ways to get back at him."

"That's what I'm saying," Taylor said.

"Here's a good trick," I said. "You get one of those hair removal creams, like Nair or something, and you squeeze it into the top of his shampoo bottle. When he washes his hair, big chunks of it will come out."

"I thought of that," Taylor said. "I even thought of a way that I could get into his house to do it. But then I was like, no, he's got a little sister, you know, and what if they, like, share the same shampoo bottle?"

"Good thinking."

"I heard that doesn't work, anyway."

"Oh, it works," I said. "Believe me. It works." Because Sophie had done that to me once. I lost half my hair and had to shave the rest of it off. I looked like a skinhead for a month.

"It doesn't matter, anyway, because I did something way worse."

"What did you do?"

"I stood behind Chip one day when he was opening his locker. And I memorized his locker combination. I said it to myself, like, a hundred times in my head. And, after school, I tried opening it, just to make sure I got it right. And it worked. I totally got into his locker. Then I shut it and went home. Then, I went back to school the next day and I told Sandy Kelleher what I did to Chip's bike lock. Because Sandy's, like, this total gossip whore. If you tell her anything, you tell the whole school. So, next thing I know, Chip is after me. He's calling me a jungle bunny and making monkey sounds at me and yelling at me in the halls and being a huge dickhead. I didn't say anything back to him. I just bit my tongue and took it. And the next day, which was yesterday, I brought a knife to school."

"What kind of knife?"

"One of my stepfather's old hunting knives. He doesn't use it anymore. He said I could have it. So I took it to school and, halfway during first period, I got a bathroom pass and went to Chip's locker and put the knife in it. Then I went to Dean Glenn and started crying and told her what Chip had said and also added that he said he was gonna bring a knife to school and stab me and I was worried for my life. So Dean Glenn, who's the only black woman in the school besides me, says, 'Let's go take a look.'

"That's when they found the knife and expelled Chip."

"Holy shit," I said. "Remind me to never cross you."

"It's pretty bad, huh?"

"Yeah, that's pretty bad."

"Am I a bad person?"

"No. Just make sure you don't tell anyone about this but me."

"Oh, I won't."

I smiled. Crazy kid. I shook my head.

Taylor said, "At least he can't call me a fucking nigger anymore."

I got up and grabbed my board. "I need to be getting home," I said. We started walking for the boardwalk.

"Now it's your turn," Taylor said. "What's your number one regret?"

"I don't know," I said. Though I did know. I walked up the boardwalk steps.

"Do you regret your tattoos?"

"Enough with the tattoos," I said. "They look cool."

"What about those scars in the middle of your tattoos? The ones on your belly?"

"I'll tell you about those when you're older," I said. Because I didn't even want to think about that shit. I kept walking across the beach and up the boardwalk stairs.

The wheelchair dude was there. I'd been thinking about him the whole time Taylor told her story. She'd given me an idea. I stopped when I got to the wheelchair dude and said, "Clay Barker?" Like it had just occurred to me who he was. "That's right. I knew I recognized you. Dante Jones introduced us at one of those cop parties in Cocoa."

The wheelchair dude shook his head.

"No. No. I'm pretty sure about it. You were talking about playing football for Merritt Island High. You were on the team that won state in '79, right?"

Clay kinda smiled. How could he not? He was on that team. He did win state. He didn't say anything to me. He just tried to keep down the smile.

I pointed to Taylor, standing behind me. "Clay, this is Taylor."

Taylor put out her hand to shake his. He shook hands and said, "Is Taylor your first name or last name?" he asked.

"Fuck you," she said.

"Listen, man, I was gonna have some drinks with Dante next Monday night. Why don't you come down and hang with us? We're going to Duke's. Around seven."

Clay said, "I don't know."

I knew he'd be there, though. It was his job. So I said, "It's up to you, man. We'll be down there either way. Maybe I'll see you then."

Clay nodded. Taylor and I walked away. All I could hear was that nagging id screaming inside my head.

22
The Way of the Barnacle

Helen invited me over to her house. I got excited. Turns out, I had the wrong idea.

I went over to her house. She had a little two bedroom bungalow down around Duke's. It wasn't much bigger than the half of a duplex Bart and I shared, but she had a garage. I always wanted one of those. That's where Helen and I went. Not inside the house. To the garage.

Helen unlocked the side door. She said, "Remember when you used to do all those sculptures? Before you ran off on me?"

"Yeah."

"Do you still do stuff like that?"

"Sorta, yeah," I said. "I have a whole pile of that shit over at Duane's."

"Who's Duane?"

"The guy I used to work for."

"Did you just get fired again, Danny?"

"Not fired, exactly. Duane just said I couldn't work for him anymore until the guy in the wheelchair stopped watching me all day."

Helen nodded. "Who is that guy?"

"A private investigator."

"Why's he following you?" Helen paused. "Wait," she said. "Don't tell me. I don't want to know."

She opened the garage door but didn't go in. She said, "Anyway, you shouldn't call your sculptures shit. I like them. My ex-husband loved them. I had a few of those sculptures lying around from the last time you lived here. He sold them for, like, hundreds of dollars."

"Hundreds of dollars! How many did I leave behind?"

"I don't think you understand," Helen said. "He sold them for hundreds of dollars *each*."

"Damn," I said. Because Helen and Sal sold those things, too, but for usually for between twenty and fifty bucks each. I couldn't imagine some sucker paying hundreds of dollars for one. "I wish he was still around."

"He is," Helen said. She opened the door to her two-car garage and turned on the light. One side of the garage was piled in junk. Old lamps, sheets from a tin roof, a metal bed frame, metal everything: magazine racks and chairs and table legs and balcony railings and all kinds of shit. It was all pushed up against a wall. The rest of the garage was pretty clean. Helen had her pickup truck there. She had her bicycle. A washer and dryer. A tool bench. My old acetylene torch and set-up.

I walked over to the tool bench. A bunch of my old tools were still there. My shears. My mallet. A vise. Some pliers. Some clippers and center punches and metal files. Even my old welder's mask. "You kept all this stuff?"

Helen shrugged. "I figured I could get some money for it. But I didn't know who to sell it to. I couldn't bring myself to take it to a pawn shop."

"I'll buy it," I said.

Helen smiled. "You don't have to buy it, Danny." She walked over and sat on the tool bench. Her feet dangled. She pointed at the pile of junk. "My ex-husband left all this stuff here when he moved out. He doesn't want it. I figured you could do something with it."

I walked over to the pile. There was some good stuff there. And Duane had a buddy who ran a body shop. I figured I could get some scrap quarter panels and fenders and shit like that off of him. You could never hammer that stuff flat again, but you could get some nice textures out of it. It all seemed easy enough. It all looked like possibilities. It was kinda beautiful. "I could do something with this," I said.

"I get half," Helen said.

"What do you mean?"

"I mean I get my ex-husband to sell your stuff, and I get half of what we make. He'd get a commission. I get half of what's left over after that."

"You can have it all," I said.

"I don't want it all," Helen said. "I want half."

I shrugged. I didn't care about any of that. I didn't really believe that her ex-husband could get any real money from anything I made. I kinda wanted to get to welding, though. I mean, I wanted to hang out with Helen, sure. But really, I wanted to start welding.

Maybe Helen saw this in me. Who knows? She got up from the workbench and handed me a key. "This unlocks the side door," she said. "It won't unlock any other door in the house. You can use the garage whenever you want. Roll my truck into the driveway if you're welding."

I nodded. She smiled and started to walk away. I said, "Thanks, Helen."

Believe it or not, this actually changed things. Now that I wasn't working for Duane, I had a lot of time to spend welding for myself.

Since Helen had set all this up for me and since she owned Duke

Kahanamoku's and since she dug that whole Pacific Island kitsch, I came up with a tiki theme for the stuff. I fashioned the balcony handrail into metal bamboo shoots. I hammered the tin roof sheets flat and cut them into strips and wove them into mats that I could use with the bamboo and make all kinds of shit. I turned the bed frame into a picture frame with wiry waves and diamond-shaped strips of metal and I framed her Duke Kahanamoku painting. I made actual tikis out of old fenders and lamps. It was weird to see metal versions of all that stuff. I kinda liked it.

The more I worked, the more abstract the tiki theme became. It was just a starting point for all kinds of weird shapes and designs.

Helen seemed to like the stuff. Or she acted like she liked it, but she never did anything with it. She just lined each sculpture up against the garage wall, right where the metal had been originally. She did take the painting and frame to Duke's and hang it up there. Everything else, she just piled along the wall.

Still, I got kinda obsessed with all that scrap metal. For a month, it was just about all I did. I'd pick up dead bodies at night, sure, and I'd surf with Taylor a few times a week. But mostly, I hung out in Helen's garage, welding all this shit. Helen usually wasn't around. Usually, it was just me and my metal and my flame.

Helen came out to check on me one afternoon. I was using a tin woven mat and an old magazine holder and trying to rip off Picasso's painting about the three hookers. I don't know why. It wasn't coming out how I wanted it to and I was getting frustrated and thinking about torching it all when Helen called out to me. "Doing okay, there?"

I turned off the torch and lifted my mask. "Hey," I said. "What's up?"

"I heard a lot of banging," she said. "Wanted to make sure everything's okay."

I put the torch on the tool bench. I loosened the vise and let my latest pile fall to the floor. "It's all a bunch of shit," I said. "A waste of time."

"You gotta stop running yourself down, Danny."

I shrugged. I took off my mask. "Do you ever wonder what you want to do with your life?"

"I'm kinda doing it," Helen said. She looked like she felt bad for saying it, but she went on. "I have my own bar. My own house. No bosses. No landlords. It's not bad."

"I guess so," I said. "That's not bad at all." I started to put away my tools. Helen walked over to the tool bench and sat on the middle of it, just to my right. From where she was sitting, I couldn't put my tools up and I couldn't go back to work. I took a step away from her.

"What about you?" she asked. "Do you ever wonder what you want to do with your life?"

"All the fucking time," I said.

"And what do you think about?"

I shrugged and said, "I don't know. You know, I thought I'd be dead by now. I'm turning thirty in a couple of months. I thought the booze and drugs would kill me by then."

Helen shook her head. "You never did enough to kill yourself."

"I don't know. Brother Joe did. I felt like I was on the same track."

"Wasn't your brother in his forties when he died?"

"Yeah. But still..."

Helen wasn't having it. She dealt with boozers for a living. She knew. She said, "It takes a lot to kill yourself. Especially by thirty. Look at your friends. Look at Bart. He drank enough to die by thirty. And Sophie did enough drugs. You never did half as much as them. If they're both doing fine, where does that leave you?"

"Exactly," I said. I felt bad even talking about it with Helen because she was a bartender and people dump their problems on bartenders all the time. Especially Helen, because she was kinda nurturing. She actually listened. That's dangerous for a bartender: to actually listen. I figured I'd let the subject drop. I pushed a bunch of tools to the back of the bench and sat next to Helen. "I appreciate you letting me use your garage."

"Don't mention it," Helen said.

"But, really, I appreciate it."

"Well, really, I get half."

I looked at the metal against the garage wall. Both the stuff I'd welded and the stuff I hadn't welded yet. "Half of what? You haven't even tried to sell it."

"I just like the way it looks there," Helen said. "You took a bunch of junk and welded it into something worthwhile."

I nodded. I knew Helen was trying to give me some advice, there.

23
Twilight of the Idles

The time for my showdown with Clay Barker, Wheelchair Dude, was well overdue. I was having problems making it happen, though. For one thing, I couldn't get Dante to come have a beer with me. I'd made the mistake of telling him what I was up to, and he'd said, "Deal with your own shit, Danny. Leave me out of it." And, nagging id or not, I couldn't find a way to beat up a guy in a wheelchair and not feel like a bully. So Clay kept following me around and I kept trying to figure out a way to deal with it. And, finally, I figured out a way.

I was locking up my bike outside of Duke's when I saw Clay in the parking lot, waiting on me. There was nothing unusual about this. I also saw Bart and Sophie pull into the parking lot. This was unusual. At this point, a plan occurred to me.

I unlocked my bike and walked over to Clay's van. I opened the side door and put my bike in. Clay said, "What the fuck are you doing?"

I climbed into the van and made my way to the passenger seat. "Let's head over to Sully's. It's on Brevard Street, between 1st and 2nd Streets North."

"I know where fucking Sully's is," Clay said.

"So what are you waiting for?"

Clay gave me a long stare. I guess he was sizing things up in his head. I was already in the van. I wasn't acting violently, but I also wasn't going away. So what choices did he have? He could call the cops. He could pull a weapon on me. He could try to talk me out of the seat. Or he could just go to the bar and see what was up. He chose the bar.

I checked out his van while he drove. Seven or eight different paperback crime novels lay scattered around the floor. All of them were old, noir types. Early twentieth century stuff. The type of books that Brother Joe had handed down to me and I kept going back to again and again. He even had Jim Thompson's *Pop. 1280* on the floor. It was the very same novel I'd been reading when Sophie freaked out all those years ago. I picked up Clay's copy. "I love this book," I said.

"It's Thompson's best," Clay said. "Trust me, I've read them all."

And, with that, my nemesis became my buddy.

My plan was simple: get Clay drunk at Sully's, get him to confess who he was working for, and, when I knew for sure it was Libra's parents, call them and tell them to get him the hell off my trail. It was so simple, it was almost retarded. Well, maybe not "almost."

Clay and I took a table at Sully's. I went up to the bar and ordered a pitcher of beer for the two of us. We sat together and drank and talked about books and football and shit like that. I didn't ask him why he was following me and he didn't volunteer. We didn't talk about any personal stuff. We just drank and chatted about shit that didn't mean anything. Just like men normally do at happy hour.

The first pitcher dried up. I purchased a second. I thought about getting shots, just to expedite the process, but really, I wasn't in a hurry. I kinda liked Clay. I didn't mind drinking with him at all. And, anyway, he made his big mistake halfway through the second pitcher. He went to the bathroom, which in and of itself isn't a mistake. But he left his cell phone on the table when he went.

As soon as he'd wheeled around the corner and out of sight, I picked up the cell phone. I wasn't very good at working those things—I'd never had one myself—but it was all logic. Just point arrows and follow directions. I got into his list of recent calls, and, sure enough, there was the 520 area code and Libra's mom's cell number. I figured, why not give it a shot? and hit the call button.

Libra's mom picked up on the second ring. She said, "Hello, Clay."

"Hello, Mrs. Fulton," I said, my voice cracking like a teenage boy's. "This is Danny McGregor."

The line went dead.

I put the phone on the table and looked around Sully's. The scene never changed. The same few regulars sat at the bar, drinking their regular drinks. The bartender played solitaire in a lonely corner. Bart's basketball machine sat unused while he drank at Duke's. The ghost of Joe took an empty stool, ordered an empty beer, faded away. I waited for Libra to join him, but no such luck. I put my hand on my glass of beer, and it started shaking. My whole body shivered. Hearing Libra's mother's voice again, having her hang up on me… There was a time once when that happened all the time. "Hello, Danny, Libra home?" "No, she's…" Click. No chit chat. No time for me. Which was fine. I never really wanted to get to know her anyway. But when so much of my past was turning to ghosts and I heard the voice of a ghost from the past, it put something in my blood and gave me the shakes.

Clay wheeled back from the bathroom. I set his phone on the table and slid it over to him. He picked it up and pushed some arrows, then looked at me all scared and betrayed.

"I think I just got you fired," I said. "Sorry about that."

Clay set his phone on his lap. "If you were sorry, you wouldn't have done it," Clay said. He wheeled back from the table and out the door.

I let him wheel away for a second and forgot that he was the guy who'd been following me for months, taking pictures of me, getting me fired from Duane's, all that. I felt bad for him. I also remembered that my bike was still in his van, and I couldn't let him get too far.

For a few awkward moments, I made empty apologies and pulled my bike out of his van and locked it up against the handicapped parking sign. Clay lifted himself into his van and got situated behind the steering wheel. I waved to him. He waved and backed out of the parking lot.

This would be the end of Clay, but I knew Mrs. Fulton wouldn't give up that easily. Sure enough, within a week, the Samoan would be on my trail.

In the meantime, I went back into Sully's to finish the beer and wrestle with the latest ghost coming to life: Sophie Dunn.

24
Run Away, Danny

Rewind four years.

The stabbing.

Four significant things happened between the summer when Sophie and I broke up for good and the summer when she stabbed me.

First, she went off the deep end. She'd been bluffing in that backyard when she told me she was really in love with Bart and sick of me. A part of her still felt like she needed me. Our breakup was bad news for Sophie. She sold her car and bought enough cocaine to kill a normal person. It almost killed her. Her dad stepped in just in time, fronting her the ton of dough to go to rehab.

Second, Sophie came out of rehab six months later. She came out sweet as could be. It seemed like she'd finally taken care of her shit. She acted like an angel. Bart started dating her.

Third, Bart still hadn't taken care of his shit. He spent most of his time living at my pad. Since I was spending most of my time at Helen's, I didn't mind. When I wasn't around, Bart slept in my bed. When I wasn't around and he and Sophie were dating, they both slept in my bed. I didn't care. Or, to be honest, I did care, but I did my best to convince myself I didn't care.

Fourth, things went well between me and Helen. I switched over to night shifts at the bar so that we could hang out together more. Helen bought me an acetylene welding unit and let me use her garage to weld metal together. She sold the sculptures. I wouldn't take the money she made from them, so she saved it. When she had enough, she bought a longboard to replace the one that Sophie had ruined. I surfed a lot.

I even found a new copy of that Jim Thompson book and read it, cover to cover, with no incident. So I guess five significant things happened.

Then the summer started heating up. Hurricane season came around, and it was only a matter of time before hurricane Sophie struck again.

I'd had a crazy night at work and just wanted to go home and sleep. It was about midnight. Bart and Sophie were sleeping in my bed. Actually, I don't think they were sleeping. I think they heard me come in and quick pretended to sleep. The light was still on in my room.

I walked in and said, "Sorry, guys. You gotta go." I picked up their clothes from the floor and tossed them on the bed. I left the room to give them time to dress.

Bart came out first. He had just his shorts on and his t-shirt in his hand. "Dude, you mind if we crash on your couch?" he asked.

I thought about what they'd probably been doing in my bed and didn't want them doing that on my couch while I tried to sleep. I pulled out my night's tips. I peeled two twenties off the stack. "Listen," I said. "Why don't you and Sophie get a room tonight?"

Bart took the forty bucks and nodded. Sophie walked out of the bedroom, fully dressed. She walked past me, bumping into me but not looking at me. Bart followed her. I went to bed.

Apparently, Bart and Sophie took the forty bucks and went to a bar. They drank for the last two hours that bars were open, then came back to sleep on my couch.

I slept through all of this. I was sleeping when, in the middle of the night, someone cuddled up behind me and started kissing my neck. I turned, half asleep, half expecting to see Helen, and saw Sophie there in my bed. I sat up.

"What the fuck?" I said.

"Shhh," Sophie said. "You'll wake up Bart."

"Leave me alone," I said. "This isn't right."

Sophie jumped out of bed. "You're an asshole!" she said. Really, she screamed it. Loudly enough for Bart to hear and wonder what Sophie was doing in my bedroom, calling me an asshole. "What are you now? My pimp? Buying me hotel rooms to fuck your friends. Asshole!"

She stormed out of the room.

I went back to sleep.

Another hour later, Sophie was back. I was dreaming that something was wiggling around in my belly and it hurt enough to wake me up and Sophie was kneeling on my shins, stabbing me in the gut. She'd gotten me twice already. The knife came down a third time. I grabbed her shoulders and threw her off me. She bounced into my dresser and came back. I jumped off the bed. Sophie swung the knife at me. I hopped out of the way. She tripped over the edge of the bed and fell onto it. I pulled the bed sheet over her and pulled it tight behind her back. I knelt on her back and grabbed the fitted sheet and tied Sophie up. She struggled. It wouldn't take her long to get free, but she was caught for a while.

I looked down at myself. I was losing a lot of blood. Every time my heart beat, I'd lose more. My boxers were soaked red. The bed sheets were covered in blood. I grabbed a pair of shorts off the floor and my wallet and a t-shirt and ran out the door.

The hospital was only about three or four miles away, but the drive seemed to take forever. I struggled to stay awake the whole way. I just kept bleeding and bleeding. It was too much. I fell asleep at a red light. I couldn't let that happen again. No one else was on the road, anyway, this late, so I just ran red lights and drove straight to the hospital.

I pulled up at the hospital and parked about twenty feet from the emergency room. I can't believe I was clear headed enough to do this, but I took my wallet out, grabbed a health insurance card that I'd swiped from my roommate Rick, just in case, put the card in my pocket, and stuffed the wallet in the glove compartment. I got out of the car and passed out before I could take two steps.

I woke the next morning in a room with two other beds. They both had patients in them. The old white guy kept coughing. The young black guy watched a western on TV. I lay there, looking at the ceiling, trying to piece together everything. I had to take a leak, but any movement at all hurt. I looked left and right to see if they'd left me a bedpan or even a thunder mug. Nothing. So I just kept lying there. I figured I'd wait until the pain in my bladder was worse than the pain in my stomach and move then.

It didn't take long.

I hoisted myself out of bed and to the bathroom. When I got back, there was a nurse there. She said, "You're not supposed to be out of bed, Mr. Williams."

Mr. Williams? It took me a second. I had to remember that I was supposed to be Rick. Let his insurance cover this. "I'm sorry," I said. "I had to pee."

"It's okay," the nurse said. She helped me back into bed. "Just ring for us, next time."

I nodded. I fell back asleep before anything else could happen.

The next day, a cop showed up. This couldn't be a good sign. He called me "Mr. McGregor." This was a worse sign. He said, "Who stabbed you, Mr. McGregor?"

"You got the wrong guy," I said. "I'm Rick Williams."

"We spoke to your roommate, Mr. McGregor," the cop said. "We know who you are."

"..."

"We want to know who stabbed you."

"..."

"Who stabbed you?"

"..."

"Why are you posing as Rick Williams?"

"..."

"Who's your drug dealer?"

"..."

"How much money do you owe your dealer?"

"..."

"Mr. McGregor, we need you to answer these questions if you want us to help you."

I closed my eyes. I kept singing the Circle Jerks song in my head. "Innocent, till proven guilty. Deny everything. Deny everything." I faked sleeping until I really fell asleep.

That night, around two A.M., I woke up. No one was around. I tried standing. It worked out okay. I tried walking. That worked, too. I tried on the clothes of the old man sleeping in the bed two down from me. They fit well enough. The slacks were high-waters, but the guayabera fit just right. His shoes were too small, so I had to steal shoes from my other roommate. I felt bad doing it, but I figured that my hospital bill had to be up around seven or eight thousand dollars by now. Plus, the cops would be back in the morning. I needed to get while the getting was good.

I moseyed down the hallway, into the elevator, out the lobby, and into my Galaxie. My wallet was still in the glove compartment. The car hadn't been searched.

I headed first to Brother Joe's. It was the safest place I could think of. I didn't want to go home because I didn't know what Bart and Sophie were up to or what everyone would have thought when they went into my bedroom and saw all that blood and Sophie tied up in my bed sheets. Surely, they'd be able to put two and two together. The cops had told my roommate Rick that I'd been stabbed. Sophie would've been wound-free. Even if Sophie denied stabbing me, the evidence had to be clear. Still, I wanted no part of it.

Joe lived in a duplex off of 7th Street South. It was far enough from my place that no one would likely be driving by and see my Galaxie out in the front lawn. It was also the apartment that Joe and I had lived in when I was in high school. I was bad about carrying keys in those days, so I'd learned how to break in.

I didn't want to wake Joe and figured I could still get in the old way.

I parked the Galaxie and walked around the side of the house. I climbed the chain link fence into the backyard, popped the lock on the kitchen window the same way I'd done dozens of times, pulled a trash can around to stand on, and crawled through the kitchen window. My stitches scraped along the aluminum frame of the window as I squeezed through. One of the stitches broke. A little blood dripped out.

I didn't care. It was still the middle of the night and I was tired. I went to sleep on Joe's couch.

Joe woke me at about six A.M. "What are you doing here, Danny?" he asked. He had that tone of voice: too soft, a little high-pitched lilt, like a bad actor trying to sound compassionate. Only Joe wasn't acting. He was trying to control his anger. I knew this tone of voice a little too well. The fact that Joe wouldn't sit down only made things seem worse.

I sat up, scratched my head, and took a look at myself. Here I was, waking up on a childhood couch with my blood crusting on a stolen guayabera and my ass jammed into golf pants that obviously I'd stolen because why on earth would I buy plaid slacks two sizes too small for myself? What did I expect from Joe? "It's a bad scene," I said.

"I can see that," Joe said.

And this wasn't an interrogation with a cop, here. This was Joe. I needed help. So I spilled the beans, blurting it all out with no details. Just, "Sophie stabbed me and I skipped out of the hospital so I wouldn't have to pay the bill."

Joe nodded like this was about what he'd expected to hear. "And what? You need money to pay off the hospital?"

I shook my head.

"What are you gonna do about that?"

I shrugged.

"How'd you get them to even treat you in the first place?"

"I passed out in the parking lot," I said. "I guess someone found me there. I had Rick's health insurance card, too."

"Why'd you have that?"

"I saw it lying around the apartment one day about a year ago. I figured it would be a good thing to have, just in case I got in an accident or something, so I stuck it in my wallet."

"Good thinking."

"Thanks."

"I was being sarcastic," Joe said. How was I supposed to know that? He still had on that I'm-doing-everything-I-can-to-not-explode-right-now voice. He said, "And what about Sophie?"

"What about her?"

"Why'd you let her stab you?"

"I was sleeping."

"That's a lousy excuse," Joe said. He gathered together a pile of books and lifted them off the recliner. I read the spines of the books as if I were going to change the subject. Ask him what he'd been reading lately. Joe sat down. "We all knew this was gonna happen. You knew it was gonna happen, didn't you?"

"How would I know?"

Joe shook his head. "Damn it, Danny, it takes a special kind of stupid to live life the way you do."

And what could I say to that? He was right.

Joe told me that I'd have to move on, that I couldn't stay at his place, that I had to deal with this shit myself. He said it in that soft voice, holding back so much anger that I couldn't be mad at him. Later, I got angry. Later, I felt betrayed by my last bit of family. At the time, though, we just handled the events of the morning. Joe called his boss and said he'd be an hour late for work. We had breakfast at Miguel's—eggs over easy, black beans and rice, cuban bread—then Joe ran me by my place. No one was home. I ran in real quickly, grabbed some clothes, some cash I had hidden in my closet, some random cassettes, and a few books.

Joe said, "Is there anything else you need?"

I shook my head.

He dropped me off at the Galaxie and left for work. I went back into Joe's apartment and grabbed a little metal monkey that I'd welded for him in shop class in high school. It wasn't the prettiest thing—out of proportion, squatting, holding two machetes like a little tough guy. I'd made it for Joe when I was sixteen and I was real proud of it then. Joe really liked it, too. He bragged about it to his friends. He'd get drunk and sit in his recliner and stare at that little monkey. He used to rub it for good look. Originally, I'd painted a bandana on the monkey's head, but Joe rubbed the monkey so much for good luck that the paint had worn off. Now, the monkey was dull from the oil on Joe's hands. I knew it was cruel for me to take that monkey from Joe. I guess that's why I did it.

I left his apartment and sat in the Galaxie and thought about driving down to Helen's. I looked at my watch. It was still before eight A.M. Helen worked nights, so I knew she'd still be asleep. I decided not to go see her. I don't know why I decided this. I'm an idiot. I started up the Galaxie and hit the road.

Because that's what I do when things go sour. I run away.

25
A Special Kind of Stupid

It's a bad omen when an old lady crashes her moped right in front of you. I learned this one afternoon as I rode my bike back from Helen's.

I'd been in her garage all morning and I was on my way home for some lunch. At about 5th Street South, this old lady on a moped whipped out in front of me, completely cutting me off. She didn't even see me. She drove about halfway down the block and started swerving. Not big, fluid swerves or drunk driving swerves, but these short, wobbling swerves. I don't know if she tried to right herself and jerked the handlebars too hard or if she just let go of the handlebars and they swung around on their own. Either way, the moped went down and the old lady went down with it.

A big SUV was at the stop sign in front of the old lady. The car didn't drive off. The brake lights stayed on and the reverse lights came on and off real quickly. Then the hazards. So I knew that the woman in the SUV was parking. I peddled as fast as I could up to the scene.

I got to the old lady before the SUV driver got out of her car. I stood my bike on its kickstand, just so that any new cars would see it and stop before they got to us. I knelt down next to the old lady.

She was passed out. I could see her stomach rising and falling in quick breaths, but her eyes were closed and her jaw was slack. I had no idea what to do. I shook her shoulder. "Hey, lady," I said. "Are you all right?"

Of course she didn't answer. She was out cold. And so of course she wasn't all right. I blew in her eyes—one of Bart's homemade death tests. Her eyes blinked, but she didn't come to.

The SUV driver called out to me. "What's going on?"

I couldn't see the driver. I felt like an ass just yelling to the back of a vehicle, but I said, "This lady passed out. Must be the heat."

The driver finally got out of her SUV. I didn't look up at her. I kept my eyes on the old lady.

I didn't know what to do. The moped was lying across her legs. I stood it up and parked it behind the lady, right by my bike. I knelt beside her. She was a strange looking old broad. Make-up caked on her face. Crazy orange plaid pants and a homemade shawl that should've been unraveled and turned back into yarn. Combat boots. A strange sight all around. She was breathing. I looked at her mouth. She didn't seem to be choking on her tongue or anything. I didn't have anything with me. No water, nothing. It was as hot outside as, well, Florida is in June, so I didn't have a jacket or anything to put under her head. I thought about taking off my sweaty t-shirt and bundling it up and putting that under her head, but that seemed kinda gross. I thought about talking to the lady, too. I couldn't think of anything to say.

The driver, meanwhile, had been rustling around in the back of her SUV, looking for something. I glanced up at her a couple of times. I could only see her legs and ass. I kinda wanted to stare, to see the way those seams stretched in her polyester slacks, see the way those legs reached all the way to the ground. I told myself to focus; stay in the now. I had no idea what the driver was doing. A car cruised past, but didn't slow down or help out. The SUV driver found what she was searching for and ran up to me. She handed me a bottle of water. "Give her this."

I looked up at the SUV driver. I'd know those small ears and that smooth brown neck anywhere. Her face was older and her body was rounder, but it was unmistakable. She even rocked the same soft afro that she'd worn back in high school. Things suddenly got that much stranger. I said, "Rosalie?"

"Yes, Danny," Rosalie said, like I was an idiot and like it wasn't weird that, after not having seen each other since high school, this was how we should meet again. "Give her some water."

I looked at the old lady. "Her mouth's closed," I said.

Rosalie grabbed the water out of my hand. "Just hold her head."

I cradled the old lady's head in my hands. Rosalie squeezed the lady's nose. The lady opened her mouth and let out a quick breath. Rosalie poured a little water into the lady's mouth. She gave the lady a second to breath, then poured a little more water. And just like that, the lady woke up. She swatted me away. I let go of her head. It didn't drop. She pushed Rosalie out of the way and stood up.

"Hold on a second there, sister," Rosalie said. She handed me the water.

"Get away from me," the lady said.

"An ambulance is on the way," Rosalie said.

"I don't need an ambulance. I'm fine." The lady walked over to her moped. Rosalie followed. The lady waved her off. "I'm fine," she said. "Leave me alone."

"You're not fine. You passed out. You need help."

"I'll sue you," the lady said. "I'll sue both of you. Don't ever touch me again." She got on her moped and started peddling.

"Look, at least drink the water. You're dehydrated," Rosalie said. But by now, the engine of the moped had kicked back on. The old lady started driving away.

I pulled my bike over to the curb, parked it there, sat down, and drank some of the water. Rosalie turned to me and said, "We should go after her."

"Fuck it," I said. "She knows what she's doing."

Rosalie walked back over to her car and grabbed her cell phone out of it. She called the hospital back and called off the ambulance. Explained the whole situation. Then she sat on the curb next to me. "What'd you do to that old lady, Danny?"

I handed her the water. She took a sip. "You know me," I said. "I make women swoon."

"That was nuts," Rosalie said.

"Yeah." I looked at the pavement where it had all gone down. It was just pavement. Nothing of that little drama remained.

Rosalie stared ahead, too. After about a half a minute, she said, "Hungry?"

"Yeah."

"Want to get some lunch?"

"Yeah."

Rosalie stood. I locked my bike up to the stop sign. We got into her car and took off.

We had lunch. We talked about the old lady. We caught up on old times. We ate tacos. We told jokes. At the end of it, Rosalie said, "Come on, I'll drive you back to your bike."

Only she didn't drive me to my bike. She took a wrong turn on Woodland and drove all the way down past my pad and past 3rd Street North and parked in the driveway of a house there. "I just need to make a pit stop here," Rosalie said. She got out of the car.

I stayed in my seat. Rosalie waved for me to follow her. I did. She unlocked the front door. "You live here?" I asked.

"Of course. Where did you think we were?"

"That's strange," I said. "I live a block away."

"With Bart. I know."

"But I never see you. I didn't even know you moved back to Cocoa Beach."

"I see you all the time," Rosalie said. "Riding your bike around town. Going surfing." She opened the door and went in. I followed.

"Why didn't you ever stop to say hello?"

"I'm married now," Rosalie said. She walked into the family room. The place was a mess. Clothes everywhere. Videos scattered in front of the television. A pile of papers on the coffee table. A cereal bowl left over from breakfast. Stuff like that. Rosalie gathered a pile of clothes off the couch, threw them onto the clothes piled on the recliner, and said, "Have a seat. Want something to drink?"

"I'm all right," I said.

Rosalie went into the kitchen. "Well, you're having a drink with me," she said.

"Really, I'm all right."

I could hear Rosalie breaking open ice cube trays and opening and closing cupboards and clinking glasses in the kitchen. I guess I was having a drink.

Rosalie said, "I married Paul Stromme from high school. Do you remember him?"

The name didn't ring a bell. "No."

"He remembers you. If you see him, act like you remember him."

"Okay." I started idly folding the clothes next to me on the couch and stacking them on the table. I don't know why. I'm not usually like that. I guess I just didn't have anything else to do. "How'd you two hook up?"

"At a real estate seminar up in Jacksonville. About four years ago. I didn't remember him from high school, either."

"What were you doing there?"

Rosalie poked her head out of the kitchen. "I'm a realtor," she said. "You don't think I wear these business suits 'cause they look cool, do you?"

"It looks good on you," I said.

"Quit folding my dirty laundry." Rosalie went back into the kitchen to finish making the drinks. I kept folding. It was mostly dirty t-shirts with big prints of American flags and wolves and largemouth bass and stuff like that.

"Is Paul a redneck?" I asked.

"Kinda. He fishes a lot."

She came back out of the kitchen with our drinks. The seat on the couch next to me was open now that I'd cleared the laundry off. Rosalie sat there. She tucked her feet under her and faced me. I took a sip of my drink. Gin and grapefruit juice. Heavy on the gin. I tried to put the glass down, but there was no room on the coffee table. I held onto my drink. Rosalie looked at me and twirled her hair and said, "So where were we?"

I knew that look in her eyes. I knew that hair twirl. "We were talking about your husband," I said.

"Oh yeah, him," Rosalie said. She sipped her drink, pushed some crap off the coffee table, and set the drink down. "Forget about him."

"It's hard to, with his clothes all around and everything."

Rosalie reached out and touched the back of my head. Her fingernails ran down through my hair. "Don't be mad about my husband."

"Why would I be mad?"

"Because I always feel like I'm cheating on you," Rosalie said. "Since we never officially broke up."

I knew a line of bullshit when I heard it. "Officially?" I said.

"Never even got to say goodbye."

Which was true. Rosalie and her family picked up and left

pretty quickly back then, between our junior and senior years of high school. And seeing her there on the couch again, talking about high school, close enough to smell her, feeling her fingernails in my hair, feeling her knee brush up against my leg... For tiny moments, I felt that old high school feeling. That flutter of early afternoon and skipping school and heading back to Brother Joe's when he was at work and Rosalie and I having sex until it was almost time to get caught. "Don't try this," I said.

Rosalie took my drink and put it on the table. "Try what?" She scooted closer. Her eyes locked on mine. I wasn't ready for it. I hadn't been with a woman since Libra, and I hadn't even come close to dealing with that. And I was hung up on Helen. And Sophie was back in town. And I felt like I'd been steadily fucking up for so long that it was time to stop.

But then again, Rosalie always got her way with me.

She ran her fingers through the hair on the top of my head and rested her hand there, massaging my scalp a little. When she did this, my glance fell down to her chest, where a button of her blouse had come undone. Her red lace bra cut a wavy line across her cleavage. I tried not to stare, but I knew a little. I knew that that button hadn't come undone on accident. I knew the score, here. I thought, come on, Rosalie, what are you doing to me?

She put a finger under my chin. I lifted my head. She came in for a kiss and I let it happen. Before I knew it, she was pulling off my t-shirt and undoing my belt and I was suddenly naked on her couch, not even quite realizing that I'd given in. I felt kinda silly, all white underneath where I usually wore my baggies. My goofy hard-on staring up at me. "How is this fair?" I said.

"You're right. It isn't. Come on." Rosalie led me into the bedroom.

There was very little foreplay. Her clothes seemed to fall off of her like a dream and she stood before me naked, perfect breasts, stomach pretty flat but a new roundness to her hips and thighs. Here was my high school girlfriend turned into a woman. The age and extra pounds did her well. Our bodies more or less took over. We fell into that old rhythm. This was something that Rosalie and I had always been good at. Lord knows we practiced it enough in the bedrooms of these little Woodland homes.

The air conditioner pumped overtime, but with the heat of sex and the humid Florida summer, we were both pouring sweat. We slid and glided against each other. Rosalie took control, putting my hands where she wanted them, guiding my mouth to all her tender spots. At times, it was too much. At other times, I'd think of Rosalie's husband and feel guilty. Or I'd think of Libra—the last woman I'd done this with—how different every aspect of it was. And I'd remember that Libra was dead. These thoughts would rip my right out of the moment. To Rosalie's credit, though, she never let my mind drift far enough to lose my erection. I pinballed between guilt and horror and pure pleasure. The sex seemed to go on forever. Not that I was complaining. It was just way more than I could've anticipated. Finally, Rosalie pulled out all the stops: flicking her tongue on the soft spot of my neck, grazing her thumb across my nipples, grinding on me, saying the dirtiest things, demanding I come until I came.

When we were done, Rosalie rolled off of me and said, "There's that goodbye I never got."

If that's what it was to her, that was okay with me. I wasn't sure what it meant to me.

Almost immediately, though, Rosalie was up. She toweled off, dropped the towel on my chest, and started getting dressed.

"Is your husband gonna be home soon?"

"No. He's gone for the week. Fishing." Rosalie tossed my shorts to me. "But my daughter'll be here any minute."

I sat on the bed and put on my boxers. "You have a daughter?"

Rosalie looked at me like I was crazy. "Of course," she said. "Aren't you two best friends?"

This took me a second. I figured she meant Taylor. I didn't know where Taylor lived, but she always did take a right at Woodland when I took a left. So this would make sense. But still, I didn't understand. "How could you be Taylor's mom?" I asked. "She's, like, what? Twelve or thirteen."

"She's twelve."

"Okay, how could you have a twelve-year-old daughter? I mean, shit, weren't we dating twelve years ago?"

"Twelve years and nine months ago, yeah," Rosalie said.

I didn't see that one coming. Damn near knocked me out.

An hour later, I was still trying to get Rosalie to marry me. My point was that if I was Taylor's father and she was her mother, then we should do what was right and become a whole family. Rosalie's point was that she already was married, already had a family, and… Well, it took an hour of me harping on her before Rosalie finally laid it out for me. She said, "There's no nice way for me to put this, Danny, but you're a loser."

"What? I'm not a loser." Or, more to the point, only *I* get to call me a loser.

"What do you do for a living?"

I didn't answer. What could I say? I pick up dead bodies? Then, I could've made the point that I'd been working at a metal shop and making good money and that was a respectable job, but I'd just gotten fired. And why had I gotten fired? Because my boss got sketched out by the private investigator who'd been following me because I'd left my last girlfriend dead on the train tracks in Flagstaff. I convinced myself more and more that Rosalie had a point. I said, "Fuck you."

"Typical loser thing to say," Rosalie said.

I tried to think of a comeback, but right then, Taylor walked in. She dropped her backpack on the floor right by the door and said, "Danny? What are you doing here?"

"He's trying to get me to marry him," Rosalie said.

"What?" Taylor asked. "Why?"

" 'Cause he's your goddamn daddy," Rosalie said.

"Oh, Jesus fucking Christ!" Taylor said. She started crying. She grabbed her backpack, stormed back into her room, slammed the door, and locked it.

Rosalie looked at me like it was all my fault. Which, well, a lot of it was. She said, "I think you should leave."

And, don't you know it, I was thinking the exact same thing.

26
Crazy Broads and Dead People

I parked the Space Coast van under an awning of red and blue swirling lights, slipped on a pair of rubber gloves, and walked out into the 3 A.M. carnage. A few fireman and cops stood around waiting for Bart and me. I asked the nearest cop, "Where's the body?"

"Where isn't it?" the cop said. Everyone around him laughed.

I looked down the train tracks and got a sense of déjà vu.

Bart stepped next to me. He had a body bag in his hands. We headed down the tracks. About fifty feet down, we found most of the stiff. He'd lost his head, half an arm, and his foot. The rest was slumped in a bloody pile right in the middle of the tracks. I picked the corpse up. Bart held the body bag open for me. I slid the corpse in. We set off down the tracks to find the head, arm, and foot.

There wasn't much of a moon shining down on us. The only real light we had were the swirling ones on top of the fire trucks and cop cars. As we searched for the rest of the body parts, the fireman and cops started to take off. One cop would stick around, but now that Bart and I were on the job, there was no need for the rest of them.

It was all overgrown around the tracks. Weeds and hubcaps and fast food bags and empty cans. Still, I found the foot on top of a little bush. I bent down to pick it up. As I stuffed it in the bag, Bart tapped me on the shoulder. I turned to look and saw that he didn't use his own finger to do this. He used the dead guy's. I stared down the severed arm that Bart was tapping me with. "Goddamn it, Bart," I said.

He was all grin.

I pulled the arm out of his hand and stuck it in the body bag. And right then, at that moment among the moonlight and weeds and body parts I was stuffing in a bag, it all hit me. I started crying.

Now, I never cry. I don't know why not. I just don't. I didn't cry when I heard that Brother Joe was dead. I didn't cry at his little grave marker. I didn't cry when I saw Libra on the tracks or during that forty-nine-hour bus ride when all I could think about was Libra. I didn't cry when Sophie stabbed me or when I left Helen or any of the dozens of times in my life when it probably would've been healthy to let a tear fall. I never did it. But there on those train tracks, with a stranger's mangled corpse in my body bag and Bart and a few cops and firemen looking on and a missing head floating around in the weeds somewhere nearby, I started crying like a little girl.

I don't know if Bart noticed. He said, "I'm gonna borrow a flashlight from those cops." He headed back up the tracks.

I paced up and down the tracks, looking for the head. Bart got the flashlight and came back and we both looked. I wasn't really crying in the same way any more. Tears were still dripping out, but I tried to ignore them. And, as for the head, we couldn't find it anywhere.

By now all the cops and firemen were gone except for one. He was getting impatient. He yelled something from his car, but he was too far away. I couldn't hear what he was saying. Bart had an inkling, though. He said, "That cop's right. Fuck the head. Let's just take what we got and go home."

"No," I said. "What if some kid finds the head tomorrow morning?"

"Then he can bring it in the M.E." Bart handed me the flashlight. He turned and headed back to the van.

I kept looking.

I found out later that the cop had recognized Bart from the days when Bart was a basketball star. The cop had gone to Merritt Island High School when Bart and I were at Cocoa Beach High. They played against each other a few times. This gave them something to talk about when I kept looking for the head. Later, this is probably what kept me from getting arrested.

I walked farther down the tracks. I went as far as I thought the head could possibly have flown. I thought to myself, I have to change what I'm expecting to see. It won't look like any head I know of. It'll be different. I have to open up my mind to that.

And there it was. Crushed. Mutilated. Hardly a head at all. But still human flesh and blood. I picked up the head and sat down on the tracks. I held it in my hands and just cried and cried.

The cop pulled out his bullhorn. "Bring in the head," he said. "Quit fucking around. Bring in the head."

Bart yelled out, "Come on, Danny."

And I just cried.

Not for too long. Maybe twenty, thirty seconds, then I pulled myself together. I stood and dropped the head in the body bag and headed down the tracks.

By the time I got back to where the cop and Bart were, I wasn't crying anymore. I had the body bag zipped up and draped over my shoulder. Bart opened the back of the van. I heaved the stiff on the gurney and we strapped it in. The cop stood behind us and watched.

"Who was this guy?" I asked the cop.

"Just some bum," the cop said.

"How do you know?"

"Didn't you smell all the booze on him?"

"I smell booze on Bart. That doesn't make him a bum."

"Look," the cop said. "You do your job and I'll do mine."

"But I want to know. How do you know he's a bum?"

"Don't fuck with me, son," the cop said, even though we were the same age and he knew it.

"Did you check for I.D. or anything? Did you take fingerprints? Dental records?"

This was what I asked for: dental records. As if I hadn't been holding the crushed head in my hands just three minutes earlier. As if there were any teeth or jaw left.

The cop said, "What is this? Who the fuck do you think you are?"

"I want to know. How do you know who this guy is?"

By now, the cop was pissed. He had one hand on his gun and the other on his walkie-talkie.

Bart stepped in. "I'm sorry about this, Gene," he said to the cop. He grabbed my arm. "Come on, man. Let's go."

I wouldn't budge, though. I just kept asking the cop how he knew that the dead guy was a bum. Or how he pretended to know anything about the dead guy. Or why he and the rest of the police department had no intentions of investigating this shit. When I said, "What? Are you too busy busting keggers? Too busy copping a feel off of high school girls when you do?", the cop got pissed. He threatened to arrest me.

Bart physically picked me up at this point and started dragging me to the van. At the same time, the cop got on his walkie-talkie and radioed for back-up. I took the hint and left.

The next day, all I could think about was the corpse on the train tracks. And, of course, it wasn't the dead guy's corpse I was thinking about. It was Libra's.

I couldn't bring myself to leave the house. I could barely get out of the recliner. Bart tried to talk to me. I just shrugged him off. The phone rang a few times. I didn't answer it. The television was on, but it would be a mistake to say that I watched it. I just stared straight ahead, seeing mostly that Betty Boop tattoo and that severed leg.

At about three o'clock, there was a knock at the door. I assumed it was Taylor wanting to go surfing. This sent another jolt through me, a sudden reminder that I was a dad. Shit. Things got complicated so quickly. I opened the door and there was Helen.

"Hey, Danny. Got a minute?" she asked.

I stepped aside and made a sweeping motion to welcome her in.

She handed me a Styrofoam take-out container. I opened it. It was a plate lunch from Duke's. Teriyaki beef, rice, potato-macaroni salad. One of my favorites. "Thanks," I said.

Helen sat on the couch. I walked into the kitchen, stuck the plate lunch in the refrigerator, and grabbed two beers out of the crisper.

"Bart had lunch at Duke's today," Helen said.

"Yeah?" I handed one of the beers to Helen and sat in the recliner.

"He told me all about that dead guy last night?" Helen said.

I nodded. I leaned back in the recliner and propped my feet on the footrest. I turned off the television. "Who's watching Duke's?"

"Shaggy," Helen said. "No one comes in this time of the afternoon anyway."

"So you came by to see me."

Helen shrugged. "I owe you one, Danny. You saved my ass that one night. Remember? When you waited tables?"

I nodded.

"So I figure I owe you."

"Thanks," I said. "I appreciate the lunch."

Helen took a sip of her beer. "Do you want to talk about it?

About the dead guy last night?"

I shook my head. I took a sip of my beer. It was the last thing I wanted right then. I put it back down on the end table and scratched my head.

"What was it about that guy?" Helen said. "Why did he get to you?"

I shrugged.

"You really don't feel like talking, do you?"

I shook my head.

"Then I'm gonna tell you a story," Helen said. That was fine with me. At that point, I'd rather hear someone else's shit than think about my own. And I liked Helen's stories.

"Go ahead," I said.

Helen said, "I have this friend Elena. She's a girlfriend of mine from college. She lives down in Costa Rica. She and her husband work for a little resort, renting out bungalows on the beach. Her husband is crazy.

"Now, you know I think most boys are crazy. But this guy is really crazy. Certified crazy. Spent time in a mental institution. For real."

"And why are you telling me this?" I asked. Because you never know with Helen. This could be her way of saying I was certifiable.

"Just listen," Helen said. "I visited with Elena and her husband for a week down there. This was earlier this year. Just before you came back to Cocoa Beach. And, while I was there, they surfed a lot. You know I don't surf, so I mostly sat on the beach and read. When they were done surfing, I would tell them that I had watched them surf. I hadn't really, though. Not much. But why hurt their feelings, right? When they came in from surfing, I'd say, 'Oh, those were some nice rides you got.' And they'd be all happy. It made everything a little nicer.

"Maybe that's what I've learned from all my years bartending: how to tell nice lies."

"That's a good thing to tell me," I said. Not that I didn't know that she told nice lies. I knew that. It's just different when you hear it straight from her mouth.

Helen said, "Anyway, I did watch Elena and her husband while I was down there. And when I knew them in college, they were always fighting. Not anymore. At least not when I visited them. He'd be so considerate of her. He'd do dishes after dinner. He kept their little bungalow really clean. I even saw him iron one of her sundresses before she went to work."

"Hell of a guy," I said.

Helen nodded. "So it would seem. So I asked Elena, 'What came over your husband? When did he get so sweet?'

"She said, 'As soon as we found the red bus right.'

"That's what they called their surf spot: the red bus right. There was a red Volkswagen bus in the jungle right off the beach. That's where the name came from.

"So why am I telling you this, Danny? I keep thinking that you just need to find your red bus right. Not a surf spot, exactly. Just a spot where you can find peace." Helen paused here. She looked me in the eye to make sure I'd been listening. I had.

"That's a nice story," I said.

"Well, anyway, that's why I opened up my garage to you. I thought maybe you could find some peace there."

"I appreciate it."

Helen looked at me. I wasn't being condescending or anything. She had told a nice story. I did appreciate her letting me use her garage. I just wasn't in a talking mood. This clearly frustrated her. She stood and said, "Well, if you don't want to talk, don't talk." She carried her mostly full beer into the kitchen and set it in the sink. She walked back into the living room and over to me. She put her hand on my head and mussed my hair. "Come to the bar later, if you want to talk."

"Libra," I said.

"What?"

"It wasn't last night's stiff. It was Libra. That's the problem."

"Who's Libra?" Helen asked.

And now the cat was out of the bag. I wasn't sure how to tell Helen or how much to tell her. I let out the information in little bits. I said, "Libra was my girlfriend in Flagstaff."

"Okay."

"She got hit by a train."

"Oh, no. Did she live?"

"No."

"Oh, shit."

"I found the body."

"Whoa. Good christ."

"I didn't tell anyone."

"What?" Helen asked. "What did you do?"

"I just left," I said. "I just freaked out and left."

"You didn't tell the cops?"

"No. I just left."

"Who do you think found her? Who reported it?"

"I don't know," I said. "I don't know. That's why I'm freaking out. I just figured someone would've reported it, you know. I just assumed that. Now, with that stiff last night, I'm worried that she's been a Jane Doe this whole time. Maybe people don't even know she's dead."

Helen looked at me, stunned. She didn't know what to say. How could she? Years of bartending wouldn't prepare you for this kind of confession. Nice little stories wouldn't give answers to problems like this.

I said, "For a while, there was a private investigator following me around. You know that wheelchair dude?"

"Clay. Yeah, I know him."

"But I ran him off. I thought he was following me because Libra's parents wanted me arrested. Now I'm thinking that maybe they don't know. Maybe they're looking for Libra."

Helen stared at me. She abandoned her nice little lies and said, "That's fucked up."

I nodded.

"And it gets worse," Helen said, "because lately, a Samoan guy has been hanging around Duke's looking for you."

27
Seeing Scars

ITINERARY FOR A SETUP

2:31 P.M. Sister Janie will call. From her very first, "Hey, Knucklehead," be suspicious.

2:33 P.M. Agree to go over to dinner at Janie's that night. Understand as soon as you agree that you've made a mistake. That you were supposed to have been suspicious. Too much shit is going on in your life. You're not thinking straight.

7:09 P.M. Get on your bike and head for Janie's. You were supposed to be there at 7:00, but you won't be able to get yourself to leave until 7:09.

7:13 P.M. Ride your bike up Janie's driveway. The garage door will be open. Notice: one BMW convertible that looks suspiciously like a Mazda Miata and one Land Rover, Janie's. There is also a Volvo station wagon in the driveway. Ask yourself how many cars two people need. Also notice again how big Janie's house is. You could fit five of your apartments into this house. The same number of people live in your apartment and this house. Grumble about what's become of your sister.

7:14 P.M. Knock on the front door. Powell will answer. You've known Powell for years and you still don't know if Powell is his first name or last name. By extension, you don't know if your sister's last name is Powell or not. Don't bother cursing yourself for skipping out on their wedding. The waves were good that day.

7:15 P.M. Powell will offer you a glass of wine. Don't accept. You've never been a wine drinker. It's always seemed like a rich man's game to you. You're not thirsty, anyway.

7:16 P.M. Enter Powell and Janie's living room. Janie will be sitting in an antique wooden armchair, drinking wine. You haven't seen her since the day she picked you up at the bus station, almost six months ago. Even though she hasn't seen you in six months and has only seen you once in the past four years, she won't get up to hug you. She's never been the hugging type. She'll only say, "Knucklehead!"

7:16:05 P.M. Notice Sophie sitting on the couch. Scream curses in your head.

7:17 P.M. Sister Janie will tell the story about how fat you were when she picked you up at the bus station. Six months have passed since then. You've been surfing nearly every day and riding your bike a lot and eating right and working manual labor that whole time. You've lost those extra pounds. Janie won't notice. Sophie will say, "I don't know. Danny looks the same to me." Powell will offer you a drink again. Ask him what kind of whiskey he has.

7:19 P.M. Powell will disappear into the kitchen to prepare dinner.

You'll be stuck in the room with Janie and Sophie. Janie will not be drunk, but you'll recognize a bit of a wine high in her eyes. She'll start telling embarrassing stories about your childhood. Look in the kitchen. See that Powell isn't cooking so much as reheating pre-prepared food that he'd picked up at the grocery store. Relax. Dinner will be ready in ten minutes.

7:24 P.M. Janie will say, "Hey, Knucklehead, do you remember the Robisons?" Nod. The Robisons were the foster parents you went to live with after your father died. You were four years old. Janie will tell Sophie, "We'd lived with the Robisons maybe, what? Two weeks? When Mr. Robison died. We all had to go to the funeral. Danny and me and a couple of other foster kids. And we're at the funeral. It's an open casket. And Danny's looking at the body. Just staring at it. Oblivious to the line of people behind him. He even had his hands on the side of the casket, trying to pull himself up for a better look. And he asks Mrs. Robison, 'What happened to his feet?'

"She says, 'What?'

"Danny says, 'What happened to his feet? How come you can't see his feet? Couldn't he afford shoes?'

"Oh, Jesus, did that get Mrs. Robison fired up. She gave Danny such a beating. I've never seen a kid take a beating like that. You remember that, Knucklehead?"

Yeah, Janie, you'll think, I remember that. Thanks for bringing it back up.

7:32 P.M. Dinner will be served. Eat quickly. The sooner it's done, the sooner you can leave. Janie will be in rare form. You won't be sure if she's trying to set you up with Sophie or humiliate you. Maybe both. She'll drink a lot of wine, though, and laugh a lot.

7:41 P.M. Notice that Sophie will handle the situation with a lot of grace. She'll look at you sympathetically and give Janie polite smiles. Wonder if Sophie is really as crazy as you made her out to be in your mind. Try to remember if Sophie has always been this pretty. Have her eyes always been this root beer brown? Did her left cheek always dimple like that when she smiled?

7:46 P.M. Powell will start in. What are you doing with your life, Danny? You're not still picking up dead bodies, are you? Do you think there's a future in that? Don't you have a daughter to think about now? Wonder how Powell knows about Taylor. Remember that you told Janie on the phone, earlier that day. Make a mental note not to tell Janie anything anymore.

7:47 P.M. Decide there's one of two ways you can respond to Powell: you can be a smart ass or you can go on the offensive. Because, obviously, ignoring him won't work. Say to Powell, "Are you still working at the Space Center?'

Powell will say, "No. I'm working at Lockheed now."

"But you're still an engineer? You're still working for the defense department?"

"Yes. And making a good living at it."

"So you're basically working on bombs. Missiles. You're working on ways to kill as many people as possible from as far away as possible. So you're creating dead bodies all over the world and you're getting on my case for picking dead bodies up?"

Powell will grow strangely silent.

Janie will scold you: "You're being inappropriate, Danny."

You'll suddenly feel like a kid again. But not in a good way. Decide that you don't need to be where you are. Thank Janie and Powell for dinner and walk away. Do it abruptly enough so that no one will have time to protest.

7:49 P.M. Sophie will come out into the front lawn and catch you as you're unlocking your bike. She'll say, "Sorry about that." Shrug. She'll say, "Let's get a drink. Just me and you." Agree to go.

7:54 P.M. Lock your bike up to the post outside of Sullivan's. Sophie's Volvo will already be in the parking lot.

7:55 P.M. Join Sophie at the bar. It's fairly empty. Sophie has wine. She's ordered a beer for you. Some kind of fancy brown British beer. Take a sip. It'll taste good.

7:59 P.M. While Sophie is talking about Atlanta, think about the sex you used to have with her. Remember the mornings when she'd grab your erection and say, "We can't waste this." Remember the way she'd bite down on the side of her bottom lip when you did things right. Invite her to play a game of darts before you drive yourself mad.

8:48 P.M. After a few games of darts and another brown British beer, you'll start to feel good. You'll start to forget everything. Sophie will seem remarkably put together. You'll start to feel like her bad times are all part of the past. At that exact moment, Sophie will say to you, "Why'd you leave me, Danny?"

Even though the answer seems obvious, tell her anyway. "You were just too mean to me."

"I was going through a rough time," she'll say. "I broke a lot of things that meant a lot to you. I'm sorry about that."

Say, "Don't apologize."

She'll say, "No. I'm sorry about that. But couldn't we have worked it out? I was never that mean. I was never mean to you like Janie is."

Point out the obvious: "You stabbed me."

Sophie will look hurt. She'll look at you like, *how could you say that to me?* She'll shake her head. She'll say, "No. I don't believe it."

Try to make sense of this. How could she not believe it? Try to see things from her perspective. Could she have been sleep-stabbing? You've gotten up and walked in your sleep before. One time, you even sleepwalked outside of your trailer and took a leak against the side wall. You didn't remember any of it until Libra told you the next morning. Could this have been what Sophie was going through? It seems unlikely. But there's also blackout. Even you've blacked out. Even you have drank so much that you don't remember whole chunks of a night. You can't remember even when you're reminded. Bart and Sophie were very drunk that night. They drank more after you saw them. It's very possible that she was in blackout when she stabbed you, that she has no first hand memory of doing it at all. Tell her, "I have about ten thousand dollars worth of medical bills to prove it."

"I'd like to see that."

You won't be able to show her the bills. The hospital has found your new address and phone number. They are hounding you again. But you don't exactly carry the bills around with you. Be honest. You just throw them away when they come.

8:51 P.M. Lift up your shirt. Tell Sophie, "You can see the scars." Sophie will bend down to look at them. She'll rub her fingers against them. She'll stand back up and look you in the eyes and start crying. Give her a hug. She'll put her face in that soft spot between your shoulder muscle and your chest muscle. Her tears will soak your shirt. Her breath will be warm against your chest.

8:52 P.M. Realize that it's ridiculous to comfort the woman who stabbed you. Especially when she needs comfort to deal with the fact that she did stab you. Let go.

8:53 P.M. Sophie will lose a little grace. She'll leave abruptly. Too abruptly for you to react. Stand there with darts in your hand. Ask yourself, what's next?

28
Joe and the Samoan

The next thing was the fucking Samoan. Or whatever he was. He was a big, fat guy, built like an offensive lineman, taller than me and I'm usually the tallest guy in the room. He looked Samoan. Helen called him Samoan. So I took him at that. And, anyway, the most important thing about him was that he was stalking me. Everywhere I turned, the fucking Samoan was right behind me.

It didn't make sense to me, to be honest. If Libra's parents were going to be this obvious about having me tailed, why didn't they keep Clay Barker on the job? I liked Clay. I would've ridden around with him and made it easier on everyone. But this fucking Samoan, man…

I hopped on my bike and headed down to Helen's garage. There, I could close the door and narrow my world down to a dim room and a single flame welding metal. Everything else would fade away. On the ride there, though, the Samoan followed me in his car.

He couldn't have been more obvious. Even at my fastest, I only went maybe twelve or thirteen miles an hour on that bike. Which was normal. But for a car to ride behind me at that speed caused all kinds of problems. Other cars honked at the Samoan, yelled at him, made crazy passes around him. The Samoan seemed undaunted.

He just rode behind me. Blank expression. Sunglasses on.

I tried to ignore him until I got to Helen's. Once I was there, I locked myself in the garage and did my best to forget.

My latest sculpture was on the workbench. This was my favorite so far. I'd taken old fenders and banged them out into a big bowl, and I'd cut up the edges of the bowl so that it looked like flames. In the center of this flaming bowl, I was welding together a figure that was seated like Rodin's *Thinker*, only, of course, my thinker was a monkey. I had him sitting on his haunches, one long arm on his chin and one wrapped around his leg and, hopefully, when it was done, the monkey would look guarded and scared of his thoughts. And the world would be burning around him.

That was the idea, anyway. So far, I only had a frame of a monkey sitting there. This was the day I'd give the monkey skin and a face. I had a busted chimney flue to make the skin out of. I took out my clippers and got to work.

Joe came into the garage as I got started. Or the ghost of Joe. Or my imaginary friend Joe. However you want to think of him. He would come by now and then when I welded. We'd chat. It helped me deal with his death.

I cut the flue. Joe walked by my pile of sculptures. He ran his finger along them. Ordinarily, I would've warned against this. Most of the sculptures had sharp edges and could cut you. Joe was beyond bleeding. He touched the sculptures as he walked down the line. "You've been busy," he said.

"I have."

"This is a whole lot of metal. A whole lot of work." He stepped back and looked at the sculptures as a whole. "How much money would you have made if you had spent this time welding for Duane instead of making these sculptures?"

"I don't know. A couple grand."

"How much do you think you'll make off of this stuff?"

"Who cares?" I said.

"Humor me," Joe said.

"I don't know. Helen and her ex-husband set up a gallery show for me. Helen said her ex-husband had friends with money. Maybe I can make some decent scratch. I don't really care, though."

"Of course you care," Joe said. "Everyone cares. No one wants to spend this much time and heart on something and not make at least a little dough."

I nodded. Fair enough. I wrapped the metal around the monkey's leg frame. A couple of snips to adjust it just right and a weld down the back and the skin looked pretty smooth. Of course, there should be hair. I should do something there. But first things first. I picked up the flue and started cutting the skin for the next leg.

Joe walked over to the workbench. "Another monkey," he said.

"Yep."

"You remember that monkey you made for me when you were in high school?"

I nodded.

"Whatever happened to that thing? I loved that thing."

"I think you know, Joe," I said.

Joe looked at the floor, at the metal shavings and his white bare feet and the way his tan stopped a few inches above his ankles. His legs got this way from years of working landscaping. It looked like he forever had on a pair of socks. "It's hell raising a kid," Joe said. "You should try it some time."

I kept cutting the flue. "I'm a dad, now," I said. "Turns out Taylor's my daughter."

"I heard," Joe said.

"How could you have heard? Who else talks to you but me?"

Joe looked at me. "Sometimes I just float around in your brain, picking up bits of gossip."

I shook my head in short, tight jerks, as if I were trying to shake Joe out of my mind. His ghost or whatever he was still stood in front of me.

"That's some shit," he said. "What kind of dad are you gonna make? You're almost as bad as me."

"You were a good dad, Joe," I said. I looked down at his white feet when I said it. I think Joe nodded. I kept making the monkey's skin. Joe changed the subject.

We chatted like that for the next few hours. Helen wasn't around. No one could see what I was doing in that garage. No one knew that I spent hours talking to dead people in there. Sometimes it was Libra, but usually it was Joe. There was no harm in it, anyway. It kept my mind occupied while I welded the skin on my thinking monkey. The ghost of Joe even modeled the pained expression I put on the monkey's face.

By early that afternoon, the monkey was more or less done. I'd probably think of other shit to do to him. I'd probably tinker a little more before leaning him against the wall to sell. For the time being, I felt done. I started cleaning up and thinking about the Samoan.

He was sitting outside of Helen's garage, just as I'd expected. Helen's truck was out of the driveway. That meant she must've seen him as she left for work earlier that day. I couldn't have this. I couldn't have a stalker watching me and all my friends. I couldn't cause a traffic jam every time I rode my bike. I couldn't just ignore problems and wait for them to go away. I leaned my bike against Helen's garage door and walked over to the Samoan.

I didn't storm over there or anything. In my head, I thought about running over there, yanking him out of the car, and thrashing him. Giving him a good, sound beating. I was actually okay with that thought. The Samoan wasn't in a wheelchair. He was big enough to defend himself. Hell, he was quite a bit bigger than me. I wouldn't be a bully if things got physical. But I held off that screaming id and decided to just talk to the Samoan.

I put my hand on the roof of his sedan. His window was open. Fast food bags and wrappers littered the floor of his car. He had a hamburger on his lap and a forty-four ounce soda between his legs. I said, "I can't have you following me like this. Do what you have to do and move on."

He lifted the soda to his lips and drank. He said nothing. I looked into his sunglasses and saw my reflection.

"I know who you work for," I said. "You work for the Fultons. You're the second dick they've sent after me. The first one is in a wheelchair."

The Samoan laughed.

"So let's get it out in the open. What do they want from me?"

The Samoan lifted the burger to his mouth, took a bite, and chewed. I wasn't going to say anything more. I'd already laid my cards down. If he didn't start talking right after he stopped chewing, things were gonna get ugly. I waited. He chewed. He washed it down with more soda. I started the countdown in my head. Ten, nine, eight... The Samoan set his drink in a holder. I looked to see if his door was unlocked. It was. Five, four, three... "They want you to come to Flagstaff," the Samoan said.

"I'm not with Libra, anymore," I said. "I don't know where she is."

The Samoan looked at me like I was crazy. "Are you fucking kidding?"

"You've been following me. You can see Libra's not here. I don't know where she is."

"Libra's fucking dead," the Samoan said.

And I knew that. Of course I knew that. But he didn't know I knew that and he knew good and fucking well that Libra and I had dated and even been serious and lived together and this is how he told me that she died? *Libra's fucking dead?* What kind of bastard was I dealing with? I'd had enough of this guy. I yanked his door open and grabbed him by the throat and ripped him out of his seat.

He was too heavy for me to lift out of the car, but I had a hold of his throat and heaved with enough force that he followed. He stumbled out of his car. I tripped him and forced him down before he ever got a safe footing. He hit the ground, flat on his back. I put my knee on his chest and leaned most of my weight into it. My first punch went for his nose. It's a good place to start when the guy you're fighting is surprised. I missed and hit the sunglasses. The frames flew off his face. A left followed that right, though, and my left hit his nose. It wasn't as hard as I wanted it, but it was hard enough to hurt my hand and bust open his nose. His eyes teared up. Both of his hands went up to his face. Blood seeped between them. I leaned over and punched the hands on his face a couple of times. He kicked back. His knee missed my sack by inches. I couldn't have that. He was down and I was up. There was no reason for me to punch. I jumped off him and started kicking him. The first couple of kicks went for his ribs. He tried to crawl away but I kicked his arms out from underneath him. My toe hit his nose on one of these kicks. He gave up at that point. He curled into the fetal position. It did me no good to keep kicking him. That was that, as far as I was concerned. He wasn't fighting back anymore and I'd made my point.

I checked his waistband and ankles for weapons. None there. I rolled up the window to his car, pulled the keys out of the ignition, locked the door, and shut it. I threw the keys about twenty yards down the middle of the street. This way, if he had a weapon in his car, he couldn't get to it before I was gone. I kicked him one more time. Not hard. Just enough to keep him down. "There's your answer," I said. "Give it to the Fultons."

I walked back to my bike. The Samoan didn't move. I rode away, wishing he would've fought harder so I wouldn't feel so bad about what I'd just done.

29
It's More Fun If You're Scared

I had no idea how to be a dad. I'd never had one myself. Or, at least I hardly remember him. And, as far as fathers go, I was a pretty shitty one. I didn't even meet my daughter until she was twelve years old. I made her cry the first time we met. When I found out she was my daughter, I spent a week avoiding her. And now I wanted to do something and I had no idea what to do because all I'd ever done with Taylor was go surfing and the ocean was flat, flat, flat.

Still, I had a plan. I figured we could borrow Bart's car and go south to where the waves were better. So I woke up early on that Tuesday morning and I called a surf report down in Sebastian Inlet and the waves weren't great, but you could ride them. As soon as the surf shop around the corner opened up, I went over and bought some soft surf racks for thirty bucks. Then I called Taylor.

Rosalie answered the phone. She'd been acting weird toward me, which was totally understandable, considering. Rosalie and I didn't talk long. I just said hello and asked for Taylor. Rosalie went and got her.

"What are you doing?" I asked as soon as Taylor picked up.

"Sleeping."

"Let's go surfing."

"There's no waves." Taylor sounded groggy, like she might fall back asleep in the middle of talking to me.

"I'll drive to where there are waves. Get here in fifteen minutes."

"Okay," Taylor said.

She was at my apartment ten minutes later. Still sleepy, but ready to go. I asked her if she'd eaten. She hadn't. We went inside and I fixed her a bowl of cereal. While she ate, I went outside and strapped her board to the roof of Bart's car.

With the sun still hanging low over the eastern horizon, Taylor and I headed south down A1A in search of waves.

It was tough at first. I didn't know what to say and Taylor was so groggy that she wasn't talking. I felt kinda trapped in that car. I'd only driven a few miles when I pulled off A1A onto 22nd Street. Taylor said, "Where are we going?"

"You have to check this out," I said. I pulled into Helen's driveway.

Helen worked nights, so I was careful to be quiet. I unlocked the side garage door, flipped on a light, and stepped inside Helen's garage. Taylor followed me. By now, almost a third of the garage was taken up by the shit I'd welded together. I pointed that out to Taylor.

"What is all this junk?" she asked.

"It's stuff I made."

"Why?"

"I don't know. I guess it's like art to me," I said. "Helen set up a show for me in a gallery in August."

"Who's Helen? Is she your girlfriend?"

"No. She's the woman who set up the show for me. This is her garage."

"Why'd she do all that for you if she's not your girlfriend?" Taylor asked.

"I don't know why I'm talking to you about this," I said.

Taylor looked at me like, *no shit. I don't know why you're talking to me about this, either.* She looked at all the metal welded in front of her. She kinda shook her head. She walked along the line of stuff. Against the wall, over by the garage door, was one of the first things I'd done when Helen let me get started. It was basically a picture frame made out of metal but shaped to look like a bamboo frame. In the middle of the frame was a metal mat that was supposed to look like it had been woven out of palm fronds. And on top of the mat was the silhouette of a turtle. I'd taken a roll of soldering wire and held it over the mat and held the flame to the wire and let little metal drops fall onto the mat until all the drops formed a turtle. I guess Taylor liked this one. She knelt down in front of it and reached out to touch it, then pulled her hand back. "Can I touch it?' she asked.

"Of course."

Taylor ran her fingers across the drops of metal. I knew what it felt like for her. Cold and smooth. Unnatural and fluid. Kinda bumpy but it all made sense in a weird way.

It took us about an hour to get down to Sebastian. Taylor napped a lot of the way. I listened to music and drove along the ocean, checking everything out. I hadn't been down this way since I was in high school.

The water was pretty crowded when we got there, and unless things had changed drastically since I was in high school—which they hadn't—the crowd wouldn't be too friendly. I didn't care. It was all worth it. There were waves. I stood on the shore with my board under my arm and looked at the water. Taylor stood next to me. "What are you waiting for?" she asked.

I watched a few waves roll in. "Check it out," I said. "You see where that group of guys is sitting there? Look a little bit to the right of them. See how the wave is starting to break there? I think if you stay out of the crowd and ahead of the drift, you'll get better waves."

"I have no idea what you're talking about half the time," Taylor said.

"Just follow me."

I walked down to the water and paddled out, past the crowd of shortboarders and to the spot that I'd noticed from shore. Taylor followed me. Within a minute or two, a set rolled in from the east. The shortboarders paddled in our general direction. Taylor lined up for the wave. I said to her, "Let this one go." She stopped paddling. The wave broke in front of us and curled down the line toward the crowd of shortboarders. Taylor watched it go. She looked at me. I said, "Go now."

Another wave was coming in, only no one was jockeying for this one except Taylor. She was in the perfect spot. She caught the wave just as it was breaking, stuck her feet on the board, and took off down the line. It looked like a shortboarder might try to cut her off, but she gunned her board right at him. Playing chicken. And of course she'd win. I didn't watch, though, because another wave was building right around me, and that one was all mine.

Taylor and I caught a few set waves like that. Every time we'd paddle back out after a ride, more of the crowd was around us. This always happened to me when I went surfing: I'd stand on the shore and look for a spot where the waves were breaking and no one was catching them. I'd paddle out to that spot and get a couple of good rides and suddenly, everyone was around me, trying to catch the waves that I found. It didn't bug me, though. It actually made me feel good. Like I was the wise man in the line-up.

I could tell it bugged Taylor to be stuck in the crowd. She'd fight the other surfers for waves. Or she'd catch the wave and still some hot dog would cut her off. It was frustrating for her. Finally, I told her, "Don't go for the first wave of the set. Let all these hot dogs fight for it. Go for the second or third."

"But what if there isn't a second or third?" Taylor said. "Then what?"

I told Taylor something that Helen had told me: "Compassion breeds courage." It's some Taoist thing. Like, if you have the compassion to give up the first wave to someone else, it gives you courage to wait for the better waves. I tried to explain this to Taylor, but she wasn't having it. She just kept fighting for the first wave.

After we'd been out for about an hour, I noticed a set building on the horizon, bigger than all the sets that came before it and breaking farther out. I started paddling east as fast as I could. Taylor followed me. The waves came at me pretty quickly. I knew I wouldn't be able to get out there soon enough to ride the set. I only wanted to get out far enough quickly enough so that I could duck dive under the waves. I paddled like mad and the waves kept coming and the first one broke right in front of me. I thrust my board down into the water and ducked down with it. Most of the wave rolled right over me. As soon as I popped up, another wave crested above me. I paddled straight for it. I wouldn't be able to turn and ride this big sucker, either. I ducked under it. When I came up, a third wave was in front of me. It was gonna break pretty close to me. I had about a fifty/fifty chance of making it. But, what the hell? This was as good as it got. I turned my board and went for it. The wave looked like it was gonna break right on my head. That's okay, I thought. It's more fun if you're a little scared. I paddled just a little and already felt the momentum of the wave. As soon as I did, I stood and stayed low. The wave was breaking right on top of me. I free fell a couple of feet but kept my balance and stayed in front of the break. It was perfect. No one else had gotten out this far this fast. I had the wave of the day all to myself.

When it was over, I paddled back out to the spot where I'd been waiting for waves all day. One thing I knew about surfing in Florida was that, when a swell is building, you'll occasionally have those big, outside sets. Every now and then, if you're very lucky, you'll be able to catch one of the waves. Like I just had. But they don't come that often—only once in an hour, if that—and there's no point in sitting way outside and waiting on them. Most of the crowd, who'd been wiped out by that big set, paddled out to where I caught that big wave. Taylor was out there, too. I waved to her to come back in. She shook her head. I stayed where I was.

A few minutes later, another set came in and I caught another wave all to myself. By the time I paddled back out to my spot, Taylor was waiting for me. "What are you doing in here?" she asked.

"No point in hanging out there." I pointed to where the crowd was. "You can't catch waves that are already gone."

"What are you? Yoda all of a sudden?" Taylor said. " 'Stay out of the crowd and ahead of the drift.' 'Compassion breeds courage.' 'You can't catch waves that are already gone.' What is this?"

I shrugged. I didn't think I was trying to be all fatherly. I thought I was only talking about surfing. Not about life or anything. But I guess that's not how Taylor took it. I said, "Look, we're just surfing here. There's nothing to it."

"There you go again, Yoda," Taylor said. Already, though, she was lining up for the next wave.

Taylor was awake for the drive home. We talked about waves we caught and surfing and all. She kept asking me if I thought she was getting better. Of course she was. I told her that. But I think she just wanted to keep hearing it. And it was good for me to know that, even with this big gorilla of fatherhood in the room, Taylor and I would still go surfing together.

I played a few cassettes on the way home. It was all punk rock and Taylor didn't really dig it.

After a long stretch of no one talking, I turned down the stereo and said what both of us were probably thinking. I said, "I can't believe you have a loser like me for a dad."

"No shit," Taylor said.

I looked over at her. She wasn't smiling like she was kidding around. I wasn't really kidding around, either. "At least you have a stepdad. He seems like a pretty good guy."

"He *is* a good guy."

"Still," I said. "All that time you spent without a father... imagining who he was. Hoping he was cool or, I don't know, rich or something. And then he turns out to be me. Fuck, that sucks." I paused, thought about what I'd just said, then checked myself. "I mean, I'm cool with it. I'm happy that you're my daughter. Just, for your sake, I wish you had a better dad."

"Me too," Taylor said. Still not kidding. And why should she be? What kind of joke would all this make?

I didn't know what else to say. I just kept driving and hoping something would come to mind. I thought about telling her that I didn't know about it. I hadn't known about it until she did. But, hell, she knew that. And what else was there to say? We drove along A1A, through the dunes of Melbourne Beach. Seven- and eight-story condos lined the ocean like so many orangutans on an African savannah.

Finally, Taylor said, "Remember when you swore you'd beat up my father if you ever met him?"

"Yeah."

"Well, what are you gonna do now?"

I shrugged. "It's a pickle, kid," I said. Because what could I tell her? I spent most of my life beating that guy up.

30
Still Dirty

I still had to resolve things with Sophie. She wouldn't just run away and not come back. That's my trick, not Sophie's. She'd want to talk about things. She'd want something she could call closure. It's just the way she was.

She called a few times and left messages, but I didn't call her back. She showed up a few times at my haunts. I did my best to avoid her at every turn.

She caught me on the phone, though. I'd been expecting a call from Helen. The phone rang and I answered it without letting the answering machine pick up first. Sophie was on the line. She asked me to go out to dinner with her.

"I don't know, Sophie," I said. "I'm kinda busy."

"Busy doing what? Did you suddenly get a real job?"

"That's it. Pick on me," I said. "That's a good way to get what you want."

"Don't be a jerk," Sophie said. "You're not busy. You love sushi. Come to dinner with me."

I tried to think of an excuse and decided I didn't need one. I said, "I don't really want to."

"Dinner's on me."

Which did make the offer more tempting. The only thing better than a sushi dinner is a free sushi dinner. Still, I'd have to have that dinner with Sophie. "I don't know."

"Bring your medical bills, too," Sophie said. "I'll pay them."

And that was an offer I couldn't refuse. I still owed the hospital close to ten grand for that little stay after Sophie stabbed me. I had no intention of paying it, but it haunted me. I wanted that monkey off my back. Besides, Sophie would keep calling until I had dinner with her, so I figured I may as well get it over with. "Pick me up at seven," I told her.

Sophie showed up dressed to the nines. She had on this sheer white blouse and hiphuggers and fancy shoes. It was all so tight and close to see-through that I couldn't help thinking about her naked. Damn. This was going to be a long night.

Sophie said to me, "You look good." But I didn't. I was wearing an aloha shirt, shorts, and flip-flops. I hadn't even shaved. So, of course, this meant Sophie was fishing for a compliment. I didn't offer one up. I just smiled and nodded and we headed to her car.

On the way to the restaurant, Sophie tried to get me to talk and mostly I just realized how much she knew about my life. She asked me, "Anything new?"

"Nah," I said. "Same old."

"Still hanging out with that little surfer girl?"

I shrugged. Okay, so Sophie knows about Taylor. She knows I'm a dad. I said, "We don't hang out. We just go surfing."

"Been welding at all?" Sophie asked.

"A bit."

"Anything interesting?"

I shrugged.

"Any monkeys?"

"A few."

"Doing anything with your sculptures?"

Aha. So Sophie knew about the gallery exhibit that Helen and her ex-husband had set up for me. That's what she was waiting for me to tell her about. I said, "No."

"Anyone selling them?"

"Not right now. No."

Sophie pushed her hair behind her ears. "You're impossible," she said. She turned up the music and we rode the rest of the way without talking.

As soon as we got to the restaurant, Sophie went to the bathroom. Of course, I was suspicious. Years of dating Sophie made me suspicious every time she went to the bathroom. Especially at a joint like this sushi restaurant, because the bathrooms were the kind that only one person went into at a time, so Sophie could snort whatever she wanted in private.

I took the table and waited. I told myself, you're gonna eat, you're gonna be polite, you're gonna hand over your medical bills, and you're gonna leave. That's it.

Sophie came back from the bathroom. I couldn't tell if she'd taken a bump of coke or not. We ordered our food and Sophie started chatting. She told me about her job. She'd been working at this fancy French restaurant in Cocoa Beach. Chez Jean's Bistro. "My friend Gretchen called me in Atlanta about the job. She said I just had to come down and work for her." So Sophie waited tables there and made a lot of money. She wanted to be clear that she'd come down to Cocoa Beach for the job and not because I was back in town. I wasn't sure I believed her. It didn't matter. She said, "I'm moving back to Atlanta, anyway. I'm cleaning up my act."

"I didn't know your act was still dirty," I said.

Sophie glared at me. "Don't be a jerk," she said. And she kept talking. She told me about her mom and living in Atlanta and on and on. I listened and tried to figure out if she was so chatty because she was nervous or if she was coked out. It was hard to tell with Sophie.

When the sushi came, she picked up her chopsticks and arranged all of her rolls and nigiris in a half-circle around her plate. There was a definite order to it. The arrangement started with California rolls and made it's way up to the raw fish nigiris.

"What is that?" I asked. "A ranking system?"

"I like what I like," she said.

She started eating the California rolls. And to watch her do it… There was something childlike and vulnerable about it. Something very cute. But sincere, too. She had a definite pattern. Eat a roll. Take a little bite of pickled ginger. Put down her chopsticks. Sip her green tea. Pick up her chopsticks. Repeat.

She didn't seem to notice me watching her. She just ate. I looked at those slender fingers on her chopsticks, the bare shoulders I could see through her white blouse, that soft face ready to break into a smile any second. I'll admit it. I wanted to have sex with her so badly. I wanted to forget the past and the future and everything and take her into the bathroom and lock the door and just…

I bit my lip hard. Almost hard enough to draw blood. I looked back down at my plate. Forget it, I told myself. Just eat your damn food and get out of here.

After dinner, Sophie went to the bathroom again. That convinced me. She was snorting coke in there. Everything added up: working a job where she made a lot of cash, planning to go back to her mom's in Atlanta, talking up a storm, going to the bathroom twice in thirty minutes. Her act was still dirty.

When she came back, she said, "Hand them over."

I reached into my back pocket and pulled out an envelope. I hadn't even opened it. It had come a few days earlier. Usually, I just threw those bills away. I hadn't gotten around to tossing this one in the trash. Lucky, I guess.

Sophie picked up her fork, which she hadn't used when she ate, and used it to open the envelope. "Is this going to give me a heart attack?" she asked.

I shrugged. "Probably."

Sophie's lips got tight. She exhaled through her nose. "Here goes." She pulled the bill out of the envelope. I watched her eyes flicker back and forth as she skimmed down it. "Wow," she said. "That's a lot of stitches."

"Yeah."

Sophie flipped through the pages that itemized everything in my hospital stay. She rubbed her nose with the back of her hand. She mumbled, "So fucked up. So fucked up."

I nodded.

Sophie took a deep breath, gave me the smile that she'd give one of her tables when she was just about to take their order, and said, "Well, that's doable. I thought you really had ten thousand dollars worth of bills. This is barely over nine thousand. And you probably didn't have insurance, did you?"

"Of course not," I said.

"See, and the hospitals charge more if you don't have insurance. My dad can call them up, spout off some legal precedent or something, and get this down to six grand." She sighed. "Not so bad."

And, for her, it wasn't. Her dad would pay for it. He was a lawyer. He told me once that he charged two hundred and fifty dollars an hour. I did the math. He could have this covered in three days' work. As opposed to the months it would take for me to earn that kind of money. Plus I'd have to pay full price.

Still, it was good of her dad to cover it. I told Sophie that. I asked her about her dad, too. I said, "I bet he liked to shit when you told him you stabbed me."

"I don't know if he shit, but he wasn't happy."

I smiled. I liked her dad. He was a character. I said, "How is old Hank, anyway?"

"Henry," she said. "He's good. He asked about you."

"Yeah? What did you tell him?"

"I told him that you were all in one piece."

I rubbed my belly. "Is he still in Orlando?"

"Yeah. He's doing stuff for Disney over there. Last time I visited, maybe two, three weeks ago, he took me with him to see a client. The guy lived in this town called Celebration. Ever heard of it?"

I shook my head.

"Dude, it's crazy," Sophie said. "Disney owns the whole town. They built it. It almost looks like a cartoon suburb. No cars in front of the houses. No trash cans. Everything matches. Even all the doorknobs were exactly the same. I felt like I was on acid. Like Mickey would come by in a wizard hat and sweep me up into the stars at any second. You should go over there."

"To Celebration?"

"No. To Orlando. To see Dad."

"Is he still dating that floozy? What was her name? Starshine or something."

Sophie wiped the polite smile off her face. Her lips got tight again. She said, "Just Star. And no. They broke up."

"Did he find someone younger?"

Sophie picked up the bills, folded them, and stuck them in her purse. "Yes," she said. "As a matter of fact, he did."

"Is she younger than you?"

"Don't be a jerk."

I tried not to laugh, but I didn't try too hard. A little one squirted out. "She is younger than you, isn't she?" Sophie's tight face answered me. I said, "That sucks."

The waitress came back with Sophie's credit card and the bill.

Sophie tipped the waitress, signed off on the credit card slip, put her card back in her wallet, and stood up. "That's enough, Danny," she said.

And I hoped to hell she was right.

31
Picking Up Stiffs

The stiff was at a condo in Cape Canaveral. I knew the building well. I'd helped build it more than ten years earlier. It was one of the first jobs that I actually welded on.

We took the gurney to the elevator and rode up. I told Bart, "It's weird. I don't think I've ever been inside something I built. Not when it was finished."

"Really?" Bart said. He couldn't care less.

Probably because of this, I said, "It's weird to think that, if that weld I laid down ten years ago isn't still holding, this elevator shaft could crumble below us." I smiled. "It'd be an ironic way to die, huh?"

"Sure would," Bart said. This kind of shit didn't creep him out at all, I guess. We just rode up to the dead guy's floor.

There were a few cops still hanging around the dead guy's condo. Two of them were outside on the balcony, watching the moonlight shine down on the ocean. One cop was inside. It was Dante Jones. We all said our hellos. He pointed to the recliner in front of the TV. "There's your man," he said.

"Who found the body?" Bart asked.

"His wife," Dante said. "We got her out of here a while ago.

She's with the neighbors."

Bart nodded. I walked over to the corpse. I hadn't noticed at first because his back was toward me, but when I walked around in front of the recliner and caught a glance of the guy, I kinda laughed. "Oh, Jesus," I said.

Bart came around and stood next to me. He pointed at the dead guy and said to Dante, "Did you guys do this to him?"

Dante was all grin. "He did it to himself."

"For fuck's sake," Bart said.

"You don't know how right you are," Dante said. Because the dead guy was sitting in his recliner, facing the television, with his pajama pants down around his ankles. He still had an erection and his hand was holding on tight.

Bart said the obvious. "Went down beating off, huh?"

"You could be a detective," Dante said.

Bart pointed at the VCR over the television. "Looks like someone already took the porn. Evidence, huh?"

"How the fuck can you tell?" Dante asked.

"I have the same VCR at home. There's a little thing that lights up when a tape is in."

"Damn," Dante said. "Maybe you could be a detective."

"Did you steal the tape?" I asked Dante.

"Fuck, no. I don't want to watch white people fuck."

I looked at Dante. He was smiling, but I could tell he was serious. The other two cops came in from the balcony. Dante introduced us. The two cops hung out. As Bart and I wrestled with the corpse, I caught occasional glances of the two cops, standing there, grinning, laughing. Telling jokes about the guy who died beating off, but stealing the dead guy's porno so they could beat off to it. It's a strange world we live in.

As I pulled the van out onto A1A, Bart said, "Hell of a way to go, isn't it?" This was our little ritual. We always talked about the corpse and the way the dead person went down. These conversations were my doing. Obviously, death spent a lot of time on my mind. Whenever I went to pick up a stiff, I'd check out the room and try to figure out what they'd been doing right at the end: what their last meal had been, if I could tell, if the dishes were still in the sink. Or I'd look to see how much dirty laundry they had amassed before dying. Weird little things like that. I was most interested in what they'd been reading in the end. I'd heard somewhere that Elvis went down reading *Another Roadside Attraction* by Tom Robbins. Not a bad last book, I figured. And, since we were in Florida, a lot of the old guy's had copies of Carl Hiaasen or Randy Wayne White books on their nightstand. For some reason, those books depressed me. I don't know why. I hadn't read anything by either of those guys. Sometimes I'd flip through them while Bart steadied the gurney, but that was about it. The last book Libra read was *Kitchen* by Banana Yoshimoto. I remembered because she was really digging it. She kept saying to me, "You gotta read this when I'm done." I tried a few times, but I couldn't get through it. Not that it's not a good book. What I read was pretty great. It's just too painful for me to read. I hope Libra got a chance to finish it, though.

Bart wasn't interested in this stuff. Instead, he and I talked about the means of death. It was like we were trying to figure out the best way to die. The best ways not to die were easy. You don't want to go out in a crash of any kind: motorcycle, car, plane. You don't want something to hit you and kill you: a train, a car, the sidewalk. Or, basically, you don't want any accident or violent death. If your body is working fine and some outside force takes you down, that's the worst. We agreed about that. The best way to die was still a mystery, though. That's what we debated.

I said, "I don't know. I guess it's not so bad."

Bart looked at me. "Are you kidding me? How embarrassing

would it be to die jerking off? You wouldn't be ashamed?"

"I'd be dead," I said. "Look at this guy in the back. Does he look embarrassed?"

"What about his wife, though?"

"What about her? She had to know it was going on. She found the body by midnight, which means she wakes up in the middle of the night sometimes and goes out into the living room to check on her husband. And he dropped his pants all the way down to his ankles and watched a porn with his wife in the other room. She had to know what was up. And if she was really so embarrassed, why didn't she take his hand off his dick?"

"I guess," Bart said. "I'd just like to have a little more dignity. I'd like to think a bunch of people aren't standing over me, making jokes when I'm dead."

By now, I was driving down State Road 528 over the Banana River. The moon was a day away from full, and you could see the lights of the Space Center up north. The VAB all lit up. The islands in the Banana River. The water sitting still and flat as glass. I'd actually been thinking about the dead guy from the moment I saw him sitting there, hanging onto his last dead erection. Because I kinda envied the guy. He had a steady, long term relationship with a woman. He had furniture that wasn't fancy, but it all matched and it obviously hadn't been pulled off of a curb somewhere. He had a decent pad with a balcony that overlooked the ocean. He was obviously retired. I thought, shit, if I could get to that point: where I wake up in the morning next to a woman I love enough to swear I'll spend the rest of my life with her, and I don't have to go to work that day, and I could walk out onto my balcony and look at the beach and the waves rolling in and read a book and hang out and do whatever the fuck I want, I'd take it. I'd probably even be happy about it. I wouldn't necessarily want to go out with my dick in my hand, but shit, that old guy was probably eighty years old. If I could still get it up at that age, if I was still beating off to pornos at eighty, well, what the hell? I guess it ain't so bad at all.

I told Bart all this. I said, "The thing is, it's not what you're doing in the end. It's what you do leading up to the end that's important."

"I guess," Bart said. He shook his head. "I'd still like to go out cooler than that old guy."

"Yeah, me too," I said.

But that old man had me thinking again. Because I'd been taking care of all the shit from my past. I'd dealt with Sophie and I'd been doing my best to deal with Brother Joe's death and Taylor was surfing with me again and all that. I'd even gotten rid of the Samoan and the wheelchair dude. And it felt good to face all that stuff head on. But I hadn't gotten very far on my original question. I still hadn't figured out what I was gonna do with my life now that I realized that living fast wasn't leading to dying young.

32
Where the Waves Break

You've been waiting for hurricanes. Keeping your fingers crossed. Hurricane swells are the best thing about living in Florida. You remember some of the best days of your life by the names of the storms: when Hurricane Fran blew in so big that you couldn't even paddle out in Cocoa Beach. You had to go down to Cape Canaveral, where the waves are always smaller, just to catch something a mortal man could ride. Even then, only veterans of a lifetime of storm swells made it out to the line-up. You had the waves all to yourselves. And there was that hour of perfection back in 1995, when Tropical Storm Chantal was directly east of Cocoa Beach, sucking in a great big offshore wind, standing up the most perfect waves you'd ridden up to that point in your life.

Storms like this are what you live for. They usually start coming in by June. This year, you have to wait until August for the first big storm. It's a hurricane. Meteorologists have named it Alberto. Alberto is your new best friend.

You don't call Taylor to surf with you. You're not sure if she's ready to ride a hurricane. Besides, sometimes you have to do things just for you.

You take your shortboard, obviously. The longboard is new

and it's fun on small days, but you can't take a longboard out into Alberto. You also ride your bike down to 16ᵗʰ Street South. The waves are better there. They break over a little sandbar. If you position yourself right, you can find the spot where the wave will peak like an A-frame and you can go left or right on it. It makes you feel like a kid, this bike ride with your board tucked under your arm and the wind blowing you around.

The beach is packed when you get there. Every kook in the county comes out for the first hurricane swell. Dozens of surfers look out at the waves. They're big. And they're breaking way outside, twenty or thirty yards east of the sandbar. When the waves hit the sandbar, they close out. It's nothing but walls of white water from the sandbar to shore. This is enough to get your heart pumping. The adrenaline drips into your bloodstream. You let out a deep breath. Fucking A.

There are definitely more surfers on shore than in the water. Most of those in the water are struggling in the whitewash, just trying to get to the line-up. Most of those surfers won't make it out. You're pretty confident that you'll make it out. This is where you're from. This is who you are. Hurricane swells are in your blood. You strap on your leash and walk down to the water.

At first, you think about timing it. If you can start your paddle out between sets, it may be easier. But it doesn't look like the waves are breaking in sets. It looks like one wave after another. A tough paddle out regardless. So you just go for it.

It's not easy. One wave after another hits you. Sometimes as many as ten or twelve waves in a row. You have to duck dive so much that you hardly have time to paddle. Even when you are paddling, there's so much power pushing you back to shore that you feel like you're not gonna make it. You're breathing heavy by the time you're ten yards from shore. The ocean doesn't relent. It seems to be telling you, "This is serious shit. Go back in." But you're not gonna do that.

Now and then, there is a break between waves. Surfers who don't know better pause to catch their breath during these breaks. Not you. You know better. As soon as there's calm water between waves, you paddle faster and harder. All you think is: go, go, go.

The waves keep getting bigger the farther out you go. They get meaner. There's a lot of power out here. You have to duck deeper and deeper with each wave. You stay under water longer. You go through spells when you think, I'd really like to breathe, now. Then you think: go, go, go.

It takes almost twenty minutes to get out to where the waves break. You're pretty winded by the time you get there. You sit on your board and look at your watch. Don't do anything for one minute, you tell yourself. Catch your breath. You're out here, now. There's no hurry.

While you're taking these deep breaths, you notice that there's only about a dozen surfers in the line-up. There's plenty of room out here. Plenty of waves for everyone.

Your mind starts drifting immediately. You're thinking in metaphors. It feels like the last several months have been one long paddle out in a hurricane swell. You kept getting hit by storm wave after storm wave. As soon as you surface from one, another one hit you. You started with Brother Joe. You had to deal with that, so you ducked. As soon as you surfaced, Libra was dead, so you ducked. As soon as you surfaced, Sophie was back, so you ducked. Then Taylor, so you ducked. Then Libra again and Sophie again and everything. And you never caught your breath during the calm spells. You paddled like mad the whole time. And now you're out where the waves break. All of that white water is behind you.

A minute passes. You've caught your breath. You've watched other surfers ride waves that were well over head high. You've seen the long left lines. This is the shit you live for. You're ready. A set starts to roll in. It's coming right for you. You turn your board toward shore and go for it.

33
Surfing the Hurricane

When I finally got to the place in my life where the waves break, there was an art exhibit. It was a solo show. Mine. A few artists showed up early and asked me how I'd managed to get a solo show. Hell, I didn't even know what they were talking about. I didn't even know it was a big deal until I saw the envy in their eyes.

It was a big deal, though. Helen and her ex-husband Jonathan had worked hard on it. They got the newspaper to interview me. They caused a buzz in a scene that I didn't know existed in Cocoa Beach. The owner of the art gallery took me seriously. She talked to me like I was important, not just some old barnacle who welds a bunch of shit out of metal and picks up dead bodies at night. She bought a couple of cases of wine and snacks for everyone. When I first showed up at the exhibit, about a half hour early to help set up, she offered me a glass of wine. I asked if she had beer. She said, "No, but I'll get some." And she left for the store right away. It was crazy.

A few minutes after the actual event started, Lester showed up. I knew it was a big deal when he showed up. Wearing a button-down shirt, no less. I hadn't seen him since the next door drunks moved out of that apartment next to me. That was about five years earlier.

He walked up to me and said, "Look at you. Big time."

I guess he was talking about the exhibit, because I wasn't looking big time. I didn't even have the right clothes to wear that night. I had on jeans and one of Brother Joe's old bowling shirts. It said, "Central Florida Soil and Sod," on the back, but it looked nice enough from the front. I figured that, if I just kept my back close to walls, I'd look fine. I said to Lester, "I've got some golf clubs in back, if you get the itch later."

Lester smiled like he had the itch now. He pulled a beer out of his pocket.

I pointed to the table with all the snacks. "There's free beer over there," I said.

Lester dismissed it with a wave of his hand. He said, "So what the fuck? I read about you in the paper and everything. Turning junk into art. That's pretty cool."

"Thanks," I said. "It was mostly Bart and Helen, though." I told Lester that Bart had coached me on how to be interviewed. He'd learned all that stuff when he was a college hoops star. He told me that all news is basically a sales pitch, so you want to keep things simple. Make one point again and again. And Helen had told me to focus on the fact that I used to be an iron worker, and that where most people see trash, I see possibilities. That my goal was to take the trash and turn it into art. Bart told me to really focus on only that one point. I could say that I was welding the detritus of my life, or trying to transform junk into beauty, but the point I really wanted to get across was that I was making trash into art. I saw what Bart was saying: white trash kid becomes an artist. Learns big words. Makes Horatio Alger proud. I could sell that. It seemed like the least I could do, after all the work Helen and Jonathan had put into this exhibit. But I didn't want to try to suck Lester into the sales pitch. I was just happy to see him. So I told him all that back story.

He said, "Keep that to yourself. The story's better if I don't know it."

Actually, it was stories I wanted to hear, so I asked Lester what had become of his whole sick crew. Lester had stories. He told me a couple of them, about Sally and Swoboda and Alex and all the next door drunks. He said Sally might stop by later, but I knew that, if she didn't catch a ride with Lester, she probably wasn't coming. It wasn't too important, though, because Jonathan and the gallery owner wanted to introduce me to so many people that I hardly had a chance to talk to Lester or anyone else. Luckily, Lester found Bart and they had a chance to bullshit.

Jonathan and the gallery owner wanted to introduce me to the people who were buying my stuff. They all asked the same questions: how'd you get to be an artist? This must be a big deal for you, a solo show? Who influenced you? What inspires you? What's the main point you're trying to communicate?

I kept my answers simple and consistent: I guess I've always been creative; it's a huge deal to me; modernists, surrealists, Pacific Islanders; friends like Helen; look beyond the trash. Look for possibilities.

I guess it was all true, but it felt like a sales pitch. I'd been coached by Bart and Helen. I felt like I didn't know shit, so I did my best to bluff a good game.

Taylor and Rosalie stopped by. Rosalie's husband was with them. Seeing him didn't ring any bells. I didn't remember him from high school at all. I acted like I knew him, though, because I felt guilty for sleeping with his wife. Because I appreciated that he raised my daughter. I shook his hand and smiled and he said, "I remember when you were the best surfer in town. Remember when you beat Benji Clarke in that one Easter contest?" I acted like I didn't remember at all. Like I didn't eat that shit up every time someone said something about it. Like I hadn't quit surfing contests right after beating Benji because I knew I'd gotten lucky once and it wouldn't happen again.

Taylor said, "I can't believe people came out to see all this junk."

Rosalie scolded her and apologized to me.

But there was no need. She didn't have to apologize to me about how my own daughter acted. Besides, a little part of me agreed with Taylor.

Taylor said, "Thanks for taking me out in that last hurricane."

I was glad to see a little sarcasm from her. She was Rosalie's and my offspring, after all. If she wasn't a little bit of a shit, I would've been suspicious. I said, "Don't worry. Hurricane Debby might do something for us."

Because there was another storm building down in the Caribbean. It didn't look like it was gonna come up north far enough, but we'd get some decent waves. Not full-on hurricane swell waves, but something big and something Taylor could handle. And she lightened up toward me as soon as I made that promise.

As I was talking to Taylor, Sal walked through the door. Flagstaff Sal. My old buddy the mechanic. At first, I didn't believe my eyes. But it was him. I'd recognize that brown buffalo anywhere. Taylor told me about going down to 3rd Street North during that last hurricane swell and watching all the surfers. I tried to listen, but I couldn't take my eyes off of Sal. He circled the room, waved to me, and left. I shook my head, tried to rattle my brain. Was it a ghost?

Sister Janie and Powell showed up. They took a long walk around the exhibit. By this time, a lot of the pieces had sold. The sculptures were still on display. The gallery would keep the stuff out for three weeks, whether it sold or not. But, by this time, more than half of it had little red "sold" stickers next to the title. I think this impressed Janie and Powell more than the stuff I'd welded.

I was talking to a lady who'd bought the piece that, in my head, was the rip-off of Picasso's hookers. She was happy as could be and I was happy, too. Janie leaned in between us. She touched my arm and said, "You did good, Knucklehead."

"Thanks," I said.

Janie pursed her lips like she wanted to smile, but she didn't quite pull it off. Powell shook my hand and said, "Congratulations," and the two of them left.

They didn't buy anything. I was kinda glad about that.

When the rush of people died down, I snuck over to chat with Helen a little. She was leaning up against an empty, white pedestal. Her ex-husband and another guy were standing by her. I said hello to them. Jonathan said, "Danny, I want you to meet my boyfriend, Tim."

The other guy stuck out his hand. I shook it. "Nice to meet you, Tim."

"Don't look so surprised," Helen said.

Though I didn't think I looked surprised because I wasn't surprised. I suspected that about Jonathan all along. And I'd noticed the way he and Tim had been hanging out earlier. I ignored the comment and said to Jonathan, "I really appreciate all of this. It's, uh..." But I couldn't think of what it was.

Jonathan said, "Fucking strange."

"Yeah," I said. "Yeah, it is."

Tim told me about his first art show. Jonathan said that it had sold out on its opening night. Tim tried to downplay that. He was a humble guy. And my show was doing pretty well, but it wasn't gonna sell out. I didn't really care, anyway. All this welding was just something I did. Therapy or something. A way to stay sane. Or at least as sane as I could be. I didn't expect anything to come out of it. Every time anyone tried to compliment me, I reminded myself who I am: a white trash kid from Woodland Avenue. A protégé of

Brother Joe's with a head full of machete monkeys and the world on a toilet. I didn't tell Tim and Jonathan this. I just chatted with them until their wine ran out and they went for a refill.

At this point, I said to Helen, "Thanks for doing all this."

"I get half," Helen said.

"Really, you can have it all," I said. "You earned it."

"I don't want it all," Helen said. "I want half."

"Okay."

Helen had been like this toward me lately. I think it had something to do with Libra. I think that, when I told Helen about freaking out and leaving Libra on the tracks, Helen was done with me at that point. Or maybe not entirely done. But just disgusted with me and thinking that, if things had gone differently, it could've been her on the tracks. That I would've left her again.

I couldn't blame her. And the truth was, I'd actually given up on trying to date her again. I didn't even want to sleep with her anymore. Not really. I just wanted her to stay the person who believed in me a little. So I told her that, in my own roundabout way. I told her, "I don't think anyone but you would've thought to put all this shit in a gallery. Thanks."

"Quit calling it shit," she said. And: "Look who just walked in."

I looked over at the door. Sophie was standing there. By herself. She was a little sweaty and most of her hair was pulled back in a ponytail. She'd changed clothes since work, but I could tell that she'd come straight from the Bistro. She didn't seem to notice Helen and me staring at her. She just walked along, looking at each sculpture.

Sophie took a long time with each one. She'd run her hand above it, like she wanted to touch it, but she never did. The art gallery owner walked over to her and said something. Sophie spoke with her. I watched. Helen said, "I think she's gonna buy something."

"It's that Miro rip-off," I said.

"Quit calling things a rip-off. That looks nothing like a Joan Miro painting," Helen said.

But it did. I'd made a little wire-mesh dog standing on a hill made out of a piece of an old quarter panel. And there was a ladder going nowhere. And at the top of the ladder, I'd fashioned an arm from an antique mobile, and hung a half moon off of it. Sophie reached out for the moon. The gallery owner said something. Sophie shook her head. The owner nodded. Sophie reached out and touched the moon. She smiled.

"She's gonna buy it," Helen said.

"I don't think so," I said. But sure enough, Sophie pulled out a checkbook from her purse and wrote a check for the gallery owner.

"Holy shit," Helen said.

I nodded. Jonathan and Tim came back. "What are we looking at?" Tim asked.

"Danny's ex-girlfriend just bought something," Helen said. She looked at Jonathan. "It's Sophie."

Jonathan's eyes got big. "Crazy Sophie? Where? Which one?"

"Shhh," Helen said.

And I didn't like the whole gossipy aspect of this. I didn't like people staring at Sophie like she was a sideshow or something. Sure, she had her faults. She'd made some mistakes like the rest of us. And maybe one of her mistakes went over the line. Once. But everyone lived. I lived. I'm stronger for it. Sophie's better for it. She paid my medical bills. I couldn't hold a grudge forever. And, to tell the truth, when Sophie took me to dinner that night, and we ate sushi and she just kept talking and I could see all that light in her eyes and her mouth would half-smile when she thought of something funny to tell me and her fingers fidgeted with the napkin ring like she was still nervous to hang out with me, like it was a first date again and she was doing all she could to show her best side. I tried to be aloof that night. I tried to stand back. I did stand back, but in my mind, boy, don't you know I was thinking about sleeping with her. Don't you know I remembered exactly how it all felt when we were both spent and naked and she lay on top of me, sweating, catching her breath. Or how she looked in the morning when I woke up before her and she slept next to me with her chest rising and falling in little short breaths.

So I didn't like to hear Helen and Jonathan and Tim all saying shit about her. I didn't like that dirty look that Bart was casting across the room at her. There was nothing wrong with Sophie being there. She was just trying to support me. She was trying to make things right. And, really, was anything so bad that we couldn't make it right?

I excused myself from Helen and Tim and Jonathan and walked across the art gallery. All around me was metal that I'd welded. Trash that I'd made into something that meant something to people. It meant something to me. And in front of me was Sophie: disheveled from work and a few hundred dollars poorer. She looked up at me then, with those root beer eyes. I went to her. Maybe I was right back to making the same mistakes. I didn't care. I'm still Danny McGregor. And there's no point in paddling out into a hurricane swell if you're not gonna ride the hurricane waves.

34
East to Mexico

That's how my story should've ended. I had my little day in the sun. Everyone came out to see. I turned the trash of my life into something beautiful. People dug it. I got a toe-hold into an art community and got a little security knowing that people would at least consider my work in the future. It was a high point. No doubt about it. Even goddamn Janie had to admit that I'd done well. But this wasn't the end because 1.) Libra was still dead and 2.) I was still that special kind of stupid.

Three days after the gallery opening, Sal and I sat in a pair of first-class seats on a plane to Arizona. We got rip-roaring drunk. Sal's goal was to get so drunk that they'd land the plane early and kick us off. That did not happen. Instead, a few businessmen around us on the plane were entertained. They drank with us. Hell, they bought us drinks. One guy had a ukulele with him. He played and we wrapped arms around shoulders and sang along and Sal even got a stewardess to dance with him in the aisle. At one point, I wondered if this was what it would be like when my soul was shipped to hell.

Then we landed in Phoenix.

I half expected Libra's parents to be waiting for us at the gate. I half-expected cops and my arrest. No one was there, though. Just me and Sal and our new drunken friends shaking hands and saying goodbyes.

My Galaxie was waiting in long term parking. I asked Sal, "What the hell?"

"Like it? I rescued it from your front yard after you left."

"I like it," I said.

Sal opened his door, sat in the driver's seat, leaned over, and unlocked my door. I sat inside. Sal started the engine.

"Purrs like a kitten," I said.

"Not only that, but I've trained it. It can sniff out the nearest bar, no matter where we are. Watch." Sal pulled out of the airport and, as promised, drove to the nearest bar.

Three nights earlier, after the gallery showing and after Sophie had gone home and Bart had gone to bed, I got Sal to come clean. What was he doing in Cocoa Beach? He was a good guy. A good friend. And the art exhibit was a big deal to me. I won't deny that. But Flagstaff is two thousand miles from Cocoa Beach. Good friend, big deal or not, that's a long way to travel to see some welded metal. So what the fuck?

It took some prodding. I had to throw out a few dudes with the long "u." As in, "Duuuuude, this is Danny you're talking to." And finally Sal told me the whole story.

Sal's Story

After word got back to Libra's folks about what I'd done to the Samoan, they decided to take another tack. They approached Sal. They knew Sal was friends with both Libra and me because Sal had identified the body.

He'd gone to the Medical Examiner's office in Flagstaff on a cold February morning and looked at that severed leg and the crusty Betty

Boop tattoo and he said, "Yep. That's Libra's leg all right." This, of course, led to several hours of interrogation. The Flagstaff P.D. had a wide array of theories and scenarios that led to Sal pushing Libra into a train. Sal listened to the stories and looked at his brown Mexican skin and got worried and thought and thought and thought and finally said, "You can push someone *into* a train, but you can't push someone *under* a train. If you push someone into a train, the impact will throw them off the tracks. It won't throw them underneath. And you'd have to be underneath to get your leg cut off." This intrigued the detectives. Two detectives and Sal went down to the train tracks in Old Town, where no one was looking. The detectives took turns pushing Sal down on the tracks. They noted how he fell. They tried to look at it from every angle. Sal kept pointing out to them that, no matter how he fell, it wouldn't lead to him losing a leg at the hip. A few more scenarios came up. He could've tied her to the tracks. So they went to the spot where Libra had been found, and, no, that theory wouldn't work. There was no good way to tie a body down. Plus, there would've been rope at the scene. This was no *Dudley Do-Right* cartoon. The next theory was that he placed her unconscious body on the tracks. "But why place a body so that just the leg hangs over the tracks?" Sal asked. The detectives admitted there was no reason. They talked things over for a while on those tracks. Sal offered to let them push him down a few more times. But, no. There was no point. Sal clearly had nothing to do with this. He was who he said he was: a friend doing his civic duty. A good guy. Bending over backwards to help out, really. The detectives didn't even bring Sal back to the station. They dropped him off at his garage.

Sal thought that was the end of it. He had wondered a few times what happened to me. He wondered if I knew about Libra. He wondered even if I was responsible for Libra getting hit by that train, but he'd gone through all those scenarios with those cops. The evidence was clear. She'd fallen asleep on the tracks. No one to blame but herself. As far as Sal and the Flagstaff P.D. were concerned, the case was closed.

Libra's parents felt differently. How could they not? How could they believe that their beautiful, intelligent daughter got fucked up on booze and pills and fell asleep on the train tracks? How could they accept it? How could they not spend all their energy looking for someone to blame? And who better to blame than me?

After the Samoan had taken a beating from me, they approached Sal. They offered him money to go to Cocoa Beach and bring me to Flagstaff. They just wanted to talk to me, they told Sal. This was all about closure. They handed Sal a newspaper clipping about my art exhibit. They gave him a round-trip, first-class ticket to Florida. There was also the promise of a round-trip, first-class ticket for me. I could fly back to Arizona with Sal, talk to Libra's parents, give them their closure, and be back in Florida before the end of the week.

"Don't do it, though," Sal told me.

When I told Helen the story of Sal, she agreed with him. She kept telling me, "If Libra's parents only want to talk with you, they could do it over the phone."

Bart had another opinion. He was convinced there'd be a reward. He kept asking questions in the middle of conversations: what was Libra's full name? Where did her parents live? What were their names? When was Sal supposed to fly back?

When Bart got all the information he needed, he called Libra's parents and asked them about the reward. Ten thousand dollars. It lit up everything inside of Bart. He realized that he could change his life with that kind of money. He could sober up and go back to graduate school and study more philosophy and get a job in a university and quit picking up dead bodies and driving the short bus. Helen told him that he could do all this stuff without the ten thousand dollars. He shrugged her off. He did everything he could to convince me to go back to Flagstaff. He even arranged for my plane ticket and set up a time and place for me to meet with Libra's parents. He really could be a treacherous friend.

Still, I had decided to go back to Flagstaff before Bart had said a word. I'd made up my mind by the time Sal had finished telling his story.

So that was how I came to be sitting inside that old man bar in Phoenix, drinking dollar drafts with Sal. Outside, the waves of desert heat cooked up everything that couldn't run for shade. Inside, we had dark and air conditioning and Sal spending a little time with each beer trying to convince me to stay out of Flagstaff. He had his work cut out for him. I don't often change my mind.

Sal ran a finger up his glass of beer. Condensation had collected on it. He used those drops of water to wet down his eyebrows. "Best case scenario," he said. "What happens when you meet with Libra's parents?"

"I don't know."

"That doesn't sound like you. You always have some kind of daydream about the way things will work. Let's have it."

I scratched the back of my neck. I did have a daydream. I knew it would sound foolish if I said it out loud, though. I shrugged it off. We went back to drinking.

This scene repeated itself eight or nine times as we had eight or nine beers and got completely tanked. The bartender cut us off. Four stools down, an old man was asleep on the bar. Another guy made out with a transvestite hooker in one of the booths. The bartender served those three. Me and Sal, he cut off.

We stepped out into the Phoenix night and Sal said, "Fine, man, I'll take you to Flagstaff. But first, we go on a bender. We get a six-pack of beer and we drive to fucking Mexico. We have a three-day drunk. Exorcise every demon. Kill every ghost in Danny's head. And then we go face the music."

I looked down a six-lane Phoenix highway and beyond that to the molehill of a mountain that guarded the town and beyond that to the saguaro and sagebrush of the south and said, "Now you're making some fucking sense."

Sal drove the Galaxie to the first convenience store he found. We picked up a six-pack of the cheapest beer they had. Sal hunted down the entrance for the first freeway we could hit. We got on the freeway and rode it until it ended and dumped us off in a neighborhood. This was okay. We needed more beer, anyway. Another six-pack and we followed the freeway back the way we came. It couldn't be too tricky. If we were heading west, which we assumed we were, then we only needed to make a left turn and head south. We'd hit Mexico sooner or later.

The only problem was, even though we were on a westbound freeway, we were on a leg of the freeway that headed south. Our left turn took us east. We got lost. On a sober, sunny day, it's almost impossible to get lost in Phoenix. On this night, with both of our internal compasses off by ninety degrees, it was impossible not to. After the second six-pack dried out, we stopped at another gas station. I asked the clerk how to get to Mexico.

"Mexico?" he said. "You're in Mesa." Which was ten miles away from where we'd started two hours, twelve beers, and ninety miles of driving ago.

I went back to the Galaxie. "Which way to Mexico?" Sal asked.

I pointed to an all-night burrito joint across the street. "Let's get a snack."

So we ate burritos. When I was done, I crawled into the back seat and went to sleep. Sal slept in the front seat. Mexico could wait until morning.

35
One Foot on a Banana Peel

Libra's mom sat across the linoleum table from me. Everything about her seemed to be too good for this little mountain-town diner. Without saying a word, she screamed money and leisure: her deep brown tan, the blonde streaks in her otherwise coffee-colored hair, the diamonds on every finger, those sculpted shoulders that had to take hours of daily gym time. I hate to say it, but she was hot in a Mrs. Robinson kind of way. She'd been crying, but her mascara didn't run with the tears.

Libra's dad sat next to her. He was dressed in a standard business casual kind of way: silk shirt, khaki slacks, loafers. He gazed off at the rack of free weeklies by the front door. His eyes hadn't met mine once since we'd sat down.

I'd just finished my speech. It was the one I'd rehearsed again and again in my head since deciding to come back to Flagstaff. The one when I told them that I, too, had a daughter. I understood all too well how attached we become to our children, how we want to shelter them from the world, how we want to give them the best of ourselves. "If anything bad happened to my daughter," I told them, "nothing on hell or earth could keep me from striking back at the guilty party." But I wasn't the guilty party. They had to understand that. I'd broken up with Libra just like they'd wanted me to. I'd agreed with them when they said she was too good for me. I'd tried to make Libra understand that. And I was nuts for Libra. Over the moon for that chick. I was so in love with her that I had to leave her. I was so crazy about her, I wanted what was best for her so badly, that I recognized how bad I was for her. So I ended it. I'd even left town to make sure that she didn't sour things with her parents once and for all.

I conveniently left out the part about my finding the body on the tracks and freaking out. Libra's parents didn't need to know that.

At the end of my speech, what could they say? They nodded. Libra's mom, as I said, cried. Libra's dad stared at the free weeklies. I'd cut their fuse. What was left? I said, "So I hope you'll please stop sending people after me. I'm broken up enough about this as it is."

I didn't give them time to respond. Enough had been said. I walked away.

At least that's how it all played out in my mind. That was my best case scenario that I couldn't tell Sal about. It was foolish. Things didn't happen that way at all.

What really happened was this: Sal and I woke up in the car. August Arizona heat swallowed the Galaxie by six in the morning. We hadn't slept much. We weren't very sober. Sal rolled down a window and stuck his arm outside. "Mesa. Two hours of driving and we're in fucking Mesa."

"I thought you were Mexican, man," I said. "How does a Mexican drive east to Mexico?"

"I'm Chicano. And fuck you. You were sitting right next to me the whole time."

"Fair enough," I said. I rolled down both back windows, crawled into the front seat, and rolled down that window. "Let's go to Flagstaff."

For most of the drive up, Sal tried to convince me to skip my appointment with Libra's parents. He kept saying, "Do you really want to walk into a room with two wealthy, powerful people who blame you for the death of their daughter?"

And of course I didn't. But what could I do? They were rich. They were powerful. They'd hound me until I finally gave myself up. I felt like it was better sooner than later.

The drive to Flagstaff took two hours. We had a six-pack of beer for the ride. It kept the hangover away, but it wasn't enough booze to get us lost. We knew good and well where we were going.

When we got to town, I asked Sal to drive me to my old trailer. "I need to dig something up," I said. Sal nodded like it was the most normal thing. He took a few turns up the hill just west of downtown and pulled into my old, weed-ridden lawn.

I got out of the car and walked to the shed. I touched the middle support of the shed, took five steps forward, and started digging with my hands. The ground was hard and rocky. A shovel would've been helpful. I figured it would take more effort to go to the store, buy a shovel, and come back than it would to just claw at the ground for a few minutes. I didn't need to get too deep.

A guy came out of the trailer. He saw me digging in the yard. He said, "What the fuck are you doing here?"

"I used to live here," I said. I kept digging.

The guy was short, chubby, completely bald. He held an infant in his arms. The baby cooed. The guy said, "You don't live here anymore."

"No. I don't." I kept digging. The guy walked toward me. Sal got out of the car. The guy stopped walking. He and Sal stared at one another. By now, my hole was about six inches into the ground. I was close. I could feel the corner of a plastic container. It was still there. I picked up a flat stone and used it to dig. The guy started walking closer. So did Sal. I cleared the dirt around the plastic container and pulled it out.

Inside was that old monkey that I'd given to and stolen from Brother Joe. It was part of the reason I came back to Flagstaff. I wanted to rustproof that old monkey and weld it onto Joe's grave marker. I took the monkey out of the container. The head was oily, worn smooth. The plastic had done its job. The monkey was as clean as the day I buried it. I held it up in the sun.

"What the hell is that?" the guy asked.

"It's my monkey."

"It's in my yard. Doesn't that make it my monkey?"

I stood and faced the guy. The top of his head barely reached my chin. It was eight-thirty in the morning. I was drunk. I hadn't shaved in three days. I'd slept the night before in the back of a car. I'd just dug a monkey up out of this guy's yard. Now, my brown buffalo of a buddy and I were gonna leave with the monkey. I stared the guy down until some of these thoughts had time to run through his head. "No," I said. "It's mine."

The guy stepped back. Sal and I left.

I spent about an hour at the post office buying a box and packing material and packing my monkey up nice and solid. I sent the box to myself in Cocoa Beach. I said to Sal, "Get some breakfast before I face the music?"

"Why not?" Sal said.

By two that afternoon, I was still drinking. Sal had long since left me. I sat at the bar at Uptown Billiards. Libra's parents were supposed to meet me at one. They were an hour late. I'd spent a good deal of time talking about books with the bartender. But by two, nothing could distract me from one simple thought: Libra's parents aren't going to show.

At the other end of the bar sat a middle-aged guy in a suit. He'd come in at one o'clock. He read a newspaper and watched a baseball game on television and drank three cups of coffee. He didn't talk to anyone. I asked the bartender, "Do you know that guy?"

"Nope."

So I thought to myself, if he's not here to drink and he's not here to talk to people and he's not a regular and he's positioned by the door and he's wearing a suit, then is he a cop?

By my best reckoning, he was.

Was he waiting for me?

I thought so.

I asked myself, should I get this over with?

Why not?

I finished my beer, paid my tab, and stepped right into it.

36
Charged with Mayhem

That first day was brutal. After all that drinking with Sal, you suddenly found yourself in a spot where the booze dried up. The hangover came on quickly and you found out that being hungover in jail is its own kind of hell.

Now, the days are all the same. You've settled into a routine. You go to the cafeteria for breakfast, lunch, and dinner. You shoot hoops in the yard for an hour each afternoon. The rest of the time, you sit in your cell and read paperbacks. Sal brings them for you. This was an agreement you worked out with him. You give him the Galaxie; he brings you books. You've read a dozen novels since you got locked up two weeks ago.

When you're not reading, you spend a lot of time staring at the ceiling of your cell, thinking things over. Lately, all you can think about is that little story Helen told you about her friends and their surf spot. The red bus right. If you ever get out of this cell, you'll take Helen and Taylor there. You'll surf that spot with your daughter and that crazy guy. Ghosts will fade away, monkeys will stop haunting you. The past and future will dissolve into one moment when it's just you and a Central American wave. That's the dream that keeps you going.

Today will be different. Today, you're going to meet with the district attorney. This will be your second meeting. The first one scared the shit out of you. It scared you that the district attorney himself was handling this case. You figured it would've been passed down to one of his assistants. Not so. Libra's parents have a lot of pull in this little town. The district attorney sat with you and explained this. He explained to you that you were being charged with manslaughter. If you plead guilty, though, he'll knock the charge down to mayhem. You didn't even know that mayhem was a charge. Part of you thinks it sounds kinda cool. Charged with mayhem. As in: "What are you in here for?" "Burglary. You?" "Fucking mayhem." You asked what mayhem actually meant. The district attorney said, "Dismemberment, basically." That doesn't sound quite as cool. This is what the D.A. promises you, though. Plead guilty, he'll knock the charge down to mayhem, you'll get sentenced to three years, up for parole in a year and a half. You think about it. How bad could it be? The guys in the yard have told you prison isn't as rough as it's made out to be. They say you just have to fight someone on the first day. If you hold your own, people will leave you alone. More or less. And you know how to fight. And a year and a half really isn't that long of a time.

But these two weeks already feel like a year and a half.

Besides, can you live with yourself if you stand up and admit to taking Libra's leg from her?

That's what breaks your heart the most. With everyone jockeying and fighting for vengeance or power or whatever, you keep asking yourself, what about Libra? She was such a sweet kid. You really did want the best for her. Things didn't work out well at all. They worked out miserably. But this is still no way to treat her memory. You wish more than anything that you could just hang on to that one memory of her and her pink parka and that snowball in her hand. You wish you could go back to that one second at the end of the millennium when you reached out for a lifeline and grabbed that wrong chick in the bar and got a black eye to ring in the New Year. You wish you could grab Libra instead. No fights. No breakups. Just you and Libra at the end of the countdown. You could go home happy. You could stay with Libra, stay in Flagstaff. Everyone could stay alive for a while longer. You could deal with the ghosts of the past the way normal people do. You could go to therapy, rather than setting up this whole tangled web of self-destruction. Rather than trapping everyone you love into this web.

Instead you have private investigators and mayhem charges and district attorneys. So you have to focus and decide if and how to fight.

You understand the district attorney's position. He's looking at you: a poor white trash guy. You don't have enough money to post bail. You haven't brought in an attorney yet. You're probably going to have to fight this with a public defender who doesn't give a shit about you, who will encourage you to take the plea. The district attorney doesn't need evidence. He doesn't need to have a case. He knows you don't have much of a chance of fighting. Still, you won't say a word to him without a lawyer present.

The guard comes by your cell. You stand and face the wall. He opens the door. You do exactly as he says. He cuffs your wrists. He puts ankle cuffs on you and runs a chain between your wrists and your ankles. He leads you out of your cell. You walk down the hallway with your mind lost in that dream of a Costa Rican wave.

The district attorney, the arresting officer, and your lawyer are in a conference room in the jailhouse. Your lawyer smiles to you as if he's just seen you across a barroom floor. "Danny McGregor," he says.

Looking at him makes you smile, too. It's been too long. And he looks so spit-shined. He's wearing a tailored suit and leather shoes so soft you just want to touch them. He's even a little intimidating, but that's what you want. You say, "Hank."

Hank comes over and give you a hug. You can't hug back because you're in chains. You do him the favor of lifting your hands, though, so that they don't rub against his package when he hugs you.

The district attorney clears his throat. "Uh, Hank?"

Hank glares at him. No smile. "Henry, please. Henry Dunn."

This is something that always bugged Sophie: the only person in the world who could get away with calling her dad "Hank" was you. And you have no idea why the guy has always liked you, but he always has. That's why you called him after hearing Sal's story. You knew Hank would help you out. You knew you had Sal's experiments on your side and that there was no way anyone could push a body under a train and have it end up the way Libra's had ended up. You knew something beyond that, too. You knew that Hank's daughter had put a knife in your belly three times. And you hadn't pressed charges or sued or said a word to anyone but your brother. Hank knew this, too. He appreciated it. There's a currency in that.

So you had told Hank the whole story before leaving Cocoa Beach. He listened. When you were done, he said, "Go back to Flagstaff. If you get into trouble, call me. I'll get you out of it." He even gave you a toll-free number that you could use from jail.

And you knew this: you knew from the minute you got arrested that Hank could get you out. You knew he was that good of a lawyer. You knew what he'd done in the past and who he'd defended and how guilty those people were and how much less guilty you were. If you had wanted it, Hank could've gotten you out of this jail a week and a half ago. This past two weeks had been your own self-imposed imprisonment. Your time to get things straight in your head. Your time to pay a debt to a dead girlfriend you would trade your life for.

You sit in a hard wooden chair. Hank sits next to you. The district attorney and arresting officer sit across the table. Hank says,

"Let's get right down to business." He introduces himself as the guy who got a Disney executive off the hook after the exec had been videotaped molesting a little girl. Hank's told you this story before. It's not as severe as it sounds. The "little girl" was actually eighteen at the time. She was just doing her best to look younger. But Hank had handled the case and kept everything under wraps and even got the solicitation charge dropped despite the fact that the "little girl" was clearly a hooker. The story didn't make the news. It did make it into court record, though.

Telling this story tells the D. A. two things. First, the D. A. now knows that Henry Dunn is the guy Disney calls when they get into trouble. Disney. Second, it gives the impression that Henry Dunn could get anyone off of any charge, no matter how guilty. And you, though you are guilty of many things, are not guilty of manslaughter or mayhem.

The district attorney says, "I never heard about this."

"Exactly," Hank says. He takes a manila folder out of his briefcase and slides it across the table.

The arresting officer has a look of total disgust on his face. He clearly hates lawyers for the defense. You don't care. You care more about the district attorney. You watch his eyes work through the paperwork of the Disney exec's case. You see that attorney's smugness fade away. This case feels five minutes away from being dismissed. Hank nudges you with his elbow. You lean back in your wooden chair. Your hands are folded across your stomach. The chains weigh down your orange prison jumpsuit. You take a deep breath and wander off into daydreams again. They have nothing on you now.

Acknowledgments

Thanks to Mickey Hess, James Jay, Joe Meno, and Todd Taylor for touring with me to support my last book. This novel, in no small way, grew out of the conversations we had about writing on the long rides between readings. Thanks to Pat Geary, Jack Lopez, Jim Ruland, Toby Tober, and Felizon Vidad for reading drafts of this novel and giving me helpful feedback. Special thanks to Jennifer Joseph for all of her help editing the novel and for publishing it.